EC

Ecstasy Unbound

Titles by Setta Jay:

The Guardians of the Realms Series:

0.5) Hidden Ecstasy

1) Ecstasy Unbound

2) Ecstasy Claimed

3) Denying Ecstasy

4) Tempting Ecstasy

5) Piercing Ecstasy

6) Binding Ecstasy

7) Searing Ecstasy

8) Divine Ecstasy

9) Storm of Ecstasy

10) Eternal Ecstasy

Ecstasy Unbound

Setta Jay

A Guardians of the Realms Novel

Copyright:

ECSTASY UNBOUND

Contributors:

Editor: BookBlinders

Proofreader: Pauline Nolet

Disclaimer:

This book is a work of fiction. Any resemblance to any person living or dead is purely coincidental. The characters are products of the author's imagination and used fictitiously.

Warning: This book was written for an adult audience. It contains explicit sex, m/f/m ménage, and alpha males with graphic language and bad attitudes.

Acknowledgements:

First and foremost, thank you Lindy for being the best, most supportive friend in the world. For reading my most primitive works and telling me they were great when they weren't, then covertly helping to make them better. For our weekly girl days that help keep me sane. For your hours and hours of looking at "beefcake" pictures even though it is truly exhausting work. Thanks for being an amazing, wonderful friend. I could never have done it without you in my life. I appreciate you more than I could ever express.

Thank you to Pauline for always cleaning up my mistakes and comma misuse.

Thank you to Heather Palmer and Terri Molina for taking me under your wings at my very first Romance Writers of America conference in Anaheim in 2012. Then, for bringing my husband into the fold at the 2013 conference, it was a blast.

Thank you again Heather Palmer for allowing me to email you my weekly progress, and for all of the wonderful words of encouragement. It made the weeks of characters doing whatever the hell they wanted easier to handle.

Thank you to Heather, the best big sister ever! For all of our lives you were the smartest, most positive person in the family. I'm very thankful for that and for your proofing of my book. I know I didn't make it easy.

To my wonderful husband and best friend, you have always supported and encouraged me. This time you went above and beyond by telling me to quit my day job so I could focus entirely on my dream. I love you so very much! Somehow just a hug from you can ground me when I'm at my craziest. I'm pretty sure that is a superpower.

A HUGE thank you to all the readers. Without you, I wouldn't be able to do what I love.

Edict Set Forth by the Creators Millennia Ago:

"We deem you twelve the Guardians of this world. It is now your duty to ensure the fragile seeds of humanity evolve free from slavery to Immortal beings. Above all else, you will watch over the slumbering Gods, for they will one day be needed on Earth..."

Chapter 1

Paris, Earth Realm

Immortal males were ruled by their dicks.

That point was made painfully clear by the zipper imprint forming on Uri's cock. He ignored it while scanning the shadows, looking past barely clad mortals grinding together to the thumping music. He wasn't searching for a human female, he was looking for *her,* his obsession.

It was late, so most of the entertainment existed in the seating areas, where bodies slid together. Their husky moans filtered beneath the music to where he and his brother Guardian ruled the back of the club. Black leather lounges were purposely placed for the best views, even from the massive antique bar taking up nearly an entire wall. It was busy in the club, but not at the bar. Most were there to fuck, not drink. Which made sense considering the hidden club limited the alcohol its patrons were allowed to consume.

He ground his teeth together. The musky scent of sex and good booze only made it harder to ignore the building need.

As one of the twelve most powerful Immortals in the world, it would have been nice to have been exempt from the fucked-up biology that ruled his cock, but he wasn't. His need for sex wasn't simply to scratch an itch, it was a necessary form of sustenance that kept him strong.

Earth's healing energies replenished Immortals to a certain degree, like water for humans. That was the reason his kind usually kept private caverns hidden within the earth, to soak in energies where they were strongest. But sex for them was like food... And that particular meal held little flavor or enjoyment without his damned voyeur watching from the shadows, consuming him with her eyes the entire damned time they played their game. One they should've never started. He'd long ago been ordered to stay away from the Demi-Goddess and her brothers. All the Guardians had, but that hadn't stopped him from engaging in whatever the hell they'd been doing for over a century.

He flexed his fingers around an untouched glass of Jameson, wondering where the hell she'd been for the last month. It took supreme effort not to shatter it and leave to search for her.

When he noticed a waitress glance in their direction, he shook his head. The redhead looked disappointed at not being beckoned, but he hadn't even taken a damned drink of the whiskey and he doubted Gregoire had touched his either. Neither were happy to be there, which was laughable considering their collective pasts. Immortals didn't consider sex clubs kinky like humans did. They sought whatever pleasure they wanted and felt no shame in anything that got them off.

Gregoire shifted, drawing Uri's attention away from his fruitless search. Humans had been sending them seductive glances, but none seemed willing to brave his massive brother's "back the fuck off" vibe.

Uri caught sight of Gregoire flexing his fingers around his own tumbler of whiskey. The male had been scowling at the room since they'd arrived, which suited Uri just fine. He'd been too busy keeping the search for his Demi-Goddess a damned secret.

"Are you ever going to spit out what's eating at you?" Uri drawled in a low tone set for his brother's sensitive hearing. The male had been increasingly impatient and seemed angry or even pained by their physical needs in the last couple of decades.

Gregoire growled back a single word, "No," before stretching his denim-clad legs out in front of him as the male continued his intimidation of the room at large.

Uri turned his attention back to the shadows. That one word was all he'd get from his brother and he sure as hell wasn't going to push, not when he had his own damned secrets. Gregoire would talk when he wanted to. Or not.

Chances were G was feeling the extent of a long life of never-ending duty broken up by the need to fuck or sleep. All the Guardians seemed to be suffering it lately, but as far as Uri knew, he was the only one doing shit he shouldn't be doing. Shit that would get his ass kicked by Drake because their powerful dragon leader was not going to be happy when or if he found out what Uri was hiding. Shit, not only was he playing games with the Demi-Goddess, he'd also been housing a hell beast as a damned pet on Earth without telling any of his brothers. Just the thought should have made him cringe, but he couldn't muster a fuck to give.

He rolled his neck; his body felt strung tight, which meant he'd need to fuck soon whether she showed or not.

It'd been a month since he'd last seen her. Before that she hadn't stayed away more than a damned week since starting this game. She didn't get to stop now, not after over a century.

And not when she'd made him crave her so damned much.

He remembered the last time she'd watched him from the shadows. Gregoire had already left that night and in those short moments Uri had nearly fucked everything up. He'd wanted more and started going to her. The second he'd moved in her direction, he'd seen the desire flaring in her sapphire eyes, hardening his cock to new levels of pain. Then she'd fucking disappeared, teleporting away before he could get near enough to even catch her scent.

Drake's commanding voice slid into Uri's mind, *How many demon-possessed did you get tonight?* Uri'd been waiting for Drake's telepathic call. The powerful Guardian leader had been busy when Uri tried to report in earlier. The mental links shared by him and his twelve brethren were helpful as shit considering they were tasked with watching over all four fucking Realms of the world. Drake was busy in Tetartos, the Realm of exiled Immortals, while others were in Heaven or Hell.

Uri and G were currently on Earth rotation, and the Realm of Humanity had its own special issues, they all fucking did, but at least they could kill the problems everywhere else.

Six, he answered before adding, *All stuck in cells.* In the compound hidden high in the mountains of Idaho.

Mortals possessed by the demon souls sent from Hell needed to be contained, not killed, thanks to the Creators' curse against the Guardians. Any pain they inflicted on a mortal came back to them tenfold. The Creators obviously hadn't foreseen that demon possession would ever become a problem before they'd left this world. He understood the Great Beings' need to safeguard humanity from even their chosen ones, but that particular safeguard for humanity ended up creating a pain in the ass.

Problems I need to know about? Drake demanded to know through their mental link.

No, he answered easily. It'd been the usual bullshit getting the bastards in the spelled cuffs before teleporting them to their cages. He'd only needed to wipe the memories from a homeless guy who lived in the last dank alley they'd visited.

That last possessed had been loud as hell, a prick spewing all kinds of threats during the minutes it'd taken to get him out of there. The tainted demon souls gave their human host a boost of strength and power that generally destroyed the mortal body in a matter of days. Unfortunately, that wasn't soon enough, the bastards could do a lot of damage in the human Realm in that time.

How's the search for the missing females? And Cyril? Uri asked, more interested in the search happening in Tetartos Realm. A search he'd love to join because it had been initiated from Intel sent to them by his little Goddess and her brothers.

Alexandra... even her name made his cock twitch. He looked for her again and rolled his neck when he didn't see her anywhere.

Nothing yet, Drake growled. Drake trusted the Demi-Goddess' information; as the daughter of the Goddess Athena, she had powers that were shrouded in mystery.

Her information had indicated that Mageia females were being abducted in Earth and sent to the Immortal Realm. The magic-wielding mortals weren't just ending up in the other Realm, they were somehow landing in the hands of a sick bastard the Guardians had been hunting for millennia. The piece of shit son of Apollo had been hiding like a cockroach in Tetartos since the Creators exiled all the Immortals into the Realm and placed a confinement spell to keep them there.

They'd been searching for a damned year and come up empty. To make matters worse, every couple months another disappeared and that meant they were due for another soon. If the pattern held.

Any more news from Vane? Alexandra's messages had been passed to them through her brother's impressive telepathic skills. Even though they were allies of a sort, the Guardians would be duty bound to exile them if they ever came in contact. It wouldn't matter how much information they provided or how often they helped cut down the possessed problem in Earth Realm. It was a fine line. The Guardians needed the help, but they weren't supposed to allow powerful beings to live anywhere near humanity. They were all living in a gray area that seemed to be getting darker every day.

No. At this point no fucking news is good, Drake ground out. All they had were mental images of the bastard Cyril and his minions performing what appeared to be medical tests on the missing females. And Drake was right, the only time they got more Intel was after a female was taken.

Drake's irritated tone came back through a second later. *Pay another visit to the covens closest to where the females lived or grew up.* Not one of the females had been a part of a coven, or on the mandatory lists the Guardians demanded the covens keep, but they were all Mageia. The power signatures were in their homes.

We'll go before patrols tomorrow. Uri'd already checked the thoughts of the Mageia leaders on Earth as well as some of the underlings in each coven that existed near the homes of each missing female. They'd been clean.

They were grasping at straws. He guessed that if enough Mageia pooled their abilities, they *might* be able to power a spell to transport the females to Tetartos. But why would Mageia send one of their own kind to a monster and how did they know anything about Cyril. Yes, the covens knew about Tetartos Realm, but not that it housed Immortal races humans thought were myth.

The only reason they knew that much was because Mageia were

16

compatible as a rare mate to an Immortal. The Guardians had encouraged them to move to the other Realm, where they could live well and freely use magic.

Since there were no guarantees the Mageia would find a rare-as-fuck mate, Sirena, his sister Guardian, didn't give them any information that could scare those who'd wanted to make the one-way trip.

It was another gray area the Guardians were trudging in, but Mageia were treasured in the other Realm, not harmed or subjugated, which was the reason the Creators had wanted to keep Immortals from the human Realm. No Immortal in Tetartos would harm a Mageia. Other than the bastard Cyril and his band of assholes, who were hiding somewhere over there.

Uri took a long pull from his drink, noticing G's scowl deepening, an indication that the male was nearly ready to get on with their night.

Report when you're done. With those words Drake dropped the mental connection. Uri's mind went over all the questions that had no answers as he searched the area for his female.

"Drake?" G growled.

"Yeah. I gave him our report."

His brother just nodded before taking a deep pull of whiskey.

"We're going to check the covens again before patrols tomorrow."

"Still no clues?" Gregoire ground out.

"No."

17

His brother Guardian nodded and growled as he returned his attention to the crowds.

Uri glared into the grinding females on the dance floor, waiting for his brother Guardian to choose a female. They'd shared for thousands of years, for the pleasure of it as much as the increased jolt of energy that came when a mortal female indulged in something she found *kinky*.

He leaned forward, resting his forearms on his knees. The mortals might have no idea what he and Gregoire were, but they were drawn to their size and appearance as well as Uri's pheromones. They would have their pick. Or G's, as it were, because Uri couldn't care less who they fucked.

Mortals had long ago designated Gods, Immortals and beasts as nothing more than myth; any written references held only bits of truth. Most were laughably wrong. His race, the Aletheia, was the perfect example of humanity's poor record keeping when it came to Earth's ancient history. He was fully aware that his kind had spawned vampire myth, but to say those stories were flawed was a massive understatement. For one, he wasn't fucking dead. Though he had to admit the accounts of his race were better than some of those written for other Immortal races and, hell, humanity got the Gods completely screwed up.

"Are we doing this or not?" Uri drawled. Not half as relaxed as he hoped he sounded.

"Yes." Gregoire growled while giving a sharp nod to a female with short dark hair and a huge rack. His brother dropped his glass on the table between them and waited as if bracing himself for torture. Fuck. Uri shook his head and watched the female move closer in a tight black dress that barely concealed an inch of her curves. She smiled as she sauntered forward on high heels, her heated whiskey gaze darting between Gregoire and Uri with apparent anticipation. Their particular proclivities were well known in the club.

They used to fuck female after female for hours, thoroughly enjoying their downtime and embracing their needs. Not anymore. He was fully aware that G would only stay long enough for a quick release.

Uri would stay longer if his voyeur showed up, and he swore he could already detect her scent. He knew his mind was conjuring it up; she'd never ventured close enough for him to catch a hint of her. The only real fragrances around him were that of stale perfume, good alcohol and the spicy scent of sex.

"Is this seat free?" G's chosen female said in French as she leaned over Gregoire's lap, placing her cleavage on display.

Slender fingers circled the arms of G's chair as her gaze darted in Uri's direction for a split second. She flashed a seductive grin as she took a deep breath.

"He will touch you first," Gregoire growled.

Uri wasn't surprised, his brother barely touched the females they played with. Not anymore.

When she turned to Uri, he heard her intake of breath, her eyes dilating further as she moved before him, sending heated gazes between him and G. Her arousal filled his lungs and made his cock twitch. She leaned over him, with her eyes sliding over his face and down his body to the hard cock battling for freedom from the denim.

The tight black dress left little to the imagination, clinging to flared hips and slowly riding up her thighs from her bent position.

When she went to speak, he shushed her with a thumb to the bottom of a pouty red lip and then caressed her cheek before moving lower to free both plump breasts to sit above the female's dress. Her breath caught when he shelved them high and plucked at taut dusky nipples. She moaned deep, turned on from being on display or his fondling. Either way, they both knew she was getting wet. Her lower body swayed as her grip tightened on the armrests.

One hand moved to his lap, stroking his aching cock.

Others were watching, waiting for more of a show. A show they were used to when he and G were there.

"He's going to fuck you while I make use of these lips," Uri informed her.

She moaned long and low at the words, her eyes going to his brother again. The scent of her arousal amped up with her anticipation. Uri imagined that liquid was slicking the insides of her thighs.

Uri scanned the crowd again. Wanting... Yes, there she was, long dark hair flowing in waves down that perfectly formed body. Full delectable tits swelled above the low-cut black tank top she wore. He saw the otherworldly blue of her eyes and nearly growled at the blatant heat there. Her tight top was cut dangerously low, showing him a deep shadowy abyss he'd love to get lost in. Those sun-kissed mounds were full, just begging for his mouth or dick. His Goddess stayed in the shadows at the other side of the seating area, but *she* was what his cock was waiting for. It hit full mast instantly.

The need to fuck her nearly pulled him from his seat. Instead he moved a hand to Whiskey Eyes' chin, and when her heated gaze landed on him, he commanded, "Get on your knees."

A small moan lifted from her lips as the female kneeled between

20

his spread thighs.

"Good girl." She was eager to suck him off and he'd let her, for a moment, before he moved the party into better lighting. If his voyeur wanted a show, he'd fucking give her one.

He was rock hard and irritated that his little Goddess could affect him like this. He glanced over again, feeling the burn of her gaze as she watched. She was maybe five eight, making her small for her kind. It also made her a foot shorter than him. Humans moved around her, oblivious to the spell she must have used to shield herself from their sight.

Whiskey's breathing had gotten raspy as more liquid slipped from her body. She licked her red lips and he felt warm breath on the head of his dick before she sucked it into her mouth.

Looking at the dark head between his thighs, he imagined it was bright sapphire eyes looking up at him, not the brown he was seeing. He didn't see short dark hair, but long, wavy strands flowing around her shoulders, a taut, perfectly rounded ass arched out behind her in the snug hip-hugging pants she wore. Whiskey moaned, taking him out of the fantasy. He tried to center his attention back on the human at his cock, but it was nearly impossible. She had a talented mouth, but his mind only wanted his Goddess.

Thankfully, if G ever saw Alexandra, he never said anything. That would open up more problems than he wanted to think about.

With only a shared look, he and his brother Guardian began moving from their private space as several people watched the exhibition. He didn't bother to zip up as they directed the woman to one of the black leather lounges. It had been vacated and cleaned, and it was at the perfect angle for his Goddess to see just what they did to the female.

Uri leaned back, his strong legs spread over the sides while he rested against the back. His cock was jutting out of the open jeans, hard and fucking ready. Gregoire unzipped, quickly lifting and positioning the eager female on her hands and knees with her mouth closing over Uri's cock. Slowly G lifted the dress and ripped the small string that comprised her panties. The action had the female's ass undulating in need. Uri knew her folds were likely glistening and on display to the crowd around them.

"Open your mouth wide and suck him while I fuck your pussy," Gregoire commanded through gritted teeth.

The dark-haired female nodded, almost choking in her eagerness to take Uri's cock back into her hot mouth.

"You'll take all of me in that hot cunt." Gregoire's words threw her into a frenzy of abandoned sucking. Her hand left Uri's balls and went between her thighs, and the move earned a sharp smack to her ass. She moaned wildly around Uri's cock as G suited up.

Instead of allowing her frantic movements to continue, Uri placed her hands on the chaise next to his hips. "Keep them there. If you're good, he'll finger fuck your ass while his dick stretches your wet pussy."

She mewled around him and he knew she'd gotten wetter at his words. He took over her movements with a firm fist in her hair. Gregoire glanced at Uri briefly, giving warning that he was going in. With an inexperienced female, you never knew how the excitement would affect them.

Looking down at her flushed face, Uri said, "He's going to take you hard. Don't clamp down while I fuck your mouth." He moved his hands to lightly hold her jaw, making sure she didn't bite down accidently, which would not make for a good time. She managed to hold her upper body up over him as G hammered into her from behind, most likely toying with her ass, the reward Uri had promised.

He looked to the side where his little voyeur was and held her eyes while he used the unknown female's mouth. He dared his Goddess to come to him, to replace the human. It went on for long moments with the female's moans buffered by the throbbing beat of music. Gregoire pushed in and out, almost angrily fucking her, while one hand worked around. Most likely thrumming her clit. The woman's body bucked as his brother forced her into a long hard climax. Uri saw G tense behind her and heard him issue a pained grunt as the male came. She was milking his brother's dick as he sucked in the energies of the harsh release.

Uri focused fully on the female, holding her jaw as she screamed around his stiff dick. The vibrations made him that much harder. He didn't chance spending in a human's mouth. She could get addicted to the semen and the youthful side effects that came with it. Instead he gently pulled from her lips.

Gregoire flipped her onto her back. She was flushed, and her big tits were still on display over the top of the dress.

After a moment, G's breathing evened out, and the male reached into his pants and produced a bandana. He pulled off the condom and wiped up the come still pulsing free and tucked both rubber and bandana into his pocket to dispose of later. Without a word, Gregoire fastened his pants and headed towards the exit, but Uri caught something else in the male's eyes. A bleakness that had been steadily growing in the last decades.

Uri couldn't think of his brother, his cock was too fucking hard. He was far from done with the female. The human lay exposed, her chest rising and falling as she watched him, lust still sparkling in her dark eyes. Glancing to the small group surrounding them, he motioned for another female to come out of the crowd, a small blonde. The tall blond male behind her nodded his assent at Uri's cocked brow. The new female was dressed in chain link that hid very little. She walked forward with her Dom's hand at her back.

"Bend over and eat her pussy. Make sure she's nice and slick for me, and if you do well making her come, your Dom will reward you with his cock." Her male nodded, and the blonde eagerly moved to her task, spreading the dark-haired female's thighs wide. Whiskey's breath caught, but she didn't object to having another female between her thighs, lapping at her bare pussy.

Soon, the dark-haired female was writhing and moaning with abandon. Their audience grew as feminine cries filled the air. He directed them to one side, making sure he could see his Goddess and she could view everything. When Whiskey started arching her back, Uri nodded to more audience members, random people began touching her breasts with hands and mouths. He commanded another female to hold Whiskey's hands over her head. Being restrained caused her to buck into those questing fingers and lips. They were plumping and sucking at her tight nipples. Whimpers issued from her lips as her hips pushed higher into the blonde's mouth; her release finally echoed off the ceiling.

Uri looked at his little voyeur. Alexandra's vibrant sapphire eyes were dilated and her fuckable lips were parted as she panted heavily. Good. He could see even from a distance that her cheeks were flushed and maybe even the swells of her gorgeous tits. He stroked his cock, watching her reaction. Was she fidgeting? His gaze shot to her legs, long for her height. She was slender, her waist tiny, and her breasts were full and so fucking perfect it made him growl low. His eyes caught hers and dared her to come to him, but she jerked her head.

It took everything inside him to turn away from her. To play the way she wanted him to.

He watched as the Dom claimed his submissive, ripping her from the dark-haired female's pussy and bending her over the top of the chaise. The male proceeded to fuck the little blonde from behind as she whimpered and begged for more. The air thickened with the scent and energy of all the fucking. He heard the Dom's smacking thrusts as the human slid in and out of his sub's wet cunt until she cried and came. Her man pushed tight against her ass as the crowd watched. He was fisting her hair, holding her head back, when he found his own release.

Uri clenched his teeth as he suited up. The second he buried his cock in the wet, swollen pussy of the dark-haired female, he was imagining his Goddess. The audience continued touching and tasting her fleshy tits as the woman's pussy clenched around Uri's dick. He held her legs wide and shafted her slowly. When her hips grew eager, pushing to meet him, he started a faster pace. A male audience member bent to kiss her as he plucked at one tight nipple while another female sucked the other swollen breast. Her arms were still being held high above her head as hands roved her flushed skin and she writhed wildly. Her pussy was getting slicker, hotter, and all he could imagine was Alexandra's sweet body beneath him.

Uri bit back a curse as he took her deeper, thrusting until her inner muscles rippled around him. He pushed her legs up higher and went as far as he could while listening to her cries. His balls tightened up, and hot jets of come shot into the latex as he felt the human's release wrap around him, fueling his strength. His eyes shot to the shadows.

His fucking Goddess was gone.

Irritation hit hard, and he sent a sharp look through the crowd as he helped the female cover herself after tying off and stashing the condom. His muscles tightened as he fought the urge to track his Alexandra, knowing it could only lead to disaster. Gods, he craved her. Uri shook his head. He was already hard again, wanting her, not some nameless human.

He needed to get his shit together.

Chapter 2

New York, Earth Realm

Alex groaned in frustration as she reformed on her private balcony. Wind whipped through her hair, batting it against her still-flushed cheeks, but nothing about it eased the heat coming from her aching body. She tucked the long tendrils behind her ear as she glanced down at the lights illuminating the dense trees in the park several stories below.

Soft laughter filtered from the sidewalk and her eyes moved to a mortal couple strolling hand in hand. The romantic picture actually made her chest ache, so she turned from the display because she refused to fall into a bout of self-pity.

With a thought she used telekinetic power to part the French doors before stepping through to the private suite of the penthouse she shared with her brothers.

Her body was strung tight. Hours spent in her private cavern getting a little *alone* time from her brothers had done little to alleviate her tension. Even the night air slipping in from the balcony did little to cool her.

Going back to her game with Urian had been a mistake. She knew she needed to end it and had managed to resist seeking him out for a month before she'd succumbed. It wasn't just that he'd tried to change the game by prowling towards her a month ago, it was that she'd been rooted in place. She'd wanted him to catch her, and that was dangerous.

She shook her head and didn't bother with the lights as she stalked through her room toward her private bath.

She'd gotten off in her cavern, but it was a hollow climax that hadn't left her relaxed or sated. Instead, she felt anxious and needier than she'd been before seeing him.

And she couldn't do a damned thing about it.

She couldn't have the Guardian and she couldn't be with a human. It would be too easy to kill a mortal if she tried having sex with one.

Who was she kidding, she had zero interest in any mortals she'd seen. She'd spent the last century, or more, obsessing over the sexy-as-hell Urian, or Uri, as Gregoire called him. She blew out a breath as she passed her big lonely bed covered in soft white linens and wished she could lie down and go to sleep. Maybe pretend she wasn't doomed, but she knew better. Her body was strung too tight, which meant she needed to find another way to release some tension.

She really did need to spend more time trying to hone her skills, but she just couldn't concentrate on anything like that at the moment. She needed something mindless.

Her rare abilities were the nightmare catalyst that had caused her to lose nearly all of her independence, and she was determined to find a way to solve her problems. The main issue was the shield she'd created to protect herself when her head-hopping power left her unconscious body vulnerable. She'd spent centuries trying to find a way to control her power or do something about the shield, with little to no progress, and she'd never stop trying. Just not tonight.

She sighed as she hit a light switch on the way through the door of her private bath. She needed a shower before anything else. It was days like these that she felt more frustration and defeat than the determination that usually drove her.

She groaned as she sent power out to turn on the nozzles. After the shower, she'd drown her frustration with a good fight or a painfully expensive shoe-shopping binge.

After slipping out of her clothes, she stepped into the tile enclosure and let the soothing warmth of the water ease some of the tension in her tight muscles. In all honesty she wasn't sure shoes or killing possessed would make her feel any more in control of her life. Or any less lonely.

Gods, she wanted Urian. Just once. She'd wanted him to move toward her again tonight and that was why she'd left so soon. It either ended or stayed the same, nothing else would work. What the hell was wrong with her? She *knew,* thanks to her other unique gift, that she was needed on Earth, which meant she couldn't risk getting herself exiled to Tetartos.

The first time her "knowing" ability had surfaced, she'd ignored the odd compulsion. That was the *only* time she hadn't heeded it... and that error was one she was still paying for. It was nearly comical how much she suffered for not listening to her budding power all those centuries ago, so when she *knew* to take her brothers far below ground just before the Creators had come back, she didn't question it. Now she, Vane and Erik were here while the other Immortals had been exiled to Tetartos. And the Gods, including her mother, Athena, had been sent to sleep. She hadn't questioned it then. She'd acted.

Her power of being taken into another person's body was the far bigger problem. It came on with little warning and left her physical

29

body vulnerable to attack. That was the one that had screwed up everything. She'd never imagined just how dangerous it could be until her unprotected body had been brutalized within the safety of her mother's palace. If she'd listened to her knowing, she would have left the palace that day. And if she hadn't collapsed in the hallway as her consciousness floated to another, she and her baby brothers wouldn't have almost died.

Never again.

She shook her head. It had been horrible, but if she'd only taken more time to think through the shield she'd built to protect her body before putting it into place... At the time she'd been so desperate to regain control, to feel safe in her own skin that she'd linked the powerfully protective shield to unconsciousness. It had seemed logical then, and it would've honestly been fine had her father and brothers not felt the need to create a link to her shield so they would always know the minute she was vulnerable.

Back then they'd felt just as powerless as she'd felt.

She groaned. It had all been handled too soon and too emotionally because obviously none of them had understood the consequences of the link.

None of them had considered that it would go off *anytime* she lost consciousness. That included sleep. In those early years she hadn't resented having to inform her brother's when she knew she was going to bed. Not when the trauma was still fresh, but years later she'd felt the true impact on her independence. Only she couldn't seem to fix it and neither could they. That shield and link were deeply cemented within her.

To make matters far worse, decades later she realized that her shield also associated orgasms with unconsciousness. She let her head drop to her chest, willing the warm water to relieve the tension in her neck as embarrassing memories replayed in her mind.

There was absolutely nothing worse than your brothers popping in like massive beastly protectors only to find you naked…

Her face flushed and she banged her head into the tile wall at the humiliating memory. She'd been barely able to look at them for a good decade after that. Not that her brothers had fared much better; they'd been just as uncomfortable. The only good news had been that she'd made the discovery after her mother and father had been sent to sleep, or it might have been a kind of humiliating family reunion. She rolled her neck and refused to dwell on things that were out of her control.

The shield was a protection as much as a curse. Until she gained some kind of control over it and found a way to sever the link to her brothers, she was forced to inform them anytime she knew it would go off. It wasn't the end of the world. She made excuses of working on her powers or sleep when she needed *private* time.

It was all so damned isolating. She was forced to keep her distance from mortals as potential lovers unless she wanted to forgo the climax part because the shield violently repelled anything that touched the magic shell that covered her. Its strength could and would likely kill a mortal.

She blew out a frustrated breath. It wasn't as if she'd ever been attracted to a mortal, but she craved some kind of contact… Connection.

She had her brothers and loved them, but just to be close to another being in a nonfamilial way would be pure heaven. To feel flesh that wasn't her own… A strong body pumping into hers, bringing her to a real release, one that would truly sate her… She

31

groaned, because the only face that came to mind was Urian's. The only body she wanted was that damned Guardian's. He'd been the feature of her fantasies for too long now. He along with the occasional cameo appearance from the brooding Gregoire. She'd wondered for too long just how it would feel to be wedged between the two massive Guardians. Allowing them to ease away all the centuries of pent-up sexual frustration.

She closed her eyes and imagined the water was their hands, their warmth. She'd never seen them take a female between them in the basest of ways. Not the way she'd seen the humans do it, with a female held firmly between two thrusting bodies, crying out in blinding release.

She wished the big Guardians could give her that experience. She wanted everything she'd never experienced, but that wasn't going to happen. Not when she was destined to a life of compulsive voyeurism added to an embarrassing amount of battery purchases on her credit card.

Going to Uri again had been stupid.

She got out of the shower and wrapped her body in a towel before proceeding to dry her hair. If she could just focus on simple mundane tasks, maybe she'd get through the almost painful arousal and bout of depression until she was herself again.

Taking a deep breath and attempting to regain focus reminded her that she needed to check on the wire transfer from their last mercenary mission. The kidnap recovery job she and the twins had just come from in Russia had ended with her beelining straight to Uri... Being mercenaries in the human Realm kept her and her brothers from boredom. Plus, though they were wealthy in all their forged identities, she had a shoe problem. The problem being that designers just kept making more.

She had a bad feeling shopping wouldn't distract her from her current aching need.

Alex didn't understand why she was so obsessed with the Guardian. Physically, Urian was absolute perfection with dark hair a little too long and those seductive mercury eyes. He was also tall, probably an inch taller than her brother's six foot seven inches. His shoulders were wide and strong, a warrior's body with muscles she unfortunately hadn't seen in decades. He and Gregoire used to undress and take their time. Now they only stayed for a short time and rarely disrobed. She missed seeing every naked inch of his chiseled body.

She groaned thinking how much she envied those human females. Uri's mesmerizing, silver eyes drew her just as much as they did the mortals. And damn if she didn't want to lick his sexy stubbled jaw down to his Adam's apple. She'd followed him for centuries, taking stalking to a whole new, pathetic level.

She'd tried to stop on many occasions, but all she ended up doing was flooding their multiple homes with sexy peep-toe pumps and strappy sandals. Then, filling her private cave, where she went to refuel her strength with Earth's healing energies, with erotic toys she kept hidden in case her brothers ever came to visit.

If Erik or Vane knew what she did on her off time, they'd be having kittens right now.

She sensed that her brothers were home. She knew they'd gone hunting possessed when she'd gone off to stalk Urian.

The twins needed to feed their lion half's need to hunt, and the possessed were pumped up on demon powers, which made them stronger and more of a challenge than the piece-of-crap kidnappers they dealt with in their mercenary work.

Alex didn't have the same animal DNA as her brothers. She'd been born before their father had been taken and altered by Apollo and Hermes. Her lip curled with disgust remembering how Apollo had enslaved and experimented on all the Immortals those millennia ago. The monster had bred them like animals in the hopes of creating the perfect immortal warriors for his army. He would have done the same to her father if her mother, Athena, hadn't forced her way into the palace and taken back what was hers.

Alex's father, Niall, hadn't been the same after that. He'd become stronger and more primal after being infused with lion DNA, the same DNA he had passed on to her younger brothers, Vane and Erik, at birth.

Alex was decades older, but she'd adored them from the second they were born. She'd held and snuggled them as babes, played with them as cubs and loved them with all her heart. They'd been her only real companions since her mother and father kept their family hidden and secluded on Earth as they'd trained their own armies for battle against the other Gods all those millennia ago.

Erik had always been the more playful of the two when they'd been children. But after Alex had been attacked, things had changed. Two years after her violent assault, their parents had been sent to sleep by the Creators. Since *her new and powerful ability had shown her* they were meant to do something in the Realm of humanity, the three did what they needed in order to avoid exile. Her brothers had followed her lead then, trusting her unique power and the near compulsion that hit when a "knowing" came.

At the time, Erik, only two decades old yet still minutes older than his twin, moved into their father's role. He grew more fierce and serious. To balance out his twin, Vane's personality had become lighter. She shook her head.

34

Shaking off her dark memories, she finished drying her hair then reached to turn on her… What the…?

"Damn him," Alex muttered while throwing on some clothes to stalk barefoot through her suite out into the marble hallway that led to Vane's room.

She hadn't spared a glance at the beautiful Venetian textured walls. Their penthouse took up the entire top two floors of the building and was done mostly in cream with a lot of metal, including the very modern wall sconces that lined each hall.

Alex threw open the door, knowing her brother was alone in his suite. He was pretty fanatic about allowing no visitors in his private sanctuary.

"That's it, Vane! The next time you take my straightener, I'm going to plug it in and attach it to your balls."

She stood, one hand on her hip, the other out palm up, waiting for the ass to hand it over. All six foot seven feet of girly beast with beautifully straightened, shoulder-length, sun-kissed hair smirked. She glared, smiling would only encourage him; he thought he was amusing when he took her stuff.

Alex narrowed her eyes when the smirk grew. A split second later she launched across the bedroom. Vane braced in expectation of the attack, so he didn't budge, just grunted, as she made contact in her attempted tackle.

Now she smiled.

Laughing, he tossed her to the bed. "I can't believe you're flying off the handle over this. It's a hair thing. You're acting crazy."

"You have your own." She wasn't really mad, part of her just wanted some company, but she also wanted to make a point. They had plenty of money, which meant he didn't need to take her stuff. He knew it drove her crazy.

"What's going on?" Erik scowled as he leaned in the doorway, arms crossed over the wide expanse of his chest. Short black hair stuck out in every direction, yet looked perfect on him with his piercing ice-blue eyes. An aura of command surrounded her darker brother even when he was doing something as mundane as standing in the entry. The twins were as opposite in looks as they were in personalities.

Vane answered Erik with a grin. "PMS."

She mentally growled. Her brother was about to learn a lesson about taunting her when she was "crazy." Teleporting onto Vane's back, she wrapped an arm around his thick neck, ready to choke the life out of him as she grinned at her other brother.

Suddenly her smile dropped as the all-dreaded flicker of vision started, the only warning she ever had.

Erik must have seen it on her face because he ordered, "Vane, get her to the bed."

She felt air, then a bounce onto soft bedding before registering the sounds of crashing glass and crunching drywall. Vane likely hadn't cleared her shield in time and had been thrown into the wall before her consciousness, her essence, floated away, being taken into another person.

Bright spots filled the sides of her vision from the relentless stream of overhead lighting. Alex saw through the eyes of the female's body she inhabited. They were in a metal room, but she couldn't tell where. The harsh stench of sterilizing chemicals burned her host's nose, and her skin itched from the cleaning they must have given her. She was grateful their father had known the importance of showing them memories he had from his limited time with Apollo and Hermes all those millennia ago. Those clear mental images allowed her to identify the evil pair that starred in all these visions.

Elizabeth, the sadistic female who worked with Cyril, the asshole, was there. Her flaming hair swirled wildly around her shoulders as she giggled freakishly. The crazy redhead liked to taunt her victims, flashing her fangs, playing on vampire fears even though her race, the Aletheia, did not drink blood unless it was to take another's memories. Alex's host wouldn't understand that, and it would just upset and confuse her more if she tried to explain it in the female's head. Cyril ignored Elizabeth's antics and performed some kind of medical tests on the body she inhabited.

Alex felt her host attempting to tune it out. Exhaustion and the drugs in her system were muffling the sounds coming from outside her head. The cold metal against her bare back made her muscles ache, adding yet another layer of misery to being naked and having samples taken from every part of her body, inside and out. Warmth trickled down the sides of her wrists where she'd fought against the shackles holding her down.

Alex melded more closely into her host, feeling and hearing her every thought, becoming the female, experiencing every emotion, every sensation.

Tears of frustration streamed uncontrollably down her face, she could barely see her tormentors through the blur, yet the dark evil behind Cyril's eyes would forever be imprinted in her mind... Eyes that looked almost purple, but it was so dark she couldn't tell. His face was backlit by the bright lights shining down relentlessly from behind the bastard's bent head, making details difficult to discern.

Her host focused on his face and cringed at the thought that he would come across as handsome if one didn't see the inhumane indifference of a sociopath lurking behind the deceptively beautiful eyes. It was scary to think she might have found a monster like him attractive before she'd been taken and violated.

In the hours since she'd been kidnapped, neither had said why they'd taken her. Apparently they just enjoyed abusing her body in any way they could. The man was more detached and scientific. As if she were a frog or cat in some biology class, meant only for dissection, not an actual living human being.

She caught glimpses of movement and heard the occasional beeping of machines, the footsteps of med techs or whatever you'd call them, and the occasional whimper or scream of another "patient." Jesus, what were they doing to them? Why lab tests? The implications were adding to her panic. Her body was still lethargic from the drugs they'd pumped into her system, and it was almost like her thoughts were coming in slow motion. A strange voice inside her head was insisting on more information, but it was so hard to focus. She'd either lost her mind, or the drugs were overtaking her again. Were they hallucinogens? Did it matter? If the voice was a distraction her mind created for her, she didn't care, it was keeping her from the hysterics that she wanted to give in to. Sam just knew the evil redhead would love that, and she couldn't bear to make that bitch happy.

Louder now, the voice demanded her name and she mentally shrugged and decided to go along with her obvious mental breakdown. What would it hurt at this point? Her name was Sam...

When was she taken?

She'd just gotten to her apartment door. It was... Friday night after work. She remembered the shock of being grabbed from behind by strong arms before a sharp sting to her neck... drugged.

Again, the voice in her mind was whispering for more information. It was so sympathetic... calming...

She answered. She'd picked up some groceries at the store down the street from her apartment before heading home. She'd planned on a quiet weekend in her apartment.

Her address?

Sam gave the street and apartment name, but she couldn't remember more. It was lucky the apartment number made it through the fuzz in her brain.

It had been dark, and she had dropped her grocery bag when she was grabbed. It had happened so fast... She'd never even had time to try to defend herself. That first burst of semi consciousness after being drugged at her apartment awarded her a brief, hazy view of rock walls and black-clad figures surrounding her, chanting in firelight. She'd heard voices of men and women but saw no faces.

Sam recalled the faint smell of damp rock and dirt as she lay on the cold ground. The chanting picked up speed; then a bright light filled her vision. The air from her lungs rushed out so quickly it had left her disoriented, followed by pure nothingness as her body felt as if it were flying apart before reforming again. It was so fast... She came to, struggling to breathe air back into her system. Spots had filled her vision, and nausea had hit so hard that she curled tighter into the fetal position.

Sam had barely registered that all the others were gone, and in their place were two huge men dressed in leather. She vaguely remembered thinking she had to be dreaming before she succumbed to darkness.

The sharp stinging pain of a cut being carved just above the nipple of her left breast jolted Sam back to her current reality with a stark rasp. Pale gray eyes above her sparkled with madness. Light skin and flaming hair surrounded moist red lips opened to display sharp fangs within inches of Sam's face. It was a glimpse of pure evil that she wished never to see again.

In the back of her mind she realized that her male captor had gone after taking her blood and performing his grossly invasive tests. It was just another violation, like not allowing her clothing. She'd been naked since she'd woken up here. It was painfully obvious she was no more than an animal to them.

A split second later she felt warmth moving through her veins and realized she'd been dosed through the IV in her arm. She welcomed the darkness, the only peace she could find, away from monsters that shouldn't exist...

Chapter 3

Scottish Coast, Earth Realm

Moonlight illuminated the dirt path as Uri took in deep, cleansing breaths of fresh salty air. He tilted his face up to the brisk ocean breeze cooling his skin, which still smelled like sex. He hadn't had time to shower since Havoc had made it clear the hound's needs were urgent.

Rolling his shoulders wasn't doing anything to release any of the tension in his body, mainly because shoulders weren't the fucking problem. The issue was his damned dick, the bastard was never fully sated anymore. He should have stayed at the club and taken another, but when his Goddess had gone, he'd lost interest. He'd been too busy fighting the desire to track her down and pull her sexy body beneath his.

He wondered what she was doing now. His mind conjured up a fantasy of his Alexandra spread and bare in candlelight, lying across a stone altar in one of the ancient temples. White silk curtains billowed out toward the sea as she moaned and writhed. Her dark hair fanned out around her smooth naked flesh as sexy half-lidded eyes beckoned him. In his mind he watched her back bow as she worked frantic fingers over her clit in a greedy attempt to gain release.

He groaned at his vivid imagination and then bit off a curse. Now he needed to lose a damn hard-on before taking the hell beast to hunt bad guys in the city.

A dose of reality did the trick, because there was no way the Goddess was alone and pining for his touch. His mind was fucked up. She was the most gorgeous female he'd ever seen, which meant she likely had several mortal lovers, so why she played their game remained a puzzle.

Why the hell was he so damned obsessed with her? It was going to drive him insane. They'd never once spoken, not even before the Exile. All they knew of each other was the game.

He shook off the thoughts and questions. He had to deal with the hound's needs and get a damned shower before crashing for a few hours.

He'd allow Havoc a few more minutes to root around in the dirt before taking him into a city. Cities were the perfect feeding ground for the animal's needs, but the pup was always cooped up in his place day or night depending on Uri's patrols, so he took more time to get the animal some fresh air in whatever time zone was dark at that given moment.

He knew he was playing with fire letting the beast out in public, even at night. He was forced to plant a different image into the mind of any human that saw the hound. If Havoc's eyes weren't bright crimson and his fur a slick-looking black, humans would've likely mistaken him for a Doberman the size of a Great Dane, but the red eyes were definitely too otherworldly for daylight hours.

As long as the pup kept his hellfire to himself, Uri could keep him out of sight and everything would stay fine. He doubted Drake was going to see it that way though, which was something he needed to deal with at some point.

For now, the animal needed to feed off evil energies to survive. Once Uri had figured out Havoc wasn't inherently evil or changed by

42

his food source, they'd gotten into a sort of habit. And allowing the beast to feed off human predators lurking in dark alleyways was rewarding as hell since Uri himself couldn't harm the bastards without consequences.

He shook his head at what had become of his existence. Housing a hell beast?

Fuck.

Blowing out a breath, he watched Havoc wag his bobbed tail as he stuck his snout in the bushes. Dirt began flying a second later as the animal attempted to uncover something.

The pup had been near death when Uri'd saved his ass in Hell Realm. A dragon had just chewed Havoc's mother to bits and was making its way toward the newly birthed pup. Uri had battled the beast before teleporting onto its back and slamming his blade deep into scales and the hard bone of its skull. That was his damned job in Hell Realm. Killing the beasts before their masters sent them out to Heaven or Tetartos Realms. Yet he hadn't killed the pup; when the little creature had whined and Uri looked into his eyes, there'd been something about the beast. He hadn't fucking looked evil, and Uri caved in to some odd instinct, taking the goo-covered pup home with him.

He shook his head, wondering what he'd been thinking. Hellhounds had been a collective pain in the Guardians' asses for centuries. The beasts were all blood-bonded to the purely evil Tria, demon-spawn triplets of the incestuous coupling of Ares and Artemis, who'd been imprisoned in the bowels of Hell Realm before the Creators had returned all those millennia ago. The story was that the twisted bastards—Than, Phobos and Deimos—were impossible to kill, so they'd been imprisoned instead. It was decades later that the assholes somehow found a way to cause chaos from their cage and they'd been doing it ever since. The Tria spent their demented existence casting out hell beasts to the two Realms closest to Hell, Heaven and Tetartos, while sending demon souls to Earth. He guessed the Guardians should be thankful not to have to deal with hell creatures causing destruction in the massive populations of humans, but he wished they could just find a way to kill the source of their problems and be done with all of it.

He heard the pup issue an oddly deep whine, a sound that was a mix of dog and something far darker. Uri smiled when he saw Havoc hopping up and down in front of a tree with a small rodent frantically eying the beast from a high branch.

The animal amused him, but he knew keeping the animal had been a mistake. If anything, Uri should have taken the animal to Sirena, the Guardian healer, his sister Guardian was the scientist of the bunch. She would have loved to research Havoc.

He'd learned a lot from the experience, though, because as far as Uri could figure, the entire species of hellhounds were blood-bound to the Tria purely for the demented fucks' amusement. Havoc had proven without a doubt that the animals weren't born with some innate evil tendencies as the Guardians had assumed. The Tria had to be making them that way with their tainted blood.

Evil or not, Uri would still get his ass kicked for housing a hell beast on Earth. Not to mention he'd have to tell Drake that he'd blood-bonded with the animal himself. He hadn't had much of a choice, he'd needed to keep him in check. Aletheia had the ability to bond to anyone, but he'd never done it with a person, much less an animal. His race were universal donors of a sort, which probably had something to do with the whole blood fixation in vampire myth.

Drake would definitely torch something when he found out. Fuck, he'd kick his own ass if he could. He had no idea what was wrong with his head, blood bond? And now he was responsible for a hell beast for life. He shook his head.

All he could think was that at the time he'd probably had too much fucking Jameson and hadn't seen his little Goddess. Add in the fact that Havoc had been destroying everything in his place and a blood bond had seemed a solid plan. It was either kill the bastard or save the house.

He'd saved the house.

He had to admit it was odd, knowing the feelings of another being, seeing things through the beast's eyes if he chose. After reining in the hound with the bond, he'd felt Havoc's need to feed off evil energies. He'd been completely prepared to kill the animal if he went dark like the Gods had when they'd fed off corrupted energy.

Blade at the ready, Uri had been set to put him down. Instead he'd been surprised to learn that the hound somehow metabolized the energy it siphoned. Havoc seemed to have no inclination to feed off those with untainted auras; instead, he hunted the sickest of humanity. Those shrouded in a thick cloud of darkness. It'd taken time to adjust to seeing tainted auras through the beast's eyes, any auras, not to mention understanding what the fuck he was seeing.

The beast was pulling his weight; he just had to make Drake see that.

Havoc suddenly stopped his jumping. The hound's ears tilted high; his back went stiff as whiffs of smoke billowed from his mouth. The stance sent Uri on alert. He only did that on a hunt, and even though they were in the middle of nowhere, Uri didn't doubt the animal's instincts, so he listened and waited.

Havoc's stance became more rigid, the nubby tail high as he emitted a low deadly growl. Uri's neck itched. The beast didn't usually growl.

Scanning the area, he didn't detect anything, yet. There were no humans to torment in the middle of the night on a dirt trail, so it wasn't likely to be possessed—they haunted cities not deserted wilderness. His preternatural hearing picked up the snapping of a branch to the right.

Uri teleported to Havoc, hearing another branch break in the heavily forested area. In a blur of movement, a big bastard, for a human, barreled through at full speed, attempting to take him to the ground. Damn, he'd been wrong, this was definitely a demon-possessed; he really hated that they got a boost of demon strength. Sidestepping the charge, he grabbed the idiot by the back of his black wife-beater shirt, the thing started to rip with the momentum, but Uri got him down and pinned. He was a good couple of inches shorter than Uri, a heavily muscled, bald, black guy, with what were probably prison tats to go with his shiny eyebrow ring.

It was irritating that all he could do was detain the asshole unless he wanted to feel the pain he inflicted tenfold.

Fucking curse.

This guy really deserved an ass-kicking for pure stupidity alone. This whole thing made no sense. Did the fiend really think he could take on a Guardian?

"How did you find me?" He growled the words. The male didn't speak. Odd, the demons almost always liked to talk shit through the possessed human. Telling all about the things they would do to you after they took out your intestines, yada, yada, fuck you with your own dick...

Cocking his head, Uri looked at the defiantly silent idiot. Fuck, he didn't have time for this shit. He was reaching to his pocket to grab a pair of spelled cuffs he'd brought when the dumbass made a sad attempt at bucking to be released. Uri shook his head; the possessed was strong, but not that strong. That was when he heard more movement along with Havoc's low growl.

Uri whipped Eyebrow's body up as he heard two more come through the same tree line. Havoc took one down while Uri moved his captive in front of him to take the blow from his buddy. As long as he didn't inflict the pain, he didn't get hit with the repercussions. Uri smirked as the wind was knocked from Eyebrow, but the impact dislodged his grip on the asshole.

Back in fighting stance, he rolled his shoulders, enjoying the surge of adrenaline fighting always brought. Checking on Havoc, he saw the animal had a barrel-chested white guy in a filthy white tank top down on the ground. The hound's teeth had pierced the guy's neck as Havoc injected him with a paralyzing agent all hellhounds held. Uri grinned as he watched the possessed go limp, screeching in rage. Then the sound abruptly cut off, no more moving or talking for that guy.

Yep, the pup was good for more than just entertainment.

One down, two to go. Both Eyebrow and the new short, stocky guy started circling him. The little guy had a knife and had obviously spent way too much time shriveling his balls with steroids before getting his ass possessed. Uri shook his head, a little surprised they were going on the offensive. Eyebrow lunged first. Uri teleported behind him, toying with him to see what he'd attempt next. Shriveled Balls thought Uri was distracted enough to take a stab at his kidney. No way did they really believe they could succeed.

He blocked the knife swing instead of teleporting. A mistake. Uri pivoted to the left, but Balls held strong, and the bastard's wrist snapped, son of a bitch. He turned in time to see that Eyebrow was hoping to catch him off guard and inject him with a syringe of... who the fuck knew what.

Havoc growled deep and lunged, taking Eyebrow down. The guy was an inch from injecting Havoc with whatever the fuck was in the syringe. Uri knew he didn't have time to detain them; he grabbed Havoc and teleported home—was forced to leave before the repercussions from breaking the asshole's wrist hit. The pain washed over him just as he landed in his bed with a bounce.

Uri immediately mind-linked to Drake with the info that he'd been attacked, sending a mental image of the location. *There were three possessed; one had a syringe of something they were trying to inject me with. One guy down. I'm down at the moment. Broke a bastard's wrist.* Shit, he hated admitting that he'd fucked up.

I'll get someone out there. Get your ass in here when shit's straight, came Drake's deep voice in Uri's mind just as his wrist hit the first regeneration. Only nine more breaks and repairs to go... Perfect.

By the second break, Uri was completely irritated. Knowing he had eight more breaks before he could get to the compound would make anyone angry. He probably should have called in when he was out there instead of toying with the assholes. Suddenly, he felt a nip from the pup, followed by long wet licks to his injured wrist. After injecting him with his paralyzing agent, the beast hopped to the foot of the bed, facing the door. He smiled as he watched the pup guard him. Drake would have conniptions when he realized Uri had not only brought the beast here, he planned to keep him.

Havoc had earned his loyalty, and the thought of Drake's scowl brought a wider crook to his lips. Yeah, Drake was going to be furious.

The paralyzing agent didn't really work its full glory since he and

Havoc were blood-bonded. Still, the next break didn't even faze him. Why had they never thought to get some hellhound venom to use like this before?

Got one of your friends, came through his link with Gregoire.

Jax's confused voice came next. *Was there a fucking hellhound out here?*

This was going to be fun to explain.

Uri would have to hit his cave for an energy refuel before going in. He'd need it to deal with the ass-kicking to come.

Chapter 4

New York, Earth Realm

Alex came to, struggling for air, and then promptly doubled over, trying not to vomit on Erik's favorite boots. Her brother held her close when she rose back up, grateful for his soothing warmth.

The queasiness passed quickly. It was something that happened every time she came back to her own body after head-hopping.

Erik rocked her gently as if she were a child, not a full-grown female, and she let him. After what she had just seen, it felt nice, and honestly the offer of comfort seemed to ease him as well. He so rarely showed emotion that Alex savored the moment while gaining control of her vision, the spots dissipating. Erik's woodsy scent grounded her. Vane sat at her other side and she felt his big hand rubbing her back as he handed her a bottle of water.

Her brothers couldn't be more different, even though they were twins. But at moments like these, they were in complete accord while sweetly soothing her, and she soaked in their love.

Alex lifted the water bottle to her dry lips with shaky hands. Taking a sip, she savored the cool slide of it down her throat.

Gods, her head hurt. She was weakened from the hop into Sam's mind, but she was also experiencing weakness in her limbs from her shield's draining effects. She hated to be taken into the minds of victims, sharing their bodies and thoughts, but what really upset her was not being able to do anything to help them.

"Cyril has taken another female. I'm betting she's a Mageia like the others." She took another deep breath before continuing, "I know I say it every time, but it's so frustrating not to be able to filter through their thoughts. I could learn so much more if I didn't have to force the information to the forefront of their minds. I hate only seeing and hearing everything in current time. If I could just dig in..." She shook her head in frustration.

"You're doing what you can. Don't beat yourself up for something that's beyond your control." Erik's voice had a rough rasp that she loved; it was so much like their father's.

"I know. It's just frustrating." She sat up straighter when she realized she had good news. "I learned something new from this one. Sam is her name, and she actually saw people with black robes and heard chanting before being teleported away. I felt what was happening in the memories she shared. She was too drugged to decipher the chanting, but it had to be some kind of transfer spell. At least we know that a Mageia coven on Earth is helping send these females to Cyril and Elizabeth in Tetartos Realm. We need to get this information to Conn." Vane's Guardian contact. The Guardian was a Lykos, half wolf, who seemed to handle all their tech stuff.

Vane nodded. Since he was most skilled in telepathy, he was the one who relayed their information. Alex opened her mind to her brother, showing him every minute of her time inside Sam's head.

Vane nodded. "I'll send it over."

She felt bloodthirsty and frustrated. "I wish the bastard was here on Earth. I hate not being able to catch him ourselves. This is the sixth abduction we know of; why haven't the Guardians stopped him?"

Vane's jaw tensed before he ground out, "Yeah, Conn's lack of sharing and the 'got it covered' or 'thanks, asshole' is grating on my nerves too."

Vane and Erik had been hacking the Guardian systems for years now, and it hadn't likely put them in the Guardians' good graces, which might be why Conn wasn't sharing anything with them.

The hacking had been in the form of a prank, like stripper grams, but some of her brother's antics had to do with information gathering on what the Guardians were doing.

A year ago, when one of Alex's head hops led them to believe the victims were being sent to Tetartos, she, Vane and Erik had decided they needed to get the information to the Guardians. Tetartos was the one location they couldn't investigate without it being a one-way trip because of a confinement spell placed on the Realm of exiled Immortals.

Alex blew out a breath; she was nearly drained. Even the small amount of energy her brothers were infusing her with wasn't helping much.

A flash of anxiety ran through her, tensing her muscles and setting her nerves on edge. It was the telltale symptom that came with a *knowing*. She felt compulsion sweep over her, dilating her eyes.

They needed to find Sam. "We need to get to the female's apartment."

She looked up into her brother's fierce eyes and mentally relayed the location and apartment number Sam had given her.

Vane gave her a nod and paused before saying, "I'll get on the laptop now and see what I can find on her." He rubbed her back again before leaving the room, headed for their office. Hopefully, Conn would be able to decipher the details Alex had seen while inhabiting Sam's mind.

Erik studied her face. Concern was flickering in his pale blue eyes, and it tightened her chest. Taking another big breath, she said, "I wish I could go back to her. Get more information." Unfortunately, she had never been able to return after hopping into someone's mind.

As she got up and straightened the clothes she'd thrown on, she realized a Kermit T-shirt and yoga shorts were not a good look for breaking in to a human's apartment.

"I'm gonna go change. I'll meet you in the office. Vane will have the visuals we need by then. I'll see if I can feel anything with my psychometrics when we get there." It was a weaker skill, but she could sometimes get a vision off an object, which might come in handy at Sam's place. Unfortunately, in the other cases of missing females, their abductors hadn't left a trace. Either Alex's power hadn't worked with whoever was taking them, or they made sure never to touch anything that they didn't take with them when they left. The strong pull to get to Sam's had Alex hopeful that one of their skills would help track her and get her back.

Something would come from seeing the apartment. She wouldn't have a *knowing* if she weren't able to do something.

She rolled her shoulders as she headed through the living room, still not feeling quite like herself. She needed to shake off the effects of head-hopping fast.

Chapter 5

Guardian Compound, Earth Realm

"Why the fuck do I smell hellhound on this bastard?" Wisps of smoke came out with Drake's every word, emerald dragon eyes flashing with anger. The Guardian leader's longish blond hair moved at his clenched jaw and shoulders as he glared at him. Uri had known the seven-foot-tall Demi-God son of Aphrodite was going to be pissed off. Drake hated being kept in the dark about anything.

Uri stood just outside Tank Top's holding cell with Gregoire, Drake, and another brother, Jax. The possessed lay still on his small cot; a toilet and sink were the only other things in the tiny space. The possessed's eyes were open, but he wasn't moving. Uri couldn't help grinning at the fact that Tank Top's eyes were open, but he obviously still couldn't move. Hellhound venom packed quite the punch.

He finally answered, "Because I had a hellhound with me."

The room grew completely silent at that revelation.

Jax cocked a dark brow and smirked as he moved into the cell and poked Tank Top's leg with one boot. "I probably don't want to know the rest, but this I fucking like. The guy's totally down for the count." Jax, an Ailouros, or half feline Immortal of the tiger variety, was one of the most talkative of the Guardians. At the moment the big warrior was grinning like an idiot, his bright blue eyes glinting with amusement. The dark-haired male crossed his arms over a black tee with a chopper motorcycle printed on the front as he awaited more from Uri. They were all waiting for more.

War room. Now! Uri knew Drake's words echoed in all their minds, not just his. More plumes of smoke flowed around the dragon and filtered through Uri's lungs. The room in question was upstairs. They were in a lower level of the Guardians' stone compound built into the mountains in Idaho, Earth. The whole place had been fortified with metal, preventing anyone from directly teleporting in or out. The above floors housed fifteen suites for the Guardians' convenience. Drake didn't believe in overkill.

He didn't know many brethren that slept in the rooms there. He had his own place in Earth Realm, and there was an even bigger Guardian compound in Tetartos with even more suites if he needed to sleep there for some reason.

He ran a hand through the back of his hair as he walked. He'd stayed in the mortal Realm every damned night since the start of his obsession with a certain Goddess in Earth.

After filing up the staircase, they made it through two metal doors secured by voice scanners keyed only to the Guardians' vocals and entered the high-tech war room. It was well equipped, with computer stations surrounded by dark walls. Low lighting showcased digital screens displaying maps of locations they'd patrolled recently and areas showing more possessed activity.

Conn was already seated at the conference table, the Lykos warrior's body was clad in his usual flannel, sleeves rolled up, showing tattooed arms. The brown-haired half wolf leaned forward, clicking at his laptop, a black piercing glittered over one amber eye as he looked up curiously.

Once inside, Uri, Gregoire and Jax dropped into oversized office chairs surrounding the huge solid wood table they used for meetings. Drake continued to stand facing Uri.

"Speak! And it had better be damned good!"

"I was attacked by three possessed." Which was information he'd already shared. He was stalling. "I had to bail before I could get the syringe because I broke one of the bastards' wrists." He took a breath. "I appear to have been targeted for some reason, seeing as I was in an unpopulated area, not their usual locale." It didn't make sense. This was fucked-up news, the possessed had always seemed chaotic in their attacks before, but a syringe? That took planning.

Drake stood with his arms crossed over his chest, smoke still filtering from his lips. A sign that the dragon was not fucking happy. "Get to the part that has to do with hellhounds on Earth."

"Not multiple, one hellhound, and he's here because I brought him." Uri waited for it... His brothers just raised their eyebrows, Gregoire included.

"Are. You. Fucking. Kidding. Me? This better be your idea of a fucking joke." The contents of the room shook with the power of Drake's bellow, as Conn put his laptop screen down and moved it to the center of the table while telekinetically turning up the superpowered exhaust fans installed in every room. A necessity for any location Drake inhabited. The smoke billowing from Drake's scowling lips started filtering up through the vents overhead.

Drake was too silent and his green eyes were flashing as he waited, demanding an explanation.

"I saved the pup in Hell Realm a couple months ago. There was every chance I was going to have to kill him if he turned out to be evil. I planned to tell you before the meeting tomorrow." Uri dragged his hand through the back of his hair again, knowing it sounded crazy. That he sounded like he'd lost his mind. "The pup had just been born; his mother was dragon food and the beast almost took the pup as an after-dinner mint. He was newborn, untainted by Tria blood bond. Each day I thought he'd go bad, but he didn't." Uri then bit out the rest. "I blood-bonded with him to keep control of him when I was on shift." He was met with silence, so he stretched his legs out and continued, "The pup instinctually hunts those with tainted souls."

"Wanna tell me how you know that?" Drake growled. The tension in the air was thick.

"He needs to hunt." Uri breathed out. "I haven't let him kill anyone, and I don't suffer when he mildly injures a human." He'd wondered about that since they were blood-bonded, but the Creators curse hadn't extended from his blood to the animal. "Havoc somehow siphons off evil from the humans he hunts. My guess is he can metabolize the darkness without it draining into him. He seems to have no interest in those humans with neutral or pure auras."

Jax finally came out of his shock. "Shit, a Guardian with a hellhound for a pet. That's fucking hilarious."

"Shut the fuck up, Jax!" Drake bit out before he pinned Uri with a furious glare. "You brought a hell beast into the mortal Realm? Then you went out walking him?" Every word was spoken slowly. A challenge as Drake finished, "You have to be fucking with me, because if you're not, the mats are not big enough for the ass-kicking you will be getting for this."

Uri nodded. He deserved the ass-kicking. "I'm not kidding."

More smoke billowed. "When this is done, you and I are going to have a little time together. Are you sure the possessed didn't track the beast? And what the hell have you done about the fucking

humans seeing him?" Drake shook his head. "Fuck, I can't believe I
even have to have this conversation. You know better than this shit."

"I've altered the memories of any human that has seen him...
My guess is the possessed were after me. Havoc has no contact with
Hell Realm. There is no bond between the hound and the Tria. I'm
not sure if the demons could somehow be drawn to him..." He
looked to Sirena, who had silently entered as Drake was chewing his
ass.

His petite sister Guardian's eyes glittered with excitement mixed
with incredulity at what he'd done. Her pale blond retro-style
ponytail moved around one shoulder with her nod. "It's a possibility."

Uri continued, "The syringe, along with their initial focus,
seemed to be intent on me. The asshole was set to use it on Havoc,
but it seemed more as a last resort. The possessed haven't ever
seemed more than an irritating rash; I don't like that they seem
focused now."

"Neither do I," Drake ground out.

Uri leaned his chair back. "Havoc held his own trying to protect
my ass. He took down that piece of shit in holding, and he had
another down. If I hadn't been forced to get us out of there after
breaking one of the bastards' wrists, who knows? He's proven to be
an asset, and if he is drawing possessed, that could be a damned
good advantage. For once we might actually get the upper hand."
Looking to Jax and Gregoire, he added, "I don't suppose I was lucky
and the others dropped that syringe for you to recover? I'd like to
know what the hell was in it."

"I tracked them down the hill while Jax got princess down there
all cinched up and transported. Lost their scent at the wooded
parking area at the bottom. No syringe that I found... although it's

not a bad idea to go check again for evidence," Gregoire said in his usual monotone. Gregoire showed no outward sign he was pissed that Uri hadn't clued him in about his houseguest.

"So do I even ask what the fuck you were thinking to bring a fucking hellhound to this Realm?" Drake asked.

"I live here. He was under control. I wouldn't have let him do damage. Yeah, I screwed up. I'll own it. But I'll say it again, the hound proved damn useful tonight."

Drake appeared to process what Uri said, and probably what he hadn't.

They all sat silently before Conn spoke. "I, for one, would pay money to see the little bastard put the hurt on a possessed. After all the shit they've given us through the centuries, it'd be nice to cause them a little pain." His amber eyes glittered with anticipation.

"Hell yeahs," filled the room, mostly from an exuberant Jax.

"We *will* deal with your fuckup after you interrogate the asshole in holding and you bring the beast in." Drake was definitely not pleased as he added, "I will evaluate the animal myself, and Sirena will check him when I'm done." Drake looked at Sirena, who nodded. After a moment she was lost in thought, most likely calculating all the possibilities of having a hell beast that wasn't tainted with Tria blood. You could almost see her mind working behind those bright violet eyes.

Drake changed focus. "Jax, Gregoire, go back and look for that syringe again." Then Drake headed for the door, indicating they were done.

All grunted assent. As the others got up to leave, Gregoire moved to Uri. He waited.

59

Gregoire asked, "You said the pup's mother was killed by a dragon?"

He nodded.

As if Gregoire knew what he was thinking, he said, "We're good. It's not like I don't have my own secrets. You want some advice? Make sure you have a tight hold on the hound's bond when he meets Drake. The beast may remember the smell of dragon." His brother nodded as he headed in the opposite direction.

"Fuck." Uri growled, appreciating the warning. He rolled his shoulders, ready to go deal with Tank Top. He hated diving into the mind of a possessed, knowing that whatever he was about to see wasn't going to be good.

Chapter 6

New York, Earth Realm

Alex sat on the edge of Vane's desk in their shared office. His was always spotless, with the computer screen and keyboard both positioned perfectly on the polished wood surface.

Vane was clicking away at the keys as he shared, "I've added the California apartment building to the notes. I haven't found any correlations to any of the other victims, so far. She's not on any coven listing, but I'm betting that she's another elemental Mageia. That's the only thing the victims have had in common."

For centuries, the Guardians had required that each elemental Mageia coven maintain a list of their members and provide it to the Guardians. For the most part they were a peaceful group, but there had been times over the centuries that they'd caused problems when pooling their powers. Usually they created environmental issues.

Since the lists were already compiled, Vane just snuck into the Guardians' network and took the information they needed. Vane loved hacking a little too much, it was an advantage in their mercenary work, but he especially enjoyed tapping into anything that Conn, the Guardian tech, was working on. Conn caught him every time he broke the firewalls, and they rarely gained much information, but it was a game her brother loved to play. Before Conn barred his access the last time, Vane had managed to send over a virus that would play a creepy children's song any time Conn opened a new file. Her brother had laughed for days while planning his next virus.

"So far all I've got on Samantha Palmer is that she's an only child, moved to Orange County from Phoenix to attend UCI six years ago and never left. Works IT for a firm in Newport Beach, and according to the lease agreement, she lives alone. Her dad's an accountant; mom's a stay-at-home, still in Phoenix. None of them are on the coven listings."

"Vane and I can take care of this. Why don't you go recharge?" Erik's voice was rough and raspy.

She tried to smile. "No, I'm good. I'll go after." He looked at her for a second, and she felt him send her some more of his energy. He was smart enough to know that arguing with her was futile.

"A picture of the apartment complex is up on the screen. It should be about eight p.m. there, just getting dark," Vane pointed out.

She and Erik took a look at the photo and teleported right outside the complex. They were able to produce the illusion they weren't there before moving up the stairs. They found the apartment on the second floor. It was one with a view of the golf course.

Alex used her powers, touching the walls and door to see if she could get a feel for what happened when Sam was taken.

Nothing. She got flashes of a black hoodie and a syringe. Of Sam dropping the groceries and another picking them up. No faces, no feelings. It was all too fast.

"I'm not getting anything useful," she declared as Erik opened the lock, and they silently slipped in. Lock verses Immortal with telekinetic ability... Immortal wins. She saw Erik tense a little, but he moved on. She frowned, unsure what that was about.

Vane inhaled as he entered. "Another Mageia, unique, but I'd say earth elemental ability," he said as they followed Erik. Her brothers were powerful and could scent even the smallest differences in Mageia.

Alex looked around, not bothering to turn on any lights; there was enough illumination from the streetlights outside the open curtains.

It was a cozy apartment, with an open floor-plan, a decent-sized kitchen to the right, and a big snack bar open to the living area straight ahead. Candles were scattered everywhere and she smelled vanilla and pineapple.

She moved into the kitchen. There were pictures of laughing girls at a pool, with drinks featuring fun colored umbrellas. More images of a different group of girls were displayed in magnetized frames all over the fridge. Alex absently wished she had that, pictures of girlfriends out on the town, shopping, dancing... but to get close to a mortal was just asking to be hurt when they died.

Looking around, her chest constricted a little. Had she been missing out on living?

Shaking out of her morose thoughts, she really studied the snapshots. The one constant was a blonde female, taller than the others, with green eyes and a nice tan. There was a framed photo with a younger version of the blonde, this time with longer hair and braces, standing next to an older couple and a golden retriever, which confirmed for Alex that Sam was the blonde.

Alex might have shared the female's mind, but without a mirror, she'd had no clue what Sam looked like.

63

She glanced at Erik, who was acting strange, his shoulders painfully tense as he moved around. She looked to Vane, who just shook his head as if he wasn't sure what was going on either.

"Erik, is everything okay?" When he didn't respond to her and just moved into the other room, Vane followed.

The hair on the back of her neck tingled and she rubbed the sensation away. She was confident Vane would find out what was wrong, so she moved into the living area.

She noted how it always felt weird being in the personal space of one of the victims, an intrusion. Alex felt Sam there. Just like the other victims, there was something left inside the home, maybe it was the elemental Mageia power signature her brothers scented.

The urgency in her mind told her they didn't have much time. They needed to find Sam. She couldn't let her suffer with Cyril and Elizabeth; the thought clenched her stomach.

A roar shook the entire building and sent a rush of panic through her as she rushed to the bedroom.

"Shit, Erik, what the fuck?" Vane yelled before he slammed their brother up against the doorway leading into what had to be the bedroom. Wood and plaster cracked with the move, and some rained from above. She hoped the neighbors weren't home to hear the commotion, but she doubted they were that lucky.

Erik was vibrating against the hold, panting, his chest rising and falling so hard that if he'd been human, she'd have been concerned he was having a heart attack. Her heart was racing when he spoke one word. "Scent..."

Erik barely growled the one word that was the last semi-coherent thing they'd get from him. His eyes went cat, and she and

Vane moved at once, teleporting Erik back to the balcony of their home, where Vane carried him to the couch.

Worriedly glancing at Vane, she asked, "Did you smell anything there? Are you feeling okay?"

"I'm good."

"What exactly happened?" she demanded.

Vane seemed fine, maybe shaken under his fierce scowl. "I'm not affected by anything. I'll go back and see if I detect anything. I went in right after him. He looked kind of out of it, headed to the bed, and lifted the pillow to his nose before he started convulsing. I barely restrained him against the damned doorway." Vane made a move to leave while she sat with a snarling, panting Erik.

"No!" she demanded. "You stay out here with him. Let me go in and see if I can pick anything up. I don't have either of your sensitivities to scent. I don't want you exposed."

"Fuck no!" He ran a hand through his long blonde hair and blew out a breath, obviously realizing how ridiculous he was acting. "Fine, go and check it out. I feel fine, but you're right about me having the same sensitivities as Erik. Do not smell the pillow! Maybe use your psychometrics on it." Her ability to gain knowledge from objects was generally only useful if the item she touched was something left behind by a kidnapper or something to that effect. Sam was taken from outside just like the other victims, so her pillow was unlikely to hold clues, but she'd try.

Alex was out the door and reappearing in Sam's apartment a second later. She heard commotion outside. Shit. She needed to be fast. She didn't doubt someone had called the cops to report the roar of a wild animal and the sound of crashing walls.

The master bedroom had a four-poster bed in oak, with a dresser and end tables to match. The bed was mostly made, except where Erik had taken the pillow out, crushing it before apparently dropping it to the bed.

Alex grabbed the pillow, feeling with her mind for a reading. Pictures of Sam tossing and turning, sleeping, nothing out of the ordinary for a pillow; there was no sight of anyone other than Sam having used it.

Quickly, she teleported into the kitchen, grabbed a garbage bag and found some duct tape in a junk drawer. Back in the room, she bagged the pillow and teleported it to her private cave in case it was some kind of clue, though for some reason she doubted it. Something about that just didn't feel right, but better to be safe.

Her heart beat nearly out of her chest as she headed back home.

Something very dangerous was happening. She felt it in her bones.

Chapter 7

Guardian Compound, Earth Realm

Uri stood before Drake, barely keeping a mental hold on Havoc. He owed Gregoire for the warning about Havoc remembering dragon scent. Even in Uri's energy-weakened state, he'd managed to keep the animal from attacking Drake as they stepped into the dragon's office.

"You controlled him, and I don't feel evil from the bastard, but I'm still not fucking happy," Drake ground out.

His massive leader eyed the beast with flashing emerald eyes. The seven-foot-tall dragon son of Aphrodite was still fuming as he said, "I still can't fucking believe you brought a hellhound into the human Realm... And you will have your ass-kicking as soon as you've rested up. You look like shit." Drake pinched the bridge of his nose. "He's your responsibility. Make sure he's not a fucking menace. Now, what'd you get from the prisoner?"

Uri rolled his neck. Memory extraction on asshole possessed always made Uri sick, if not the memories themselves, then the tainted taste of their blood. He wished there was a better option, but if he used touch, the asshole demons fought off the mental invasion to the point of nearly destroying their human host's mind. It was in no way worth the mountainous headache he'd get. So blood memories it was, no matter how much he hated it.

Being the only Aletheia within the Guardian ranks sucked at

times like these. No fucked-up pun intended.

At least the Guardian curse was only for pain, not discomfort. They were safe with paper cuts, injections, smacks to the back of the head… and the quick strike of fangs to a wrist.

"Nothing useful. I couldn't find anything in his memories about seeing the syringe. He'd just joined the others about an hour before coming to find me. Eyebrow Ring seemed to know where to go, but no one told Tank Top anything." Tank Top had only been possessed a day or so ago, but his memories were sick as shit. The human was just as bad as the demon. The images of what the bastard liked to do to kids nearly made Uri lose the contents of his stomach. Then the rage hit until he was nearly vibrating with it. He'd come close to killing the bastard and dealing with the consequences.

Exhaustion was setting in as he added, "I let Havoc feed from him… the piece of shit is dead, which was more than deserved. But someone will need to do cleanup in holding, and I'm too damn tired to deal with it."

"Fine. Take that hound to Sirena for her to check him out before you go."

Uri didn't need to be told twice. He quickly turned and commanded the animal out into the hallway.

He rubbed the back of his neck and looked down at Havoc. The pup was sniffing under every door they passed, tail held high.

His mouth quirked as he remembered Tank Top's screams when Uri had brought in Havoc and let the beast have at him.

The agonized screams of the possessed and the demon both, though piercing, had been sweet music to Uri's soul. Then, too soon, the possessed died and the demon's essence was released back to

Hell.

As wound up and energized as Havoc was after he'd fed, Uri was amazed he'd been able to keep a mental hold on him in Drake's office.

After going into battle together, added with what happened in holding, Havoc had cemented himself in Uri's life. The animal was under his protection now.

Uri and Havoc finally made it to Sirena's wing, and at his knock came a melodic, "Enter."

Sirena's office housed too much monster movie memorabilia for any one space; the black furniture and shelves were covered in slasher movie masks, like the Freddie Krueger with claws showcased in glass.

"One second, I just have to finish this." She was frantically clicking at the keyboard and didn't even glance up as he entered with Havoc at his heels.

"I just want to get the last notes on my research." She favored a very fifties appearance nowadays, sometimes innocent, other times not. Today she wore horn-rimmed glasses, even though her sight was perfect. They suited her delicate features and bright violet eyes, and brought to mind sexy librarian thoughts.

As beautiful as the three female Guardians were, he couldn't help but think of them as siblings. They had all been through too much, seen too much together, most having lived through Apollo's breeding labs. Back then they'd acted more like the animals they had been treated like for so long.

All their bonds had solidified after becoming Guardians. Their telepathic links alone made them a family of sorts. Those links and their shared duties bound them closer than any blood.

But some scars of the past ran deeper than others.

Sirena might be lethal, as much a warrior as the rest of them, but her ability to find mates and do all the science/doctor crap proved the most beneficial to the Immortal races as a whole. Her calling gave her a stronger purpose, but that meant she worked nearly as much as Drake.

She was born of a rare Siren mother, and her abilities with a body's cells, being able to morph them, made her brutal in combat. It also made her incomparable in detecting the DNA markers of elemental Mageia to see which ones were potentially compatible mates for an Immortal.

For centuries she'd been luring Mageias from Earth to Tetartos. Going to that Realm was a one-way ticket for any being except a Guardian, which meant Tetartos now had fairly large covens, some with centuries-old family lines.

Finally, the frantic typing stopped. He slowly rotated his neck. Damn, he was beat.

"Is this Havoc? Oh, what a beautiful little boy you are." She looked over the desk, with glittering violet eyes framed by golden brows. Her cooing had Uri shaking his head. She could apparently use that Siren's voice to sway any being, and it looked like hellhounds weren't immune.

Havoc wagged his bobtail along with most of his back end, and his ears lowered back as he wiggled toward Sirena. She came out from behind the desk, and he began rubbing his whole body against her leg.

He'd never seen the animal act like this. It was honestly...

70

fucking embarrassing. She kept speaking to Havoc in the same tone. It was ridiculous. She was making his hellhound a total pussy. It was obvious the beast would be thrilled to be with Sirena while he recharged.

He was too damned depleted. He sent the animal thoughts that he'd be leaving, but would be back.

Behave, he sent through their bond before watching Havoc cock his head before turning back to nudge Sirena's hand so that she would pet him.

He pinched the bridge of his nose.

"I've got to recharge and hit the house for a damned shower. Drake said you'd want to do tests on Havoc. Just call if you need me."

"We'll be fine. I'll lull him to sleep for some of the more invasive tests. I can't wait! He's amazing… and you're right. I don't get any evil from him," she said, practically beaming with excitement.

Uri sighed at her exuberance and then hauled his exhausted ass out of there. As he headed down the hall, the hair on his neck prickled.

Gods, he hoped he could at least get refueled before whatever was coming next.

Chapter 8

New York, Earth Realm

"What else can we do?" Alex asked, her heart thumping.

"Fuck, I don't know." Vane was running his hands through his hair as he looked down at his twin. They'd just brought him back from the family cavern and put him in his bed. "It's like he's trapped inside his own mind." Trying to communicate telepathically hadn't gotten through. He just stared straight ahead, growling and breathing heavily. He looked furious. And pained.

It was too much.

Alex began running scenarios in her head as she paced on the thick black rug in front of Erik's carved wood bed. They'd been home for mere moments, but it felt like an eternity. Nothing was helping.

"Taking him away from the apartment didn't help. Taking him to the family cavern did nothing. We've sent him personal energy that he's sucking down as quickly as we send it," she ground out in frustration.

She felt helplessness close in around her, and she knew Vane felt the same. Neither knew what this was doing to Erik, physically or mentally.

She and Vane had both hit him with the minor healing energies they had; nothing changed. They couldn't find anything wrong with him physically. They just didn't know where the energies were going. The fact that neither of them had seen anything like this was truly freaking her out. Never again would she take her self-healing for granted. Centuries of watching the worst of her injuries heal before her eyes as the norm, then seeing this, had her feeling way too human for her liking.

She continued pacing, likely the rug would have a permanent wear pattern when she was through.

"We need to take him back to the cavern again. At least there we could refuel as we force energies into him," Vane said as he paced the side of the bed. She went to the other side and put a hand to Erik's stubbled cheek. He was warm, but she wasn't sure if he was really any more warm than normal, since his lion DNA had a tendency to make him run on the hot side.

"I agree. We should have just stayed there. I'd just hoped that being home might change something. I know I was grasping, but I'm freaking out." She breathed.

Vane nodded. "Once we get him settled, I'm going to Conn. We need to get Erik to the Guardians' healer."

She stilled; she couldn't let him do that. The Guardians would be bound to exile her brother and ask questions later. He had a good life here, his motorcycles, the females, the feeling she'd always had that they were needed to do something more to help in the human Realm. She'd rather risk herself than her brother to exile. She might have an advantage he wouldn't.

Uri's attraction to her.

"Let's wait another few hours. Let's get him to the cavern now and make sure we're both refueled first. Maybe put him in the hot springs and see if that will do something," Alex said.

73

He didn't look sure, but said okay anyway.

"Go, I'm going to change and meet you there. I'll be fast." She didn't wait for an answer, just turned toward her rooms like everything was normal.

Vane nodded as he picked up his twin. Worry was marring his handsome face and he was just distracted enough not to question her. "I'll get him in the spring."

Was she really going to Uri? This was crazy.

This would be her first time actually speaking to him. The thought shouldn't make her stomach pitch; her brother needed this, not her.

Would Uri's attraction to her be enough to keep him off balance and give her the upper hand? She had to chance it. A part of her felt far too excited.

Alex shook her head, arriving at the door to her rooms. She guessed she could only hope that Uri would want to take her, carry her off to do dirty things to her as payment for helping her brother. As long as he helped her brother first. The idea of trading her body for her brother's health held too much appeal.

She made it to her closet and in a blink of the eye changed into something sexier. She'd need all the advantage she could get at this point; any moment's hesitation in deporting her might be all that was needed.

Low-cut tank in black, with a slit in the already low collar showing even more cleavage. Perfect. She put on the sexiest black lace bra and thong she owned under it and a sleek pair of low-rise jeans that had more stretch than most, in case she needed to fight. She topped the outfit off with four-inch, black, knee-high boots.

Louboutin, her newest favorites.

Her hair was staying up in the pony she'd put it in for investigating at Sam's. She only took an extra second for gloss and mascara; she couldn't justify any more time. Practically running, she made it out to her personal patio and teleported to Uri's home in Seattle. She'd stalked him enough through the centuries to know exactly where he lived, and she fully realized how creepy that made her, but at the moment her stalkerish behavior was serving a good purpose.

She peered up at the second-story windows of a beautiful old home with a huge lawn. The smell of salt water cleared her head some. The fragrance of damp ground and moss soothed her, but her heart still felt like it would come out of her chest at any moment. Massive old oaks and pines kept the house hidden from the street and she knew them all well. She hated to admit to having been up on the strong branches more times than she wanted to think about.

Her cheeks flushed with the thought. Please let him be there.

She looked down at her sexy boots, hoping to use the confidence they usually inspired. She had to keep her head while hoping he lost his. It was a tall order. The thought of her brother strengthened her resolve. She didn't have time for nerves. Vane would question her whereabouts soon enough.

Straightening her already straight clothing, she took a deep breath. She quickly teleported under one of the huge trees in the backyard. The large lawn stretched out in all directions with a beautiful Roman fountain not far from her hiding spot. A trio of nude females were bathed from above; liquid covered silken curves of marble to pool at their feet. Her breath caught every time she looked at the perfection of the carved figures.

Alex swore she felt him there; she looked at the dim lighting in the upstairs rooms, candlelight... it was what he always used. She wasn't sure if he was alone. She really hoped so.

She'd never seen a female in his home. He seemed to favor using the clubs for his needs. The only entity she had seen in his home was a hellhound. The beast had been living there for the last couple of months, but for the life of her she had no idea why.

Maybe the beasts assisted the Guardians somehow?

Should she look in the windows from the trees? No, better not risk her boots... They were the only confidence builder she had at the moment, and if she scuffed them, she'd be pissed.

Human males always seemed to find her pleasing to ogle. They weren't the sexy Guardian though and it would totally bite if he deported her on sight. That could definitely knock a girl down a peg or ten.

Taking another deep breath, she looked around.

Her mental skills were nothing compared to Vane's, but from this distance she shouldn't have trouble reaching him. Alex sent her telepathic thoughts out... and then she felt Uri's mind. It was a bright, solid stream of power in her mind's eye. One shaking hand at her stomach, she attempted to will away her nerves.

Uri, I need your help.

Chapter 9

Cyril's Compound, Tetartos Realm

Sam had just started coming around again only to be faced with more tests and yet another injection.

They never allowed her to gain enough lucidity to get free of the damned metal cuffs, and even if she was able, she was sure they'd be on her in a second. She fought the feeling of helplessness. Beat it back, unwilling to let it take her down. She would not end up like the others, mere shells laid out on cold metal tables with dead eyes.

She would bide her time and refused to think of what more she would have to endure before an opportunity to escape presented itself. Could she bear any more? She would have to if she wanted to escape and kill the head guy. She'd started to refer to him as the Nazi Fuck. If it was the last thing she did, she would find a way to take him out along with Rabid Bitch, the redhead that liked to flash fang every time she saw her. Sam didn't care how superior their strengths were, she would find a way out of there.

She couldn't figure out their end game. Why the experiments? What were they testing… creating? The only thing she could come up with was it had something to do with reproduction, which churned her stomach into knots.

He'd injected them all with something. Looking to her left, the other woman oozed defeat, rarely calling out in anguish when the tests turned painful, and some seemed to be agonizing. She'd seen the "doctors" break bones or cut into skin, then type away at keyboards. She'd heard tight groans but rarely any screams. The young blonde on the table not too far from hers was going through that treatment while Sam watched, unable to do anything for the woman. Sam couldn't tell how old the girl was, not from her vantage point, strapped flat to a metal gurney like the rest of them.

Sam knew that was her fate, soon... if she didn't focus on escaping. There was no way of knowing how long the other captives had been here. They were all drugged and kept away from each other. One time Sam had awoken, tried to get up, fallen from her cot, and crawled to the bars. She had desperately tried to talk to the other prisoners to find out what they knew. She'd attempted calling to the cell on the diagonal from hers only to be greeted by stark silence. Moments later, a guard had come, hauled her ass back to the cot, and injected her again.

Sam had been moved between this metal examination area and her small metal cell for who knew how long... days... She focused on the details of the room even though it was like looking through a fog. Her mind fixated on anything she gazed at too long. Damn drugs. She struggled to turn her neck to study the others and their tormentors, attempting to take in any detail she could. She searched for anything that would aid her when she escaped, but nothing seemed useful.

The power she had with metal only worked if she could focus, an ability she'd grown up hiding at her parents urging. They'd convinced her she was to never show the talent or she'd be taken from them. Though her skills were paltry in comparison to the powers of her abductors, she'd use them to the best of her ability if she could just get the drugs out of her system.

She closed her eyes, willing herself to focus more closely. She would not give up. Something had to be useful. She'd been in and out of consciousness several times. The stench of chemicals wasn't as pronounced as it once was. The thought that she was getting used to it scared her.

Sam did her best to withhold a reaction as Nazi Fuck put one overly warm hand on her abdomen. She tried to appear undisturbed, but his touch felt like acid on her skin. She loathed him so much. The things he'd done to her along with the things he'd ordered... Her jaw clenched so tight she thought it might break but didn't utter a sound.

Never had she felt such hatred for anyone in her life. The desire to kill the bastard was a sickness eating away at her from the inside. She was sure her body shook with the need to do him harm. As much as she tried to hold back her reaction, she had to remind herself not to attempt anything rash. She was weakened by the drugs, had no weapon, and was outnumbered even if she did break free. She had to endure, for now.

Attempting to move into her mind, she focused on the shine reflecting off the metal ceiling, swallowing to keep the bile at bay. The clicking as he typed on a laptop sitting high on a rolling rack beside him seemed more like nails on a chalkboard in the relative quiet of the room. The Nazi rarely spoke. None of them did.

Only once had she felt that feminine presence in her head, prompting her for answers. She could only hope that in this crazy world that voice was someone, or something, that really wanted to help her. Not some mind game coming from the evil bastards surrounding her.

She forced herself deeper inside her own mind... her only sanctuary. Willing the voice to come to her again, to give her hope that she wasn't alone, that someone other than her parents was looking for her, trying to help her. Even if her coworkers or friends filed a missing persons report, what could the police do about vampires? It was all so unreal.

She was forced back to her present situation on the metal table by the feeling of warmth making its way through her veins. They'd dosed her again. She forced herself to fight the effects. Maybe with practice she could learn to combat the drugs. As a haze entered her sight and her tense muscles started to relax against her will, she remembered what happened the third time she regained consciousness. It was something she'd rather forget, but her mind kept replaying the memories... She'd felt the true reality of her nightmare in those moments.

She woke to Nazi Fuck and Vampire Bitch staring down at her.

She was laid out naked on a metal table in a cold, sterile, metal room. It was a kind of sick taunt that metal was the one thing she had power over, but with the drugs and her roiling emotions, she couldn't focus that power. This room was smaller than the previous one, where several women had been laid out and attached to machines.

She realized in her haze that she was positioned differently than before. Instead of being flat like the other times she'd awoken, her legs were in stirrups, her ankles attached securely with straps. She tried to move and free herself, but her body was weak, and she was too drugged to do anything.

The anxiety of her situation beat at her. She was open and vulnerable, and sweat started beading on her skin. The drugs kept her in a semiconscious state, feeling like every movement was made through water, every noise distorted. All she saw, through the drugged fog of her mind, were wide shoulders, piercing eyes and dark, severely short hair.

She wanted to plead for help, but crazed monsters of myth weren't likely to help her. The look in their eyes made that point more than all the horror movies she'd ever seen.

Still, she wanted to know why they were doing this, or maybe she just hoped to delay her fate. "What do you want with me?" Her voice sounded garbled in her own ears.

The Nazi cocked his head to the right and turned toward Vamp Bitch, completely ignoring her.

"DNA tests all confirm the gene is there. Have the males fill her with semen to start the process. I have work to do in the labs. Do not do any damage until her body is able to regenerate." Nothing he said made sense to her, other than to freak her the fuck out. "Males?" As in plural? "Semen?" And after he'd issued those orders to the Bitch, he hadn't even bothered to spare her a glance, just exited through a sliding door.

Her breathing escalated.

The two huge men she'd seen upon arriving came through the door. They seemed different this time. One had slightly long almost white hair, while the other was darker. Both had pale silver eyes that appeared glazed and held a hint of hatred directed in the redhead's direction. Were they drugged as well? They seemed to be breathing as hard as she was.

It was like a movie or a nightmare... All she could think was that they were going to rape her and she couldn't do anything about it. Why? To impregnate her? That thought only accelerated her breathing more.

The men pulled off their clothing and one bent as if to kiss her neck or maybe bite her, because she saw fang and attempted to flinch away. She fought against the restraints when the Rabid Bitch stopped him. "No venom." Sam had no clue what that meant, but it seemed to agitate the dark-haired male. They were both breathing hard, but the dark-haired one actually growled at the Vamp Bitch,

81

which only made the crazy woman laugh.

"No pleasure for her," Vamp Bitch sneered.

The angry glare the dark-haired guy sent the Vamp's way wasn't lost in Sam's drugged stupor. Not that his obvious derision for the bitch mattered.

It hadn't saved her from her fate.

She tried to fight the memories, looking up into the light above her head. The nightmare kept repeating over and again in her mind as the drug worked to pull her into oblivion. They'd taken her in every way possible while the bitch had taunted her. While the redhead had done things to them that the men hadn't liked.

Just as she'd done things to Sam that made her want to vomit.

She was spinning.

The bitch had threatened them, told the men to make it painful, but something had been wrong.

She hated herself and clenched her eyes shut at the memory of her body betraying her during that nightmare. They'd done something to her, because it hadn't hurt, it had somehow felt good, and that reaction made her stomach pitch.

She swore that one of the men... beings, had talked in her head. She'd either gone insane or he'd been telling her not to let the Vamp bitch win, coaching her through every second of her violation. She shook her head as angry tears spilled from her eyes. She'd actually done as the male voice instructed like some weak woman.

She closed her eyes tight and felt blessed blackness start to take her under.

Her last thought was of how slowly she wanted to kill that Vamp bitch, because her sick laughter would fill Sam's nightmares forever if she didn't.

*****

Cyril hated working with idiots. He and Elizabeth had left the labs, and now the sadistic bitch was communicating mentally with her contact in Hell Realm. It seemed the Tria's demon-possessed had been able to track the Guardian, Urian, as promised, but hadn't injected the bastard with the serum he'd created. This was what he got for working with demons. Complete incompetence.

Elizabeth spoke out loud. "Do you have anything else you want from them? I told them to continue the search and add more possessed. This time use stealth, though I'm not sure that they have the higher brain function to pull that off. The jackoffs only sent three. That would have been nothing considering Urian's ability to teleport..." Her eyes glittered, probably anticipating the punishment she'd be allowed to dole out to those idiots. They would need to feel the force of his annoyance, and she knew it.

Elizabeth averted her attention to the broken female lying at their feet while she awaited his response. The female twitched under the boot Elizabeth poked her with. The blonde had been intended as payment for the job the demons failed to complete.

He clenched his fists at his sides. "No, I've changed my mind. They've lost any hint of surprise they had, and I don't want my serum to get in the hands of the Guardians. There will be no payment, and I expect them to return the vial." He detested having his time wasted. "And, Elizabeth, make sure the Tria understand my disappointment." His voice came out just as menacing as he'd hoped, and he watched her eyes light with sadistic expectation. Elizabeth truly loved making others' lives painful. He'd leave her to her work.

83

He exited the teleport area of his compound. He had few sections designated for secreting in and out of the mountain. Those were monitored constantly, and he was confident that the metal-laced walls in the rest of the compound would prevent anyone teleporting directly inside. He saw his contorted form in the sheen of the door as he moved through and worked his way down the long dark tunnel back to his lab. He'd go through his files on the test subjects and set aside his plans for the Guardians for later. The only reason he'd attempted to capture Urian at this point was the Tria's insistence they could track him.

He heard screams coming from the room he just vacated and shook his head at Elizabeth's behavior. It didn't matter that she tortured the Mageia female. The mortal was only useful as payment to the Tria; the blonde's mind had been ruined long ago. He just hoped Elizabeth showed some intelligence by not killing her. To use her as payment they could only kill her at the time they planned to send her soul to Hell. Elizabeth knew he did not enjoy wasting resources.

Elizabeth was born in the breeding labs, like himself. Only he was born to a God while she was born of two first-generation Aletheia. Yet, somehow, she had acquired exceptional mental capabilities, one being her rare ability to contact those in other Realms. A power he'd been unable to duplicate or find within another. There were no other options but to keep her if he wanted to continue to work with the other Realms.

The problem was that Elizabeth was becoming increasingly unstable. He exhaled deeply. Maybe if he found her a keeper? He'd need to think on it. At the moment he was more interested in his latest test subject. Something about the female niggled at the back of his mind. Was she the key he'd been searching for?

Chapter 10

Seattle, Earth Realm

"What are you doing here?" The deep sexy growl to Uri's voice made things tighten low in her body. Alex closed her eyes at the sensual vibration of it before realizing it was coming to her through the cool breeze instead of inside her mind.

Opening her eyes, she saw that he was mere feet from her. Oh, Gods, he was even more edible up close. She felt the heat coming off his body in waves, licking along her skin. Her heart beat recklessly faster. All six feet eight inches of pure muscled, half-naked Uri stood almost within touching distance, arms crossed and scowling. His near shoulder-length, dark hair was wet and glistening under the night sky. It was mussed like he'd just rubbed a towel over it. The smell of his shampoo was a faint hint in the background of his own seductive scent. Enough to bring visions of him in his upstairs shower, lathering up all that glorious skin. What she wouldn't give to have been with him, soaping every hot inch of his rigidly muscled torso until she was kneeling in front of that big cock. Mesmerizing eyes of liquid silver swirled... hypnotizing her under tightly furled dark brows.

Her breath left in a tight groan she didn't have time to suppress. What was wrong with her? She felt like she was caught in a spell; it lulled her mind and heated her body. Her nipples were hard as she caught the slight tilt to his mouth and the tensing of his wide shoulders.

He had such perfect kissable lips, the bottom slightly fuller, just begging her to suck and nibble on it. Thick taut thighs were encased in loose-fitting dark exercise pants hanging dangerously low, while the pure mass of his chest and the delectable vee of muscle near his hips was exposed to her gaze. Bronzed skin gleamed with moisture in the dark, and she wanted nothing more than to lick every drop as it traveled the dips and valleys en route to the low-hanging fabric at his waist. Her eyes traveled over his eight-pack before hitting the soft material that did nothing to hide his hard cock.

She clenched her thighs as her own desire had her wet and aching. Her chest began heaving as she fought the need to move toward him.

That jolted her. She needed to get it together. She took a deep calming breath and then nearly moaned again. What was it that he smelled of? It was so much more than clean male. It was like aged port, sweet and decadent, so tempting she wanted to cover herself in it. Bathe in it. There had to be something in his chemical makeup meant to attract, because no other male had ever smelled so tantalizing.

"Keep eating me up with those eyes, little Goddess, and I'll be so deep inside that hot little pussy you won't remember what you came here for." His voice was a deep raspy growl, making her even hotter. His voice dipped lower, and she swore he stalked closer. "Unless that was what you need my help for."

She felt her body start to pitch forward as if under someone else's control and that was when guilt assailed her.

She mentally smacked herself while licking her dry lips, and heard a soft groan. Her eyes almost closed as she tried hard not to breathe in that scent, "No, I need your help." Gods, what she wouldn't give for him to do as he said, but she had to help her brother. Clearing her throat, she added, "I need your help... first." She wanted to sound sultry and she had no trouble with all the desire flooding her body.

He sucked in a breath and brought his arms to his sides. His hands flexed as he bit off a curse before gritting out, "I got that the first time. Get to the part of why the hell you're coming to me and what you think I need to help you with. Especially since you know I should be exiling your hot little ass on sight... but trust me, it won't be before I give us both what we need. What we've been dancing around for the last century."

Was it her imagination, or was his chest rising and falling as hard as hers?

Think, Alex, think. She bit the inside of her cheek to focus. "Before I tell you, I want a blood oath from you that my brothers and I will not be sent to Tetartos. You know as well as I do that you need our help with the possessed." She took a deep breath only to get assailed with that amazing dessert wine scent again. Damn him, the male was getting inside all her senses. Her nipples were so tight they were no doubt showing through her bra and tank.

There were many reasons she had for coming to Uri, all logical, not hormonal... One was that he was the only Aletheia Guardian, so he was the only candidate for a blood oath. Something she doubted he would do, but it was worth a shot. If he consented, she and her brothers would be safe from exile. There was true power in Aletheia blood, in addition to their other fluids. Ugh, she couldn't think of the other fluids. Her mind didn't need any images to go with the Intel they had gathered years ago.

He moved closer, his fists still flexing at his sides as if he were trying not to grab her. His muscles were pulled so tight they had to hurt. He ran a hand through the back of his hair, clearly agitated. "Sorry, sweetheart, but I don't do blood oaths. If you'd like to get to the request for help, you may want to get there fast. I find I'm losing patience... I plan to bury every inch of my cock inside all the slickness. You changed the rules, Goddess." The growled-out words only made her hotter. She swallowed hard while he finished his litany. "Now you'll pay the price. There won't be an inch of your flesh I haven't taken after this night is through." His eyes scorched her skin as he took in her body, slowly, from her head to the very tips of her boots. She felt as if his lips were grazing her body while his eyes cataloged every curve.

Should she just tell him what she needed? He looked ready to pounce, and Gods, she couldn't wait, but Erik needed help first. Alex hadn't gotten a word out before he moved. She just barely teleported out of his reach. Standing in front of him again, her heart pounding, she arched a brow. "Were you that eager to exile me, or was there something else you were after?"

Another growl issued as they teleported over and over, just barely missing each other in a seductive dance until her boot heel clipped a tree root protruding from the ground. All it had taken was a moment of lost concentration and he had her, taking her to the ground beneath his heated skin.

It was like being sucked into a dream. Her body went soft and her mind hazed and she vaguely realized something wasn't normal. She felt drugged and the low growl he issued only sucked her deeper into whatever this was.

He nuzzled her neck. "Fuck, you feel and smell even better than I imagined."

She nearly moaned at his words and admitted she could have *subconsciously* let him catch her, and now she couldn't move if she wanted to. Not with her body melting into his warmth. She didn't care that the ground was damp and soaking into her clothes. His body was cradled against hers in just the right spot. She moaned and writhed a little more against him, loving the friction. She couldn't stop herself from reaching up to lave her tongue over the pulse hovering tauntingly above. How was it possible for another being to taste so good, so incredibly addictive?

He growled and used a firm pull at the nape of her neck, bringing her lips up to his, taking possessive control of her mouth. He ripped the tie from her hair, and his fingers tunneled in, giving the long strands a soft yank that sent tingles down her spine. His hips thrust against her as his tongue tangled with hers. He destroyed every remaining thought as he tasted the inside of her mouth, taking her with his tongue like she needed him to do so much lower.

She was dizzy, disoriented and so wet. All she could do was submit to the demands of his mouth and roving hands. She arched beneath him, needing more than just pressure from the hard cock settled against her clit.

Panting, she ran her hands along the hard muscles of his back. She felt them twitch under her palms as she rubbed up and then down under the stretchy band of his workout pants to grab his perfect ass.

He growled low in his throat before shifting to palm an aching breast. His mouth trailed behind her ear. A firm pinch on her tightened nipple caused her to gasp into his mouth. She rubbed harder against him, too many sensations swamped her, and she still wanted more... needed the feel of his skin against hers. She pulled him in tighter, circling her hips uncontrollably as he toyed with her.

I knew you'd taste sweet. Put your arms over your head. Offer your breasts to my mouth. He growled in her mind since his mouth was busy against her sensitive neck. She cried out; she could barely breathe as he tortured her body, leaving goose bumps along her skin.

She ached to do as he commanded, but she couldn't make herself move her hands from his warm flesh.

Her body felt as if it were floating, yet tense at the same time. He nipped hard at her collarbone while pinching her nipple. "Now." Liquid flowed from her; she knew her panties were soaked and was sure her jeans were next. The thought that she was so close to orgasm brought her back to reality.

At least enough to flip him onto his back as she stared down, panting. His eyes glittered below her, just as lost to arousal as she was, pushing his hips into hers. She followed his movements as she tried to get her fuzzy brain to focus through gasping breaths.

His focus trained on her breasts, and then he flipped her beneath him again, her hands secured above her head with one of his. She noticed his fangs had descended, something she'd never seen before, and the sight stilled her, made her hotter somehow. She shook her head to try to clear it. His kind took blood for memories. Did he want hers? When she would have pulled away at the thought, he lifted her tank with his other hand, pushing her bra up with it. With a hard warning look, he demanded, "Don't move them."

Lucid thought was impossible as he rose above her, pushing her aching flesh together, and thrummed their tight tips with his thumbs. He moved down, his big body pushing hers into the grass as he took each nipple in his mouth. He sucked so hard her back bowed, and she bit her lip. She kept her hands over her head, but she was dying to tunnel her fingers in his hair. Biting forgotten, Alex felt her body melt as her head fell back on her shoulders. A soft tongue swirled against her other tight bud before he latched on to suck her almost to completion. She moaned and wiggled, getting increasingly desperate to take his cock all the way inside her body.

There was something she needed to do, but her mind had

stalled. Her body was in charge and had given itself to Uri. Oh, Gods, too good... The scorching heat of his breath left a searing sensation down her already overheated skin.

Can't focus, you smell so good. I'm going to lick all the way inside your hot little cunt until you're clenching around my tongue. Then I'll flip you onto your stomach and take you so deep and hard you'll scream and beg for more. He practically growled the words inside her mind so his mouth could continue tormenting her swollen flesh. The words alone almost set off an orgasm. All that existed in the moment was his mouth and hands tormenting her. The damp earth scent was drowned out by the pheromones he was throwing off.

He began unzipping her jeans, dipping his fingers underneath them. She was holding her breath. Waiting. He nibbled on a nipple and then sucked hard as the back of his fingers grazed her clit. She cried out, "Don't stop. So good." Her brain was fuzzy. It felt like she'd been drugged, she knew she needed to stop, but she couldn't. This was pleasure unlike anything she'd ever been able to simulate on her own. She wanted more. Wanted it all. Her moans grew louder, and she frantically pushed her body against his erection. She had to stop or warn him or something. Oh, but the feel, it was impossible to get words to form. She needed more...

"Holy fuck, man," came from their left.

Uri reared up with an animalistic snarl, pulling her up behind him, hard. She was dazed. Only coherent enough to get her top and bra in order and her pants half zipped.

Alex glanced up from fixing her clothing to the view of the warm sexy male back flexing in front of her and was immediately assailed with the need to rub up against it. Not caring if they had an audience, her awareness ended with the knowledge it wasn't the enemy, only his Guardian brothers. Those strong muscular triceps tensed in front of her, making her mouth salivate. The desire to lick him like an ice cream cone was uncontrollable. She started low in the center of his spine and moved her way to right between his shoulder blades. His muscles twitched beneath her touch as he let out a deep half growl, half groan.

In the back of her mind, she registered something wasn't right. She should be on guard. She was acting nothing like she normally would, but she couldn't seem to stop herself from curling her body against his, feeling the hot skin against her cheek. He pulled her closer with one hand, reaching to hold her by her butt. All the while he snarled at the male in front of him. Mmm, the snarling growls vibrated against her body, so good. *Need more*, she thought as she circled his waist with her hands, moving up to feel his magnificent chest. Then down, dipping under his waistband to grasp the silky skin covering his rock-hard cock. It was wet at the tip, and she swirled it on her thumb and down. The hand on her ass pulled her tighter against his back.

"Wow, man. I see you're busy, but... Drake said you were supposed to be in and weren't answering," the Guardian Jax said with what sounded like laughter in his voice.

She moved up to swirl more hot liquid over the head, slicking him; then she couldn't control the urge to lick the wet digits. Bringing the sweet scented arousal to her mouth, she lashed her tongue out to taste it and about lost her mind at how good it was. She moaned loudly as she licked him off her fingers.

"Uri?" Alex vaguely registered the deep voice of Gregoire, and he sounded oddly concerned. She knew he'd teleported to their right, but she didn't care. She moved to get in front of Uri, dying to lap up every drop of his decadent essence from his big hard body. He held her back, still growling, but now it felt like the growling was

92

coming in her head. She glanced at Gregoire, seeing an odd stillness in his eyes.

Large hands grabbed her from behind, yanking her from Uri's body. Crap, what was wrong with her? She didn't even have time to hold tighter to Uri or fight the teleport. She heard a loud roar as her body broke apart.

Chapter 11

Guardian Compound, Earth Realm

A lex's body reformed a mere second before she was thrust into a cell.

She heard the deafening clank of metal shutting behind her and whipped around. She'd been so busy fighting the roaring growls violently echoing in her skull that she struggled to focus on her surroundings. She registered the metal walls and knew that was a bad sign.

Holding her head, she tried to tune out the rage coming from Uri. She knew instinctually the animalistic fury was his, but she desperately needed it to stop so she could focus. It was painful as hell and only allowed a small amount of sanity to come through. What was wrong with her? She was a fighter; she'd never have allowed herself to be teleported against her will. She would have fought it, but it was like her mind and body weren't in sync.

Her functions felt awkward, not her own. Again, she wondered if she'd been drugged, a good erotic drug... one that ended with getting her ass imprisoned.

She took a deep cleansing breath. Oh, Gods, Erik. He needed her; what was wrong with her? How could she have ended up so far from her plan? Her stomach clenched at the thought of failing the brother that had always had her back and continued to love her, no matter what.

Her body ached more than she ever thought possible. A spot deep inside actually hurt, and she couldn't seem to dial back the sound of Uri's angry snarls. Something had to give.

Looking through the bars, she saw Drake, head of the Guardians and the cousin she'd never met. Aphrodite and Hades were the only siblings her mother, Athena, had associated with, but all her mother's dealings with them had been in private neutral areas.

"Are you even listening to me?" he growled. Drake was even bigger than Uri. The male was huge up close. Those striking green eyes, the color of emeralds, had probably made many a female swoon over the centuries. She nearly snorted, the women probably didn't even care about the smoke that emitted from his lips, which was likely from his dragon half.

Somehow those fumes smelled sweet and a little earthy. Not like cigarettes or campfires, more like ancient wood and rich soil? Familiar as if from different times. It was oddly comforting... something she remembered from her childhood but couldn't quite place.

He'd asked her something. "Sorry, distracted by the whole sitting-in-a-prison-cell thing. You were saying?" She infused the words with as much sarcasm as possible with the pain in her womb and the snarls beating at her mind. Did she detect a hint of guilt in his eyes before he briefly looked away? Doubtful.

"Cousin, what the fuck is going on? Answer me."

She'd obviously missed something else he said. Her head felt as if it was going to explode; Uri was going crazy. What had they done to him?

"...said what did you do? Until I decide you haven't done something to him, you can sit your ass in here." Drake stood outside

95

her cage, arms crossed. In other circumstances she might feel slightly intimidated, Drake was a powerful being, but right now her focus was on the snarling that threatened to crack her skull. She had really hoped to avoid Drake until she'd gotten that blood oath from Uri. Dealing with him now just sucked. Especially with how much pain she was in.

Just then her body was racked with another sharp pain followed by mind-bending arousal... Alex pulled in a deep breath. She'd never encountered anything like this. It was agonizing. They had to have been hit with a spell or something to magnify arousal.

"You're kidding, right?" she ground out. "Whatever hit us, hit us *both*. I'm not so stupid as to spell myself!" She needed relief, now, as she bit the inside of her cheek to focus her mind on anything but the pain.

She paced back to where the cot was. Where was Uri? She could hear him in her mind. Had he been fighting his brothers the whole time? Or had he been tossed into a cell, too? Alex felt as if she only had moments before she lost her ever-loving mind as she listened to him. Her chest ached. Why was she so worried for him? Not knowing what was happening was another frustration she couldn't process at the moment.

And Erik... how could she be so selfish not to have even thought of her brother? She bit off a curse.

She tried to rub the tension from the back of her neck, using breathing exercises to get through some of the pain to focus. Her head pounded, and the arousal wasn't going anywhere, and she was sure her cousin could smell it. Wasn't that just awesome? If she could just get a moment's reprieve, she'd figure a way out of this.

If she could focus, she knew she could get Erik help, and screw it, she'd *try* not to get them exiled, but it only mattered that her brother got better.

The throbbing in her womb was rapidly escalating. She fought doubling over; she'd hold out as long as she could. The thought of looking weak in front of Drake made her want to throw up, or maybe it was the dance show currently holding auditions against her pelvis. Moisture started popping out on her forehead as her sight started blurring.

"What the hell is wrong with you?"

"Just not loving my warm welcome. Shouldn't family get a comfy guest room?" she ground out through a clenched jaw. She was starting to worry she might actually vomit.

A sharp, piercing sensation hit her so hard that she did double over this time. She knew in some fundamental part of her being that she needed Uri, that he was the only one that could take the pain away.

"Cousin?" she heard Drake snarl, although it felt like he was far away. Uri was growling and snarling so loud that she held her head, as if that could quiet the noise.

"Tell me what the fuck is going on?" Was that concern she detected? He'd opened the cell and was kneeling in front of her, looking into her eyes. Yep, he indeed looked worried.

"Need Uri," was all she could manage through shallow gulps of air.

"Fuck me," he ground out as something undecipherable flashed in his eyes. Moments passed; then Drake moved back from the cell, and an animalistic Uri was hauled through a metal doorway that slid quickly closed behind them. Uri fought to get to her. Jax and Gregoire held him on either side, not easily, it appeared.

She still held her head. "Uri, too loud."

The second the words were out, the sound cut off and she staggered as her mind buzzed. Thank the Gods. All she felt was the agony in her womb while her brain processed the sudden silence. "What's happening?" she demanded as she gazed into Uri's eyes. He continued to fight his brothers to get to her, his predator eyes never leaving hers.

"What the fuck is going on, Drake? He can't even form words, just fights us. What did she do to him?" Jax ranted.

"Put him in the cell with her."

"You've got to be kidding me!" Incredulous words from Jax again.

"Put. Him. In. The. Cell." Drake's bellow sent the room shaking. The toilet, sink and cot were all secured or else they would have cracked with the power in the Guardian leader's command.

Alex had a second to stand before Uri was let in and his big frame was pinning her against the far wall. It was so good to feel the warmth of his skin again.

Instant relief. Yes, that was what she needed. He took her mouth possessively, his tongue plunging deep to touch hers, then retreating to do it again and again. She had an instant of disorientation as the agony in her womb abated, releasing her muscles from the vise that had tightened them down. She was left with only the delicious feel of his body as he crowded her against the back of the cell.

The bliss was so strong, she heard herself whimper, her mind and body completely centered on Uri.

He aggressively commanded her mouth while ripping the front of her shirt to palm her breasts one at a time, plumping them and pinching the tight nubs through the lace of her bra. His fingers provided such sweet relief as her breasts swelled further against him. The rough feel of his fingers, relentlessly abrading the sensitive skin, had her coming unglued in his arms, bucking closer as she pushed her flesh into his hands. He groaned low in her mouth and gave a firmer squeeze. She moaned while his tongue dueled with hers.

Alex was so lost in the sensation she wasn't sure if she'd heard the others exit, and she didn't care. Her skin was riddled with the gooseflesh Uri's touch left in its wake as one hand moved to make circles against her hip. Her body ached with the desire to taste and savor every hard plane of his chest and rock-hard stomach; she wanted to lick the vee that led to paradise. She felt so small, caged by his bulk. His hips anchored her writhing frame against the wall as his herculean erection bumped demandingly against her. Gods, it felt so good; that seam in her jeans hit her clit so forcefully. The friction caused her to cry out in need. He ripped at the zipper of her jeans. She heard the tearing of fabric before he tunneled his hand inside. Her clit pulsed; it was so sensitive. When he pushed a finger inside her entrance, she cried out. She was wide open as her legs straddled his hips.

Fucking bare and so wet around me, he groaned in her mind.

She touched and caressed his arms and back, mesmerized by the feel of him invading her as he added another finger. She whimpered, was lost. "No," she protested when he pulled his hand up and away from her. Instead of going back where she needed him, he ripped her bra from her body with a feral growl. She shrugged her shoulders to get free of the torn garments, feeling the cold cell wall against her hot skin.

She submerged further into sensation, drowning in his strength and the feeling of rightness. Everything narrowed down to his hot, wet mouth latched to a swollen breast while his hand slid down the back of her jeans. The feel of his fingers on her flesh was too much. Nothing else mattered. How could anything be so all-consuming? It was incredible, but not enough. She pushed her hand between them to his hard heated flesh, silk over steel, reaching up to his belly button. So different from the plastic toys that were her only experience. She stroked him between their bodies, feeling his intake of breath at the action. Her mind melted as he stroked her between the cheeks of her bottom and further to her wet pussy.

He groaned deep and loud in the small confines of the room. He nipped at her taut peaks, not enough to break the skin, just enough to make her want him to. The primal action created a similar reaction in her. Suddenly, she wanted to mark him. Her head banged against the wall as her cries grew frantic. She wanted to claim him.

Hers...

She was sure that line of thought led to disappointment. Alex knew his habits. Never had he been with a woman twice, at least that she'd seen. But her body didn't care how her heart would feel later. Instead she held on, running her fingers through his silky hair.

He growled deep, moving to her neck and nipping harder, as if in warning. She felt the sharp edge of fang, and her pussy wept. She wasn't sure she could take much more. She needed him to fill her, had to feel what it was liked to be possessed fully by a male, this male, her male.

His fingers were driving her wild. She was gushing in need. But it wasn't enough this time. "More," she panted out. She needed him naked. All she could hear besides the ringing in her ears were groans as he worked his way back up to the other side of her neck and behind her ear, tearing tremors from her body.

Alex reached for his waistband, pushing it below his erection. He popped free into her waiting hands. She had seen him bared, felt him even moments before, but seeing the solid length up close was enough to make her pussy clench. He pulsed in her hand and she licked her lips, imagining taking that thick length inside her mouth.

He must have guessed at her intentions for he groaned, then growled, "No. Pants. Off." Immortal speed and excitement had her boots and what was left of her jeans and panties on the floor in barely enough time to stand before she was laid out on the small hard cot. Her breathing was ragged. She was beyond the point of no return. She was actually going to do this. Her ache of desire was too much to withstand. She would do anything to be filled by him... possessed by him. She could force herself to hold off orgasm until after he came, to avoid hurting him. Right now, she wanted more than anything to feel his cock inside her. To finally feel what it was like to have a hot male deep inside, as opposed to firm rubber or hard glass.

"Fuck." Uri groaned as he spread her wide beneath him. Holding her knees up over his forearms, he hovered above her opening. His body was strung tight, tendons straining as a muscle twitched at his jaw. Why was he holding back? Gods, she couldn't take it anymore. She tried to move up to him, but he held her almost immobile.

Finally, Uri guided the thick head inside, closing his eyes tight. Her passage clenched around him, desperate to feel him deeper. Then, with a loud groan, he slammed all the way inside her, his control finally lost. Her entire body bowed with the impact, so incredibly full and warm. He was so much thicker and hotter than any toy she'd ever accommodated.

His mercury eyes opened, glazed as he assessed her features. It felt so right, consuming. A claiming. His shoulders were taut, and his chest heaved above her. She couldn't wait to feel it against her aching breasts. She could still see a hint of fang showing just over his lower lip. The sight was more erotic than her brain could handle. He was watching her, the eyes of a predator. She was aching and needed to feel him moving inside her. "Are you trying to torture me?" she managed to say on a whisper. That was all the encouragement he needed. He pulled out slowly as she savored the glide. Almost all the way to the tip, then back in, touching so deep into a spot only he could hit. In and out with measured strokes until she was begging.

Her body writhed against him. Her mind was gone. She gasped for breath and was barely given a second before he started pumping faster, harder, just like she needed. She heard his low growl, "Mine." The possessiveness had her heart tightening with thoughts that she wouldn't let form.

"Such a tight little cunt, all hot and wet for me. It's strangling my cock."

Her entire body tingled, and she felt light-headed with arousal so deep and demanding her walls clamped down on him. His lids lowered on a deep moan. Wriggling, she tried to meet his increasingly forceful thrusts.

"Pinch your nipples," he demanded. His firm jaw ticked along with the muscles straining all along his neck and shoulders. His thick dark hair was in wild sexy disarray, and the picture he made was too much.

She complied without hesitation, plumping her breasts up and together, pinching the tight tips as she arched higher. His gaze fastened on her hands, and he groaned. He thrust harder, looking between them to the point where her body took him inside. He let out a low hiss as he closed his eyes. Then she heard mewling sounds come from her lips as slick wet flesh smacked together in combined pleasure. Circling her hips, she knew she was going to go over. It was then she realized what she was doing and stopped touching her breasts. She stilled her hips in an effort to stop the tide coming to take her down.

Her breathing was out of control. "Uri, wait, you need to come before I do."

His eyes opened, and he growled at her. "No."

"Can't come first. My shield. Won't be able to stop. You need to come, then get away. Now. I can't hold it back..." Alex groaned out. She bit the inside of her cheek. If he kept pumping, she'd be lost. She closed her eyes against his male beauty and waited, trying to hold back. She'd never felt so full, so possessed. She wanted to feel it all, but it would hurt him.

"Come," he demanded before thumbing her clit, thrusting again and again. The overwhelming tremors hit as his pulsing cock bathed her womb. Her release hit with the force of a tsunami and she heard his groan of satisfaction, but she couldn't move or speak to warn him. She was so caught up in the mind-shattering climax. She heard the moment of impact as her shield threw him. Then her world went dark.

When her vision returned, she quickly retracted the shield. Fear for him had her popping off the cot. "Uri?" Crap, he was sitting against the cell wall, one knee up, an arm resting on top. His chest was rising and falling hard, but he didn't seem hurt. His head rested against the bars at his back as his eyes tracked her movements. Relief hit hard, collapsing her back down. She lay there so that she could catch her breath and gain some strength back.

Alex, what the fuck? What did you do? I hit one motherfucker of a protection spell teleporting to your location, Vane telepathed. The anger and fear she felt from his mind's voice brought back the ache

103

in her head.

Shit, her shield, she'd been so lost she'd forgotten about her brothers' link to it. How was that even possible? She never forgot their link. Her eyes shut tight.

She should have at least warned Vane what was happening; instead she'd lost her freaking ability to reason. Which happened practically from the moment she showed up outside Uri's home. Although, lucky her, it looked as if her failure and idiocy was coming in crystal clear at that moment.

She bit the inside of her cheek with regret. *Vane, you need to get out of here. I'm fine. I'll come to you and Erik the moment I have everything worked out.* Sitting up, she put her head in her hands; she had to push back the guilt and deal with it later. She needed a real plan, one that didn't include prison cells and a naked Uri silently staring at her. This wasn't awkward at all.

She was exhausted, not only from the mind-blowing orgasm, but from everything else in the last few hours. First trying to heal Erik and now her shield engaging mixed in with not having re-energized after hopping to Sam's mind. She bowed her head, it was like she'd turned into an imbecile.

Not going to happen, sis. It appears we're going to have a meeting with our cousin. The steel infused in Vane's comment held a world of not-good for her.

What? What are you talking about? You are not meeting with the Guardians. You need to get back to Erik. I've got everything covered! Gods, how she wished that were true. She was once again failing her family if she didn't suck it up and come up with a plan, soon. Erik needed her, and she would not be the cause of them all getting exiled. If she got herself exiled, so be it, but not her brothers.

She heard the click and slide of the door being opened, awesome. She was naked, not to mention that the room was undoubtedly monitored, something she should have thought about before. Woo-hoo, her first real sexual experience with an actual male and it was most likely being edited for porn at the moment. She had no doubt Conn would relish using this to get back at her brothers for all their hacking into his systems. She'd watched and laughed and now it seemed Karma was coming for her.

Uri was up and had his workout pants covering her important parts in the moment it took for Drake and Sirena, the healer Guardian, to get through the door. It was actually sweet, considering he'd still yet to utter a word. Not that she'd been talking, either.

Sirena, the gorgeous blonde Guardian, looked thrilled out of her mind for some reason. She practically beamed at Alex when she came in, wringing her hands, in the very fifties-inspired dress she wore. The female passed what Alex hoped was clothing for her through the bars. Uri took the fabric and nodded to her before setting it on the cot. As grateful as Alex was, she wasn't getting up now to put them on.

Drake cleared his throat. "Sirena is going to need to run some tests on both of you." Another clearing of his throat made her almost smile. She wasn't the only one completely uncomfortable as her cousin continued, "Get dressed. We have a meeting with your brother. We've given him the basics. And he's out for blood." Drake said the latter directly to Uri, indicating he was the one whose blood Vane wanted.

Alex felt heat rise to her cheeks, anger the main emotion. The long-ago memory of Vane and Erik popping in after she'd climaxed in her cave caused every part of her skin to flame up in embarrassment. Were her momentous sexual experiences forever going to mortify her? Why did they have to tell her brother? She wanted blood of her

105

own now, dragon blood, but agonizing over it wasn't going to change a thing. She willed the heat from her cheeks after she heard Uri growl low in his throat. She had no clue why he was growling.

Wait, tests? "What tests? To determine what we were drugged or spelled with?" She looked to Sirena for answers.

Both Drake and Sirena looked to Uri, sharing some telepathic details, which pissed her off. Why wouldn't they just speak out loud? Did they still think she was responsible?

She raised a questioning brow to Uri as Drake said gruffly, "You've got five minutes. We'll be in the war room when you're done talking." With that, Sirena and Drake both exited, but the freaking cell doors were all still locked. What. The. Hell?

She stood to look at her cellmate. "Well, do you wanna clue me in? You obviously know what's going on. And for your information, I didn't do anything to cause what happened to us." She was flustered, irritated at being stuck in the cell, embarrassed, and naked.

She leaned over to grab what Sirena had left while avoiding looking at Uri. He was obviously unconcerned with his nudity since he didn't make any moves to try to dress. It was unnerving that he hadn't said a word since they'd had sex. Was he angry about getting hit with her shield? Maybe he thought she'd done it on purpose. Or was he blaming her for the situation in general. For all she knew, she just didn't measure up to the human females? She shook her head, frustrated and infuriated that her brother was now in the mix.

Alex heard Uri hiss out a breath, but still nothing. She swore she'd engage her shield and throw his ass again if he didn't speak, now. She was so flustered, her movements proved uncoordinated as she tried to cover herself with his pants while trying to figure out the garment in her hands. She quickly turned and bent to pick up the shredded remains of her tank top, thinking it was the best she could use to clean up. The thought of going to a meeting, which included her brother, smelling like sex... she closed her eyes, feeling embarrassed frustration all over again.

With a deep groan, he finally spoke. "First of all, your broadcasting is fucking distracting all on its own, but bending over in front of me like that is killing me." His voice was raspy in the most delicious way. Another groan slipped from his lips as he added, "This is not something I've experienced before. Your body is driving me insane, but the situation is a hell of a lot more complicated than that."

He was pulling at his hair without any care, and it had to hurt. She absently noticed his fangs had retracted.

She needed to take care of the evidence of their coupling. She wet the material in the little sink and cleaned the best she could, her face heating.

Alex kept stealing looks at his body when that was the last thing she needed to do. What was wrong with her? All she could think of was licking him from head to... head. Not now, not while still playing porn star. She heard him groan deep before shaking her head at her own ridiculousness; she'd practically shredded the garment Sirena provided before his comment registered.

Turning around in surprise, she said, "I am not broadcasting! I haven't broadcasted since I was a child!" She was insulted that he'd think her so inept.

Focusing to get the dress on—yes, *dress*—that Sirena brought her, she just barely heard him bang his head on the wall.

This was just awesome; she had sky-high, fuck-me boots, and a short, black, fifties-style dress with a flared skirt, which was shorter on her than it would have been on Sirena. It ended just above her knees while the black patent boots with their stunning red soles ended just below the knee. She looked down, disgusted. Great outfit to try to fight her way out of a Guardian compound in, but she would.

She struggled to get the zipper up the back before turning to glance at Uri once again. Her underwear had been shredded, which meant she also got to go into the meeting commando. "Could you please get to the whole test thing and tell me what happened to us. Your vocal cords are still working, correct?"

Finally, he got up, avoiding looking at her as he grabbed the discarded workout pants. "We weren't drugged or spelled; we are in the mating frenzy, which is why I can hear your thoughts, I'm assuming... and it's why Sirena will want to test us. Sirena's been researching the mating bonds for centuries and logs all information she can on anyone going through it," he bit out as if in pain.

His features were tense, but his eyes practically snared her in their seductive clutches, such intense... possessiveness? And blatant desire?

"What?" Her breath seized in her lungs when she processed what he'd said, making her question come out strangled. Her libido was *so* on board with the promise in his eyes, but the words... "A *mating*, like the mating-spell mating?" Alex knew of the spell; it had come right before the Great Exile. It was said to have been created by the Immortal Charybdis, who'd sacrificed her own life force to create the spell so that Immortals could no longer breed Apollo's army. Only those who were *destined* for one another were deemed *mates*. Her mind was spinning, trying to process that information.

"Wait, you can hear all of my thoughts? If it's the mating, why can't I hear yours?" Could she have another flawed power?

Alex felt a connection to him, but had chalked it up to how a female must feel the first time she allowed a male inside her body. Hearing his deep intake of breath, she knew he'd heard that. Feeling for her mental shields—they were all holding—she didn't see any breaches. But Alex wasn't hearing anything from him.

Was he listening to her now?

"Yes, I'm listening now," he growled. "I'm trying to block, but it's not working. And you did hear me. When we were separated and my more... primal side was unleashed. I was little more than a beast in those moments, but the minute you said it was hurting you, somehow I blocked my mind from yours." His voice was a deep annoyed rumble as he shook his head. "It was instinctual; one minute the mental shield was just there. It had to have been formed from the need to protect you. I'll have to check it out to find a way to help you with yours, but for now there isn't time," he said as he ran his hand back through the mussed strands at the back of his neck again, making it stick out in sexy disarray.

Gods, how she'd love to know what he was thinking, because, in this moment, he looked the opposite of happy that they were mated. Not that she knew what to think of it, but the last thing she needed was to feel like some kind of disappointment.

"No! Just give me a minute. I'm processing. Son of a bitch, I'm far from fucking disappointed, and I'm sure as hell not rejecting the idea of you. I've been obsessed with you for centuries. I'm just shocked and trying to wrap my head around it." He was shaking his head, pacing now. The strong lines of that big body were so enticing with its incredible grace, like a panther or some other graceful beast.

He growled, "We have to see how to create a block for you soon. I had no idea a female's mind could be filled with so... much."

His frustration had her hackles up. It wasn't as if she was doing it on purpose, nor was she enjoying the damned outcome. She tried again to see if there was a breach in her shields that was allowing the thoughts to break through. Nothing… Her mind was spinning with the implications of what he'd said. So much so that she found it difficult to focus on the shield. It seemed she had not been alone in her obsession; the thought made something inside her pulse.

Did she dare hope that this could end well? She didn't know him, other than his sexual proclivities. And he didn't know her. No doubt she'd never be able to hold his attention permanently; he was a sexual creature who liked variety. He didn't even seem to have a type.

In the span of a single second, Uri was on her. Taking her mouth hard. Demanding her complete submission as he caged her against the cell. His entire body connected to hers, and she felt the tip of a fang, which made her shiver as she rubbed her tongue up against his, tangling and retreating in the most delicious of dances.

You are mine. Mine, and I fully intend to keep you. I never thought I'd be gifted a mate. But if you think to get away from me now, think again. And if you want me to show you just how "mine" you are, I gladly will. He sent the thoughts directly into her mind; the dominant nature of the words made her breathless.

The intensity of her desire was even stronger after having had him inside her. All that warm, solid forcefulness coming from such a powerful warrior made her lose her mind. One of his big hands grasped her hip tight while the other was on her bare bottom under the dress. His lethally talented tongue probed the recesses of her mouth, making her wild again. He took utter control of her. Holding her firmly, he explored her teeth and tongue. Then he slowly circled his hips, pushing her further into the wall. So good. She was light-headed and weak with the onslaught of renewed desire. She wanted

110

that tongue on her, licking and stroking. Alex's body arched, rubbing against the solid jut of his cock.

Uri groaned as if in pain; then just as quickly, he was on the opposite side of the cell, leaving her panting and alone, barely standing with the help of the sink. "No more. We have to get to that fucking meeting."

Yes, the meeting. Damn. Before that, she needed to get a block up. She used another scrap of material on the sensitive flesh between her thighs as she took deep breaths.

"No time for the damn shield. Let's get up there before Drake torches something, like your brother. Now that the jackass is my in-law, I'm guessing I shouldn't let that happen," Uri snapped. His irritation was probably due to the thought of being in a family that included Vane and Erik. She sighed, her brothers were trouble, but she adored them. And she needed to get to Vane now.

He grabbed her hand and led her through the now open cell doors into a hallway. They went up one level, which was secured by two sets of voice- and code-activated exits, before reaching another hallway; this one had less metal and tile but still had the dim lighting that was in the holding area below.

Alex couldn't quiet her mind, so she tried to think of soothing things. Anything innocuous enough to get her mind off heavy thoughts, things that would showcase her inexperience in blinding spotlights or share too much. Her brothers needed her.

Shoes—she began cataloging what she'd need for summer, maybe some more strappy...

Uri groaned.

Okay, Alex changed her thoughts, going to reality TV and the team she hoped to win...

Uri growled and she gritted her teeth, guessing it was a big fat "no" to those thoughts too. Why did she even care? Because everything about him distracted her.

He gritted her teeth and forced her thoughts to stay on the mundane and not her brothers. If she got deported, she'd never see her shows again. Somehow she doubted they had access to any TV in Tetartos. She would probably be ecstatic just having a shack and a cave. Oh Gods, what if they still used pallets, could she get a real bed? She was starting to get depressed. What about bug spray? Indoor plumbing? Suddenly she began mourning her jetted tub and multiple shower nozzles?

She heard his deep male laughter cut off by a cough at her narrow-eyed glare.

She didn't think she was ready to discover just how primitive it would really be. She had enough on her plate, figuring out what happened in a mating. She already felt overloaded.

His big hand engulfed hers as they walked the hallway, making her tingly. She'd seen humans doing it for centuries but had never experienced holding hands. Her face heated at how ridiculous her thoughts were, how childish, that holding hands with her mate would make her feel fluttery. *Her* mate. She bowed her head; this fishbowl that was her mind was truly humiliating her.

Uri didn't speak, just gave her hand a gentle squeeze and brought it up for a light kiss that should not have been arousing but somehow was. Better to seem a naïve child than divulge more than she wanted...

A song. She could think of something...

She started singing in her head about "milkshakes" and how they bring all the boys to her yard. The lyric ran through her head as she hummed the beat out loud until she realized Uri had slowed almost to a stop and was staring at her. Then, throwing his head back, he bellowed with laughter. She stood stunned at the sight and sound of him before she was able to shake off the thrall. It'd somehow made him even more beautiful.

"What?" she responded indignantly. Before she could think the next thought...

"Get your asses in here. Now!" Drake's bellow shook the walls. That male really needed some dragon-strength Xanax. She shook her head as Uri's laughter barked out once again while they entered the room. She walked in with him, distractedly thinking that she enjoyed the sound of his laughter too much.

Then she got a good look at the room. A few seconds scanning the space was all it took for her vision to blur red.

Chapter 12

Cyril's Compound, Tetartos Realm

Cyril heard the clink as he slammed a test vial into its slot with more force than he intended. He was still furious at the Tria's ineptitude. It had taken years to complete that special formula to use on the Guardians. Then he'd patiently shelved it for use after the mating experiments came to fruition. He'd thought to have found a way around the mating spell centuries ago, and it was his own impatience that had made him take that reckless chance on the Tria's offer.

He'd managed to stay off the Guardians' grid for a very long time in preparation for all his work to finalize. He wouldn't be so reckless a second time.

He blew out a frustrated breath. His mating spell workaround was almost finished. The current results were promising, far surpassing anything his father and uncle had done in their work against the spell. He felt the edge of success inching closer.

The last round of tests were the closest he'd come to perfection. He'd just injected the new formula into Specimen Four, and he had at least a few hours before he would see any results. Four, who'd been abused by Elizabeth and had needed the damage repaired before he could do anything further. His jaw clamped down. He hated wasting energies. Elizabeth would need to be dealt with.

Cyril's body felt tight; he was furious and needed release.

Walking out of his personal lab, he moved out and down the tunnel. It was quiet except for the guards patrolling.

Cyril made his way through a metal door spelled to open at his telekinetic touch.

Elizabeth had managed to fortify his ranks nicely with the defectors from the local covens, up until the last few years. He'd found many a use for them. Mostly in experiments on the mating spell, but many others were enhanced and used in case the Guardians ever found him. Interesting that such inferior beings held such potential as guards. The Guardians' curse against harming humans made the Mageias an ideal first line of defense.

He needed more, but Elizabeth had given many excuses for not finding more local mortals for his work. Fortunately for her, she'd been able to find an alternative option by convincing Cynthia on Earth to send over specimens in return for a youth serum. It gave him new options.

Cynthia had no knowledge of the Immortal races, had dealt solely with the Guardians, and knew only that Cyril was the son of Apollo. No mortal on Earth seemed to realize the races existed outside of myth, and that particular secret served him well in dealing with the Mageia. She had no idea that what he sent her was primarily Aletheia semen he'd mixed with added compulsion. It was to his advantage that she thought his Demi-God powers were keeping her young.

As he neared the entrance to his private rooms, he thought about his options in dealing with Elizabeth. He should have been able to find a way around using the infuriating female, but nothing had come of the experiments he'd tried. So, for now, he needed her and her unique abilities.

115

He passed the hall mirror that led to his suite; glassy, highly dilated eyes gazed back at him. It was definitely time to gain some release. Immortals were sexual beings by nature. They needed orgasm almost as much as world's energies to remain in optimum condition. Something he had neglected to schedule with how close he was to creating the final formula.

He moved through his rooms, noting that Elizabeth was spread out on a chaise of black, her pale skin encased in a silk robe of emerald, strategically open to reveal one long smooth leg. Her blood-red hair fanned out against the raised back of the chair. She painted a beautiful picture, one that he'd taken his pleasure with often over their centuries in exile. She always seemed to know when he'd gone too long, was too focused on his multiple experiments.

He would have her, but she had chosen the wrong time to disobey his rules regarding test subjects. Today it would *not* be a mutually enjoyable experience.

Against the wall lay the massive wood bed carved with dozens of bodies entwined in an ancient orgy scene. The bed had been designed for his father, Apollo. It was his most prized possession. It had been one of the first things he'd had the Mageias on Earth procure and send to him. His chest filled with pride whenever he saw it. Soon he would be more powerful than even his father.

He'd amassed his own formidable legacy. His first priority after Exile had been to create his own compound on Tetartos, away from the Immortal races that were looking to kill him for the part he had played in his father's labs. It had taken decades to complete.

Then he'd spent several more years training the pathetic Mageia covens that Elizabeth was able to mind-link to on Earth. Making it possible for those primitive beings to recover and send much of his father's possessions to Tetartos. In return for procuring the items, he educated the much inferior Mageias on how to channel their powers. He made sure those covens were wary enough of the Guardians so as to not be seduced by Sirena to come to Tetartos. They were much more useful to him in the human Realm.

"Elizabeth," he said as he started pulling off his shoes and clothes.

She eyed him seductively, lashes lowered over piercing gray eyes.

"I suggest you divest yourself of the robe and anything underneath. Then I want you on your knees in the center of the bed. Attach the neck chains and be waiting."

Her eyes flickered at his demands, but she began to comply. She had a dominant nature, and to have the tables turned was something she hated, yet she had enough intelligence not to voice her distaste. It didn't matter, her dislike always showed as a slight change in her eye color. Elizabeth's time in the labs had formed her. He knew she was a special plaything for his father and Hermes. She'd been a breeder before that, yet, somehow, managed to change the situation to her advantage. He still wasn't sure of the dynamics between the trio and how it came about. His father had permitted him in the labs infrequently, always keeping his experiments to himself. Apollo had no trust for even his own offspring. Cyril had just begun to enter his father's inner circle before the Exile.

After Exile, fearing retribution from the large numbers of those she had tormented in the labs, Elizabeth made herself as useful as possible to Cyril. He had been amused by her, at first. Maybe the fact that she was once valued by his father kept her alive in the beginning, but it was her use with contacting the other Realms that allowed her to live this long. He realized now that he had given her free rein for too long. Foolhardy. She was at first the epitome of a dutiful servant. Slowly, she became more destructive as he allowed her time to make sure his test subjects understood their place. Once his formula proved accurate, he would mate the most powerful of the females, taking the best for himself, though he doubted one would be her. Bonded couples shared powers, and he would choose well. He hardened, thinking about all he could amass.

The formula would allow for multiple mates, in a unique way his father had never imagined.

It had always infuriated him that those few Immortals that mated became more powerful while *his* true mate had somehow eluded him. He knew she had to be out there, but to have multiple powers would be even better. He'd be free to choose. He took a deep breath, needing to focus on the problem at hand.

"Do you remember test subject four, Elizabeth?" His voice sounded smooth and calm to his own ears. "It took quite a bit of time and energy to get her fit for my last formula, and you know I do not enjoy wasting energies..." The last had the effect he was looking for. She paled a shade lighter and lowered her eyes, jaw still tense.

"I apologize, Cyril. I must have gotten carried away. I hadn't realized I'd done such damage. It will not happen again." The apology, offered in a much more subdued manner without any of her normal exuberance, showcased her abundant acting ability. He only saw a slight twitch of her eyes indicating she'd rather tear him to pieces, like the she-devil she was, than apologize.

"Yes, well, that won't do. I've grown tired of your displays, so from this point on you will obey Kane."

She made a choked sound and sputtered. He knew the female had a sadistic bend toward his people. He truly didn't care, but he was sick of dealing directly with her. He needed her abilities, but he didn't need to fix her destruction. She would be someone else's problem and he didn't care what Kane, his second in command now, did to her as retribution for any time she'd tortured the male.

He breathed out. He felt far better now.

Chapter 13

Guardian Compound, Earth Realm

Alex was beside Uri when they stepped into an expansive room with computer monitors and TVs showing maps with lighted areas, all along one wall. In the center was a large, warrior-sized, wood conference table. Big office chairs housed Conn, Sirena, Jax and Gregoire while Drake stood to one side, watching them enter with his big arms crossed. The position was testing the endurance of his olive T-shirt.

All eyes were on Alex and Uri; some looked a little wide, though she didn't know, or care, why. Her gaze sought and connected with her brother at the opposite end of the big table.

That was when Alex lost it; the edges of her sight burned bright crimson at the view of her baby brother chained to a chair. His arms, legs and shoulders were bound so that if he transformed into his lion, he would dislocate both shoulders, while the metal itself prevented any teleportation.

The warrior blood flowing in her veins mixed with centuries of training, and undiluted fury and instinct hit full throttle, proving just how dangerous an angry Demi-Goddess could be. Multiple things occurred almost simultaneously: preternatural speed and strength surged through her, propelling her body forward while pushing Uri back out the door they'd come in. His big body didn't have time to brace against her Goddess strength. Surprise was her best friend in that moment.

The occupants seated closest flew back as she let her shield fly free; the impact of chairs and bodies flying against fortified walls was loud in the room. One bay of TV screens caught an errant body, crashing into a sea of glass.

With only a split second of disorientation on her side, she assessed her target. Both Jax and Gregoire were armed, but Jax's blades were more accessible for her needs. Teleporting, Alex had Jax flat on his stomach as she straddled the male, pinning his massive arms and bulk under her bare body. She wouldn't think on that now. She lifted his head by the chin with one hand while holding his own blade against the male's throat with the other.

"Undo my brother's chains, now!" Alex demanded. The thought of them hurting Vane sent her into annihilation mode. If they'd harmed one hair on his beautiful head, they'd need a bulldozer to clean the rubble left in her wake.

Surprisingly, it was Vane who spoke. His chair was still upright, just further back from the table; he'd managed to somehow keep from toppling, probably since he'd been the furthest from the blast. "Hey, sis. Much as I'm enjoying watching you kick Guardian ass, they did this so that I wouldn't tear apart your *mate*." His jaw tightened, and he bit the word *mate* out as if it was something vile, all the while glaring daggers at Uri, who had just walked back into the room.

Her breath stuttered as she looked at Uri. He was staring at her with what looked like... pride?

Damn it.

"Drake, is this true? Will you let him loose once he's gained control over himself?"

"I'd let him loose now, but we need to talk, and if he's loose, he won't be willing to do that, will you, Vane?"

121

"Yeah, maybe after I've shredded him a bit." Her brother's voice was pure menace, and his gaze was directed at her male.

Wonderful... If Vane's rigid jaw was any indication, he wouldn't be backing down any time soon.

Vane, are you okay? she asked telepathically.

I'm fine. It sounded like he was gritting his teeth, even though he wasn't speaking out loud.

Admitting defeat for the moment, because soon she'd feel the energy drain from what she'd done, she teleported to the head of the table, choosing the seat across from her brother. She could teleport inside a metal area, she just couldn't exit through it—ah, the limitations of Gods and Immortals. Alex slid Jax's blade down the table to where he was putting his chair back into place. The male was grinning from ear to ear, making her frown. Why would he be grinning? She had just held his own blade to his neck.

Judging by his expression, I'm betting he loved having you, half naked, straddling his ass, my mate or not. The growl in Uri's mental voice set things off lower in her body. She forced the thoughts away as quickly as she could manage. Being in a room full of those with enhanced senses was making her twitchy, especially since one was her brother. She watched Uri glare at Jax. The other male just snickered.

As impressive as you were, little Goddess, if Jax hadn't worried about hurting you, he could have reversed your hold, Uri telepathed, with what sounded a lot like pride mixed with irritation. A quick glance showed the cause of his ire. He was adjusting a massive erection as he seated himself next to her, lounging back in the chair he'd taken to her right. The seat put him catty-corner to Vane's seat. It was all awkward as hell. Uri was shoeless and shirtless and didn't seem to care.

He could have tried to reverse it... she sent back. Her fighting ability was the one thing she didn't lack confidence in.

The stare-off between Uri and Vane began as everyone took their seats. Sirena appeared the most amused by the whole incident. That female had so much energy, it was like she would burst. And not a silky blonde hair on the Guardian's head was out of place. Impressive, as she was one of the ones that took flight into the wall. The Guardian healer was truly stunning, causing Alex to wonder if she and Uri ever...

We were never lovers, he said before her thought was formed, and she swore his inner voice sounded smug. The answer relieved her and she didn't care that it shouldn't.

Blowing out a breath, she looked around the room. Wasn't it odd that no one seemed to take offense at the fact that she'd just held one of their own at knife point? Not to mention she had just thrown everyone, including their leader, into the walls. She just knew Drake would make her pay for that. She felt only slightly uneasy watching the others grab their chairs. The table must be bolted down.

Conn had been the one to take out the TV, and aside from shaking some of the glass out of his shaggy brown hair, she didn't see any blood. He seemed more concerned with the laptop he was checking. It was encased in some thick rubber thing. He picked it up from the broken glass, and judging by his grin, she guessed the thing still worked, although she wasn't sure how.

Conn, along with his laptop, lounged back in a seat at the table. Dark tattoos peeked out from the sleeves of his flannel shirt, and those beautiful amber eyes looked out from below the three black loops piercing one brow. She wondered if his wolf form would hold the piercings; she assumed they were made of something other than metal. That would be something to see.

Uri's growl vibrated divinely through their mental connection.

She looked over, surprised. *Jealous?* she sent, feeling curious. She couldn't help the warmth that flowed through her chest. At least they were even now. He looked mildly confused by his own reaction, and that tilted her lips.

Are you okay? Did he hurt you? What the hell happened? She felt how all over the place Vane's emotions were, but at least he had gotten it together enough to speak. Worry was at the forefront with anger and hurt mixed in as he spouted his questions. Alex understood. She felt horrible that he was caught in this mess with her.

He didn't hurt me. I decided to go to Uri because I didn't want you to take the chance of going to Conn. I didn't know Uri was my mate, but I've been drawn to him for centuries... I didn't mean to worry you; it's just... when we came in contact, everything just got out of control. I'm sorry I got you in to this. I will fix it. I'll fix everything, she said with meaning. What a screwed-up situation she'd gotten them in. How was it possible for her entire world to be flipped upside down in a single moment? Even now, when her priorities should be her brothers, she felt Uri's heat next to her and she just wanted to curl into him and rub herself all over his warm body.

She heard a low groan to her right. Uri grabbed her hand under the table, and the innocent contact heated her blood. She needed to get a grip. Get some control over her ridiculous thoughts.

You weren't forced into it? The question from Vane caught her off guard. She could hear what it cost her brother to ask. He and Erik had been there at her attack, and after. It had been hell for them all.

Uri growled and looked at her. She would explain later... no matter how much she didn't want to.

No, I wasn't forced. It's a mating. Things are... mutual. She saw some of the tension drain from her brother's shoulders, but he still shot daggers at Uri from across the table. She wanted to reassure him, but they had other things to deal with now. *It will take some time to get used to and work out. But right now we need to focus on helping Erik. How is he?* She felt lower than low for not thinking of her brother. For losing sight when she was with Uri. She loved her brothers more than anything in the world. It had always hurt to think she was the weakest link.

Not good. Nothing has changed. She heard him sigh. *We need their help, much as it pains me to ask, especially being tethered to a damn chair.* Vane's groan tilted her lips.

"Like to share with the rest of the class?" Drake's voice oozed sarcasm.

Not having many bargaining chips royally sucked. After she cleared her throat, she decided taking the offensive was the best course, so she dug in with the first thing she could come up with. "As you know, we've been essential in the fight against demon-possessed on Earth. We don't need thanks. We were happy to help, but we'd like to call in a favor now for thousands of years of assistance."

Vane groaned. Well, it wasn't like he'd offered up anything brilliant.

Uri's arm was twitching next to her. When she looked over, she saw from the glitter in his eyes he was barely suppressing laughter. She narrowed her eyes in warning.

125

Sirena, Jax and Conn had no such compunctions in yucking it up. Drake crossed his arms over the bulk of his chest and the T-shirt that clung to his frame, one eyebrow raised, challenging her to continue the tactic. She hoped no smoke was a good sign. She hated having to deliver her speech as he towered over her, but he was the only one *not* seated. A frown creased her forehead. *Intimidating bastard.*

More shoulder shaking came from Uri.

"What did you have in mind, cousin?" Alex really hoped that Drake's continued mention of their family tie was a positive rather than a negative. It could go either way with families like theirs.

"I would like exemption from Exile, for myself and my brothers, in payment for our centuries of service to the Guardians and humanity. And as compensation for our continued service, I would ask for Sirena's medical assistance, and any other assistance you can find, for a family situation."

The laughter, that had gotten louder at Alex's exemption-from-exile request, abruptly halted at her request for medical assistance.

Erik? Uri's sexy voice in her mind made her soften a little uncontrollably.

Yes.

"Request noted. Now, do *not* tell me that you have contaminated my compound. Explain. Quickly." Oh, good, there was the smoke... Nothing like pissing off the Demi-God with Guardian powers. She might end up grilled by the end of this after all.

"No, it's not for Vane or me. It's Erik we need help for, and I wasn't the one that teleported my ass here." She pinned Drake with her gaze. More smoke filled the air. She looked over to see Vane shaking his head.

"The compound's on lockdown," Conn announced, the wolf must have sent word to the other Guardians not to come in, likely as a precaution.

"Speak," Drake growled.

Alex detailed the events after her hop into Sam's head, reiterating that Vane had sent the visuals of the hop to Conn. She focused the details of the trip to Sam's apartment toward Sirena. The healer was their best bet for helping Erik. Sirena leaned forward in her chair, absorbing the details, and asked that Vane and Alex both show her their perspectives and thoughts.

Vane, being strong in telepathy, sent the detailed images directly to Sirena, even with the metal that should have affected his abilities. Show-off.

Sirena leaned back, and after a moment her expression morphed from wide-eyed to beaming. Then as abruptly as it came, the female's smile was gone, making Alex's stomach plummet. Somber, Sirena cleared her throat before relating what she'd found. "Okay, the good news is that your brother doesn't appear to be compromised."

Then Sirena looked to Conn. "Go ahead and lift the lockdown."

The healer went on, "I need to see him, but I'd say Erik shows signs of the mating frenzy. I have been studying this for centuries, and we know that the females Cyril and Elizabeth are collecting are of elemental Mageia descent. Some have DNA markers that are that of potential Immortal mates."

Sirena eyed both her and Vane before taking a deep breath. "I think that Sam may be Erik's mate."

Alex saw her own horror and confusion reflected on Vane's face.

That was bad. If it was true, her brother's mate was suffering right now. Her limbs instantly tensed. Alex's energies had been depleting almost exponentially since she'd used her shield on the Guardians. She forced herself to work through the fatigue, needing to know more about her brother's situation. The tension in the room was almost unbearable. Those seated knew how horrible this could be. Having your mate taken by a sadistic monster who was doing Gods knew what to her?

She needed answers.

"How is that possible? He never came into contact with her. Uri and I didn't know we were mated until we made physical contact." She sucked in a breath at a more frightening thought. "And she's mortal?"

Alex glanced over at Uri; he looked grim. His hand tightened on hers under the table, and she was grateful for the silent show of support. Why did she feel so incredibly connected to him? Not just sexually, it was more. Was it because of the mating? Their souls attempting to connect on some deeper level like was said to happen?

Sirena spoke again. "With those able to transform into beasts, it is easily triggered by scent because of how sensitive their olfactory senses are. Sam's unique fragrance would have permeated the closed space of the apartment. That could have started things for him. The fact that he roared and mentioned scent after smelling her pillow is telling. I have an idea why he's taking in so much energy, but it's only a guess until I examine him." The blonde paused before answering her other question. "And mortal mates can become Immortal... with a special ceremony."

Well, at least she didn't have to worry about how horrible it would be for her brother to mate someone only to lose her in a few short decades. The problem was that they still needed to get Sam away from the monster first.

"All from a pillow..." Alex said incredulously.

Sirena nodded. "I believe so. I'll need to examine him. Taking him from the apartment should have dulled some of the effects, but he already knew that Sam was in danger after your head hop. Most mated couples end up linking minds, along with bodies, in the frenzy soon after scenting their mate. I've never come across a case like this. His drive to find her would be intense, especially because of the danger. The good news is that Erik may be the key to finding Sam, as well as the others." The Siren seemed completely immersed in her own thoughts, while Alex was fading fast. She could no longer process what the female was saying.

Sirena's Guardian characteristics were clear. Gone was the ecstatic little blonde from before; she was all business. It should have offered Alex some solace, knowing that Sirena was so focused on helping her brother, even if her reasons were for the sake of research. But, damn, the thought of what Sam had already been through and what her poor brother would suffer even when they got Sam back... It was too much. The last reserves of her energy were sapped away with worry for her brother. Alex wasn't sure how Erik was going to deal with this; her heart was breaking for him.

It wasn't fair. She wanted to rail, but she had to keep it together. They had work to do.

Her sight started to get spotty. She needed to get out of there. First the head hop... then trying to help Erik... the mating... battle in this room... her shield activating twice—yeah, she was depleted.

Uri moved from his chair, sending it sailing. With lightning speed she was caught up in the solid strength of his arms. She was so far gone, she only wanted to cuddle up and let darkness have her, but she needed to help her brother...

"I'm taking her to recharge," she heard Uri announce to the room.

Vane growled at Uri, but she saw him close his eyes for a moment as if gathering himself for torture. *Sis, he's right. You need to refuel. I can see you're fried. And honestly, I can't be around your mate without wanting to beat the shit out of him. Let me take care of Erik, and you go take care of yourself. Find out information about the mating. That might help Erik when we recover his mate. I'll let you know after the doc checks him. We need you powered up so we can rescue Sam,* he sent to her mind.

His serious look killed all her protests. Guilt ate at her, but Vane was right, she didn't have the strength to be of use to anyone until she refueled.

Finally capitulating, she nodded. *Tell me as soon as you get Erik. Let me know he's okay. I'll meet back the minute I'm refueled. And... be careful.*

I've got this. Don't worry, sis. It'll be all good. He gave her a reassuring grin. It was strained, but she appreciated the effort. She hoped he'd get over his violent tendencies toward Uri quickly. They needed to work together or she didn't know how it would all be with her and Uri after this was over. Erik and Sam were the priority.

"I can walk," Alex informed Uri and the room, mostly to the room because he could hear her thoughts. The protest came out a little slurred, even to her ears. She couldn't remember ever being this depleted. She bit the inside of her cheek, thinking a little pain might help, and tried to wiggle out of his hold. She refused to look weak.

Uri answered with a growl. "Not happening."

Hell, she knew to pick her battles with her brother. This wasn't even a fight she cared to win. He could do the "I, Uri; you, small female" move, this time. She relaxed in his hold with a shoulder shrug. She wouldn't have made it two steps before face-planting, and that would have been a far worse exit.

"I'll inform you when Sirena gets us a time frame for the next meeting." Drake barely looked at them as he began barking orders to the rest of the room. As they were going down the hall, she heard Drake say, "Sirena, Jax, Gregoire, take Vane and get Erik; bring him back here. Conn, get the others. We need to be ready at the first chance of a rescue mission. This is the best opportunity we've ever had. I don't want to fuck this shit up. Conn, I still want the area where that possessed was picked up checked for evidence and that syringe. Find out who we can spare for a quick look."

Syringe? What was that all about?

*****

Sirena, I need you to watch my hellhound, Uri sent to his sister Guardian.

I actually want to see him hunt. Take care of your mate. Once Alex's brother is taken care of, I will see that he's fed. Havoc will be fine with me. Sirena's words were melodic, easing his concern.

Thanks.

Uri relaxed a little, still not able to process everything. For now his female needed to get her strength back.

131

Chapter 14

Cyril's Compound, Earth Realm

Cyril's muscles twitched with the strength he was using to control his anger. He'd been so sure the tests on subject four were going to hold. Taking a deep breath, he used all of his immense strength of will to calm himself before he killed one of his people.

Another failure. He clenched his fists; his impatience ate at him. He was close. He needed to rework the last formula. Later. The security patrol he passed on the way back to his rooms gave him a wide berth. Smart. He was moments away from doing serious damage to anyone in his path.

Taking a deep breath, he took his mind from subject four. He needed to be prepared for the meeting ahead. It wouldn't do for him to exude anything but calm. He inhaled slowly, forcing his limbs to relax, his mind to calm.

While looking through the other files before leaving his office, he decided that his latest, subject nine, might hold even more potential than subject four had. There was something there that bore more research, her numbers were good, and she was stronger mentally than the others. That, and he'd gotten an odd, tingling awareness from the blonde female. The thought calmed his annoyance. Something about subject nine definitely necessitated more testing and deeper research before taking her to the level he'd taken subject four through. She technically wasn't next in line, but no matter. He didn't, however, want to waste her potential.

He didn't have the patience for another subject to lose their sanity. It still irked him. Lack of sanity completely inhibited any chance of power melding, rendering the subject useless. Not all was lost; subject four would still be a worthy trade for services from the Tria, should he need them. It never hurt to have payment set aside for the future.

He shook his head, finally calming.

He began thinking back on the reason he had called this next meeting. Subject nine's bloodline... He would have Cynthia, a Mageia coven leader on Earth, collect what family she could. Even members over age thirty, which had been the cutoff before. He hated to waste an opportunity to get a female in optimal condition, but securing subject nine's family to preform preliminary tests on the bloodline would be worth it. Shipments required extensive time and preparation on the side of the Mageia. Their lack of power grated, but was expected from such weak beings.

He walked into his suite. A quick glance showed everything was set. "Elizabeth, contact Cynthia." Elizabeth had been silent at his entrance. Good.

Cyril saw the small glass containers holding fluid set on a side table. "I see the partial payment is here." Cynthia was dying to get her hands on those vials. Her obsession with youth was to Cyril's advantage. The shipments of her "special serum" kept her in line. The Mageia in Earth were blissfully unaware of any other Immortals besides the Guardians. That had worked to his advantage. What he'd sent her was a youth serum that he easily procured, because it was, in fact, Aletheia semen. He'd mixed some added components to enhance the already addicting quality and she was his, just as the rest of her bloodline had been. The mortal would do anything he

133

demanded to get more. She'd already provided females, and her ancestors had supplied him with an abundance of items from Earth for decades without the Guardians ever finding out.

He looked at Kane, who was standing at attention at the doorway. The Aletheia male stood glaring at Elizabeth, and Cyril felt the tension. The male's silver eyes met his when he demanded, "Kane, you will handle the transport of the vials at my command."

Cyril, as usual, would be in Elizabeth's mind as the meeting was held. He did not trust her to handle them on her own. The mind-sharing experience was taxing, with his minimal skills in the area, but it was necessary. He wanted those bloodlines, and he wanted them as soon as the Mageia contact could track and transport them.

He was close to something big. There was a niggling at the back of his mind. Something he was missing? Subject nine was important; he felt it.

Chapter 15

Uri's Private Cavern, Earth Realm

Uri took in his surroundings. He'd claimed the cave centuries ago, enjoying the dense jungle canopy outside and the waterfall, which, along with his wards, hid his space from humans and wildlife alike. He knew that some of his brothers had modernized their caves, but he'd kept his simple. His sight was better in candlelight, his eyes were too sensitive for direct sun, and even electric light was usually too much for him, forcing him to use sunglasses.

Another reason he'd chosen the cave was the small waterfall that flowed from a crevice above the room Alexandra was currently in. The waterfall brought fresh cool water into the hot spring inside, which then flowed into an underground river that in turn went deeper through a hole in the rocks, then out of the caves again. He'd carved out seating and steps within the rock around the room. The work had been soothing in centuries past.

Now she was in there. And he was in the bedroom area. He paced the ancient rug in front of the four-poster bed he rarely used. Swords and daggers lined one wall, weapons he'd used throughout the centuries.

He paced some more. His body was strung impossibly tight. Uri desperately needed relief again. And soon. He was sure that if his balls got any tighter, there would be permanent damage, and that was the reason he'd left his female in the pool area of his cavern to refuel on her own. That and the fact that he'd felt her need to be alone to process things as much as he needed the same time.

The mating frenzy was a damned nightmare. He couldn't touch her without wanting to drag her beneath him.

Alexandra, or Alex, as her brother called her, had been his dirty fantasy for so long. One he hadn't dared touch in reality. Now she was *his... his* mate. He wasn't even sure how that was possible. That he had every right to touch and take her made his cock throb in anticipation.

The fact that she was here with him gave him an odd and primal kind of satisfaction. There was a sense of rightness in providing the space for his mate to strengthen her hot, tight, little body.

Her mind had finally stilled. Her head had been a riot of conflicting thoughts from the moment they'd connected. He really wanted to know how such a magnificent creature didn't know her worth. He was sure it had something to do with an attack centuries ago, the one her thoughts had gone to in the meeting. His stomach tightened imagining what might have happened. He could guess, and if it was true, he would slaughter his way through entire bloodlines to exact vengeance.

He balled his fists. He doubted her brothers had left anyone for him to kill. They were not the type of males to allow someone to live if they dared hurt their sister. He clenched his teeth, hating that there was likely no one left for him to damage.

Her mind wound over and over, reciting her inadequacies as she saw them. That Uri wouldn't want her as a mate, or that she wouldn't be a good mate since her powers were so uncontrollable... Like hell. Fuck, though, if he didn't like the feel of her in his mind so much, he'd have been forced to knock her beautiful ass out so he wouldn't go insane from the speed and outrageousness of her contemplations.

Thank the Gods, in the last few minutes her mind had either cleared to meditate while taking energies, or she'd finally found a way to block her thoughts. He hoped to hell it was the latter as he paced the confines of the bedroom for the fiftieth time, hands running through his hair, muscles flexing tight with his need to go to her. Damn it, he had to get his own shit together first.

Uri had learned so much about his little Goddess by being in her head; he was still a little shell-shocked at how innocent she was.

She was more than he could have dreamt of in a mate. That this could have happened never even occurred to him in all the years they had played their game. A mating was sacred among the races, but it also came with added power, and as a Guardian, he'd long ago resigned himself to the possibility that the fates would never gift him with a female. Guardians were already too powerful; when his and Alex's power started to meld, they'd both become even more so. It usually happened over the span of a year, and he could honestly say he didn't care about the power.

He was too busy reeling from the fact that he had a female whose soul called to his. Not only that, but she was a fierce little Demi-Goddess who drove his cock insane, made him laugh and could kick ass.

Shit, he was torn between feeling humbled and shocked that he was not only the first of his brethren to find his other half, but he'd found one who was fucking perfect for him. He knew he was the last to deserve to find a mate, but he was just bastard enough to do anything to keep her.

Uri couldn't believe all the centuries he'd wasted, not knowing she was his. Now he understood the draw. His obsession.

He'd assumed she was using him for her own voyeuristic pleasure. That she'd been getting off on her own while thinking of him made him impossibly harder. He groaned as his dick begged him to find her and fuck her tight little pussy all over again. He had never felt such a heavenly, constricting fit in his entire life.

How was she so damned innocent? His primal side loved it. Loved that she hadn't taken other lovers, which made no sense. His kind weren't known for their possessiveness; Aletheia were the biggest pleasure seekers in all the Immortal races. Their philosophy tended to fit in to "the more the merrier" category and that went for everything. At the moment he wanted to spend a decade in this cave with only his female and no one else around for miles.

The completion of the mating bond would most likely help with some of her insecurities. Their powers would meld in the way of mates, and in the end, she would become a hell of a lot more in control of her own abilities and get a boost of his. He wasn't sure how it would work with the Guardian powers, but he knew Sirena was thrilled with the possibilities.

Uri thought about their first joining—in a fucking holding cell. She had been so hot and wet for him; it'd been like nothing he'd ever experienced.

She'd taken him inside her blistering heat, just as much in the frenzy as he, and still tried to forgo her pleasure in fear of hurting him. Perfect. When that shield had knocked the shit out of him, he'd completely understood why she'd never taken a lover. A human couldn't have taken that impact. It took a second for *his* cracked ribs to mend.

He grinned. His Alexandra had looked like pure hellfire. Beautiful and deadly. She'd taken a warrior, a Guardian, twice her size to the ground. She'd been so damned protective of her pain-in-the-ass brother. Then, seconds later, she'd regally taken a seat at the table to negotiate with Drake. She was exactly what a Goddess should be.

This would be the first such mating of its kind, a Guardian with a Demi-Goddess. Who knew what power they would hold? The Guardians were constantly battling one enemy after another in all the Realms. The added power would be a big fucking help. Especially if what he feared was true, that the Tria were getting smarter.

He was selfish enough that he just didn't give a shit what it added to the cause. He wanted her purely as a male wanted his female.

He was forced to push back the twinge of guilt he felt at being the first Guardian to find a mate.

One that would soon learn all his secrets when they blood-bonded during their mating ceremony. She'd learn all his prominent memories, things that only his brethren knew, things no one else could know.

The biggest being the facts that surrounded the Immortal Charybdis, who'd sacrificed by using part of her soul to create the mating spell preventing Immortals from being breeders for Apollo and Hermes. The Immortals thought her dead. Uri knew the truth because it had been he and Gregoire who'd saved her.

Those times were best left forgotten, but soon Alex would have that knowledge.

Uri rolled his neck to release some of the building tension.

Only a few more minutes and he'd take her in the warm water of the springs. He'd make up for their first time being in a holding

139

cell, on video, which had distressed her. And he would get those tapes from Conn before Jax found a way to get his hands on them. Conn had probably deleted them already anyway, knowing the Lykos.

He turned to the direction of the waterfall room.

Time was up for his little Goddess.

Chapter 16

Uri's Private Cavern, Earth Realm

Alex was sitting there, psyching herself out. Not sure if she should go to Uri or wait where she was. She felt uncomfortable and awkward now that she was back to full strength and her thoughts were once again her own.

Alex had explored the room while speaking with her brother. She loved the soothing sounds of water over stone and the seductive warmth from the grotto secreted behind the shimmering fall that slipped through a crevice in the ceiling. To get over there, she'd stepped over a small stream, no more than two feet wide, which disappeared into the stone wall beyond.

Shelves were carved into the stone just inside the doorway that separated her from where Uri had gone after giving her time alone. She'd noticed soft white towels and several more cutouts surrounding the room that housed simple yellow candles. Most of which he'd lit for her when they arrived. Their light created a soft glimmer that mixed with the turquoise rock nearly glowing beneath the water.

Intricately carved stone seats in many forms encircled the room. Most seemed carved directly from the walls themselves. Had he created them? She wondered at this element of the male she'd spent so many centuries enthralled with. She truly knew so little of him.

After a moment, she bumped her head back against the stone

wall, willing the damned male to come to her. She had been absently revisiting her conversation with Vane for the last few minutes.

Vane had said the situation with Erik was covered, but it killed her not being with them, doing something useful. There was nothing she could do there that wasn't already being done. Her brother and a couple of the Guardians were forcing energies to Erik, which was apparently something they didn't need her help for.

She felt stronger now, but renewing arousal was making her skin feel tight. It had to be the mating frenzy, because this was not her. She was acting insane. Instead of centering on her brother, her mind kept going to Uri. No matter how much she willed it to stay focused. No, this wasn't normal arousal, this felt more like compulsion, like she'd come out of her skin if she didn't feed her need for him again soon.

She'd thought that Uri would have helped her re-energize, but instead, he'd left her in this waterfall room to refuel on her own. She had been thankful at first because she didn't like how depleted she'd been, hadn't been comfortable with his seeing it, and truth be told, she wanted the time to process everything. She was sure he had his own thinking to do, but now she needed not only his body, but to talk. To learn what all this meant, because she was definitely out of the loop.

Nerves and her ever-present insecurities weren't helping either. She was a damaged Demi-Goddess with little control of her abilities, and she wasn't sure he'd signed up for that.

Banging her head into the wall wasn't doing anything to help her train of thought. Everything was happening so fast.

She had to admit that she was happy that Uri was hers. She wasn't sure he'd feel the same when he learned the extent of her baggage. The connection they were building was on another level, not just the wild nearly animalistic desire, but something deeper. It almost felt like she knew... him, not just what he showed to the world. Was that what happened when one found a destined mate? Because in reality she didn't know him. She knew he was a sexual creature made to hit every one of her desires.

Fantasies of his body aside, there was more to him and she needed to know what that was because she wasn't ignorant, this was permanent. They'd have to learn more about each other, aside from what the bond was making her feel. They needed to discuss expectations. He was dominant as hell, but, for her, that dominance could never seep out of the bedroom.

For centuries it had just been her and the twins. And even though they were protective asses at times, they still understood her need, her craving for freedom. But would Uri? He was a force of nature and dominant like no other male she'd seen. It turned her on more than anything to witness it... even experience it. Gods, she was wet thinking of all the things he'd do to her, but would he want to command her life along with her body? She supposed he could try, but would he find himself disappointed by her, not just her flaws, but also who she was.

If she could keep her clothes on long enough, they'd discuss it all. Not just for her, but so that she could learn everything about the bond for Erik.

She focused on the serenity of her surroundings. She was giving him two minutes; then she was going to him. It had been so calming to take her energies while in a place that held so much of Uri within its tranquil embrace.

She liked it as much as she loved her own cave and hadn't thought that possible. The cavern she'd claimed even before the Exile was located on a tiny island in the Pacific. It had gorgeous beaches to one side and rocky cliffs along the other.

She blew out a breath, deciding to check on her brothers one more time. Vane told her earlier that Sirena had been examining Erik at the time, and Alex wanted to know what happened.

How is he? Any news from the exam?

He was pretty drained, and Sirena confirmed he is in some early stage of the mating frenzy. The Guardians and I have been forcing energies into him, at Sirena's direction. Man, is she a hard-ass. You wouldn't know it looking at her, but, shit....

Good, I should be there soon.

There's nothing you can do that we're not already doing. Sirena is taking care of him, and she said she has a lot of ideas about why he's using so much energy. It was a little like gibberish to me. Drake said for you and Uri to "get your shit figured out" and be back at the compound in an hour, but Sirena said it's extremely important that you and Uri spend time working on your bond. I definitely don't want details.

She didn't give you any other information on mating?

I know more than I ever wanted to know about what you're going to do with your mate. I would clean my mind out with Drano if I could. You figure it out with that douchebag and I'll check in if we need you sooner. If not, I'll see you in an hour.

She shook her head and told him she'd see him soon. It sounded as if he was bonding with the Guardians some, which made Alex happy. And it alleviated some of the stress, knowing that Sirena was taking Erik's care so seriously. She could tell from Vane's mental tone that the healer had definitely eased some of his worries.

Alex felt the air thicken and looked up to see Uri enter the room. The dominance he exuded filled the space, causing goose bumps to rise along her skin and ending all other thought. She took a deep breath. Gods, he was gorgeous. His chest still bare, she saw the muscles from his stomach to his wide, taut shoulders flexing as he moved.

They had an hour, but she needed answers just as much as she needed his body. She wasn't sure if she could learn anything when he looked like that. All the moisture in her mouth fled to her lower extremities at the sight of him. Her heartbeat sped up watching his long strides eating the distance from the entrance to the seat she'd taken at the other side of the pool.

Uri stared intently into her eyes before taking a slow trip down her body, lingering on her lips, breasts, legs, all the way to the tips of her shiny black boots. Slowly, he lifted his head, scenting the air like a predator and closing his eyes on an erotic groan.

"You have twenty seconds to undress and get into the grotto. If I do it for you, the dress will be shredded; your choice." His voice was strained as he opened his eyes again; his jaw was tense like the muscles of his biceps.

A little thrill ran through her as she moved to heed his command, and there was no doubt in her mind that it was just that— this kind of dominance was so damned intoxicating. She grew slick with the thought of what he'd do to her.

"As much as I'm on board with being naked with you, we need to talk. I need information on the mating and we only have an hour before a meeting with Drake and my brother."

"Ten seconds... This will provide your answers."

Her stomach clenched, realizing that talking was likely

145

impossible until they fed this need. She cocked a brow. "Mmm-hmm, and how, exactly, will that work?" she asked. Getting up, she walked with what she hoped were slow seductive strides, even though her legs felt wobbly. The clicking sound of her boots sounded loud against the stone, echoing along the walls as she strode toward the grotto. She slowly pulled down the zipper at the back of the dress. Each click of the metal teeth ramped up her excitement. She wanted to feel seductive instead of inexperienced and inept. She wanted to make him burn, just a little. In reality they didn't have much time to get this out of their systems.

She looked over her shoulder as she let the dress drop, leaving her only in the sky-high boots that flowed over her calves like a second skin. Alex saw that he hadn't moved. He stood in the same position, but his body was taut like a bowstring ready to spring. His eyes were focused on her ass so intensely she felt it as a touch. His mercury gaze lowered to her boot-covered feet, and a low growl issued from his throat. The sound brought more goose bumps to her overheated flesh. She felt the mist from the waterfall now as she drew closer. Not wanting to ruin the boots, she lifted one to the nearest stone seat and slowly unzipped it. Bending at the waist, she arched her back to give him the view she hoped would stretch his restraint.

Glancing back, she saw his jaw clench tighter. The hint of fangs peeking erotically over his bottom lip made her lower body pulse.

"Two seconds and you go in with the boots on," he growled.

She felt a surge of feminine power at his slowly shredding control.

She suppressed a grin and moved faster, extricating herself from her favorite footwear, not wanting to see them ruined. Before she was even upright, he was behind her. He sifted his fingers through

146

the strands of her hair, pulling lightly, then moving the mass over one shoulder, causing a shiver to rack her body.

Heated puffs of breath touched against the sensitive skin at her neck, and her nipples pulled tighter than she thought possible. She moaned and tried to arch back, wanting full skin-to-skin contact. Instead he kept his body away. He was bending from his greater height to rub his beard stubble lightly against her throat, marking the skin with the delicious friction. All the while his big hands sat low against her hips and his thumbs moved in circles in the indents below her waist. The dual stimulation of his gentle hands and the rough abrasion at her neck blurred her vision.

"How, exactly, is this going to help me understand the mating?" Her words came out breathless.

"Our powers blend the more we bond. We'll both gain more control over our own abilities and get some of each other's gifts. I intend to work on your shielding."

"How do you know it'll work like that?" She breathed, her brain not able to fully process what he was saying.

He nipped at her shoulder. "It will... I've told your brother already, so the bastard won't come running once the shield goes up. I heard about that link when you were projecting." His words were whiskey smooth as he laved the spot behind her ear. His decadent scent made her lick her lips. Mmm, she felt her knees weaken. "As for the powers meshing, we're not entirely sure how it will work, since I'm the first Guardian to go through it." He nuzzled her flesh, making her suck in a breath. She felt as if she were in a dream as he continued, "Sirena thinks that my Guardian powers may not meld at all, something to do with it being a gift of the Creators. I'm not sure I understood a word she said about that part, but our regular gifts should definitely meld and become more controllable."

"So you'll have my powers, and I'll have your Aletheia mental strengths?" He was nibbling at her earlobe, making it nearly impossible to get the question out. Liquid painted the inside of her thighs, and her breathing came out labored.

Once the mating is complete, theoretically... Right now we're just in the beginning. When we finally complete the ceremony and blood-bonding, the melding should start coming more rapidly. He spoke into her head, as that decadent mouth was otherwise occupied, licking at the point between her shoulder blades as he held her hair firmly wrapped in a hand. "Later, we'll work on controlling the head-hopping. That's what Conn said your brother called it," he added.

She felt a hint of fang scraping across her shoulder, causing a tremor to run through her body. She swallowed as he slowly moved his way back up her neck and behind her ear.

She couldn't think straight with the wicked things he made her feel. Did she dare hope to gain enough command over her abilities? She moaned when his teeth tugged at her lobe.

Her face flamed when realization of what Uri had said hit. He'd told her brother he would be screwing her... No wonder Vane wanted Uri's blood. Vane was already aware of what was going on, but Uri's talking to him was high-handed.

"Stop thinking." His voice was a low hoarse rasp, and then his teeth moved to her shoulder while he pulled her hips back into his hard body. She sucked in a breath and melted into his body. She'd rip into him about Vane later.

He'd taken his pants off at some point. She moaned, pushing even further into his hold. Feeling the solid jut of his need pulsing against her lower back made her sex quiver in response. He was so warm and stiff against her. She wanted to feel him sliding deep inside her again.

"Out of time," Uri growled as he smacked her bottom just enough to sting slightly while leaving a delicious warmth in its wake. The noise seemed loud even over the sounds of flowing water. He lifted her, and suddenly she was waist deep in warm water, her senses completely overloaded. She tried to turn to him, but instead, he crowded her body from behind, his body moving her further to the other side of the small pool. Their movements folded the water around them, and it caressed her sensitive flesh. She trembled with the need to feel him everywhere.

She saw movement, and a thick black cushion landed on the stone edge in front of her seconds before Uri's big palms cupped her needy breasts from behind. Her back arched, pressing harder into his palms, desperately craving firmer contact against those large warm hands. He pinched her nipples lightly, teasing her, as his cock rubbed up and down against her lower back. He was driving her wild. Alex's breath came out in gasps. Her head fell back against his chest while her body pushed against his, loving the feel of his wet skin against hers.

"Stand with your feet on the seat and bend over, head all the way down. I want to see every single inch of that cunt and ass in the air." Her body burned as he lifted her up so that her legs were still submerged. She felt the smooth glide of his hands up the backs of her thighs while he growled, "Wider."

She thought she'd pass out from the anticipation. Her upper body was wet, including the tips of her hair, which now stuck to her oversensitive flesh.

She spread her legs at his demand, feeling her juices on the insides of her thighs. She was shaking as she bent forward to rest her

149

head against her arms on the thick cushion. Every added sensation served to overload her. His roving hands inched so close to where she needed them. Her body twitched at the feel of heated breath against the crease of her bottom, followed by a deliciously languid lick that elicited a low moan she was barely aware came from her own lips. Her back arched further, wanting him to have all the access he needed to give her this new kind of pleasure. The thought of his mouth pressed against her was too much; her pussy ached for it. "Uri, please." She hated to beg, but she couldn't take it anymore.

She heard his deep inhale as he massaged her ass, spreading her cheeks wide so that nothing could possibly be hidden from his gaze. There was another deep moan followed by, "I love that you're bare, love that I can see every bit of this gorgeous little pussy." His tongue slid along her slit; Gods, his breath and hot mouth nearly scorched her. He took his time, swirling his tongue over her clit, making her pant and writhe while strong hands held her motionless against his tortuous mouth.

Crying out, she knew she was close. Instead, he denied her, moving from her aching clit to suck at her folds, one at a time. Then, his mouth was gone.

"No," she cried out in frustration. Pushing back, she imagined what he was seeing. She was spread and completely vulnerable to his sight and touch. He teased her again, this time with one finger pushing just inside her opening. She pushed against it, trying to get more. He slowly added another while giving her quick lashes of his tongue. He was keeping her at the edge of sanity, madness just one long lick away. Taking his time, he kissed, licked, and sucked his way around where she needed him to be. She was desperate, begging by the time he pushed both big fingers all the way inside her.

Heated moans came out unbidden as he pumped her with his fingers. His wicked tongue slid up and laved her tiny back hole. Her

150

movements stilled at the unexpected sensation, entranced by the sheer eroticism of having his tongue on her ass.

"Someday, I'll bury my cock deep in here. There isn't a part of you that I won't claim."

She was light-headed, ready to come just with his words. He swirled his tongue once again around the small opening, then finally moved back to her clit; the nub was swollen with need.

"I need to be in your mind," he said, and she felt the delicious slide of him inside her head as she opened to him without thought. Something she'd think about later. It was more than a caress inside her head. She let him feel what he was doing to her. The added intimacy was out of the realm of any fantasy. It was dangerously seductive. The sensation was like nothing she'd ever experienced; she felt all his heat inside and out.

She sucked in a breath as his mouth suckled her clit. It was all too powerful. Her entire being was completely in his control. One last firm suck wrenched a climax from her so strong it felt like a hurricane was taking her away. Her cries echoed off the wall as her knees started buckling. Uri had her in his arms before she collapsed, holding her close.

She'd felt the release, then subsequent push back against her shield, then some kind of snapping sensation, and finally the smooth retreat of its protection. She relaxed in the aftermath. Uri had only jerked slightly, still sharing her mind but unharmed. He'd done it. Somehow he'd manipulated her shield. She turned in his arms and stared at him, completely in awe as her senses came fully back. Looking internally to her shield, she saw it as a silvery haze along with a shiny thread that linked her to Uri's mind. It had to be their mating bond attached to her shield. The mental image had her reeling, feeling the sheer magnitude of their bond.

"How did you do that?" The words came out as a shocked gasp. Gazing at Uri, she saw the tense muscles of a male in need. He was the picture of undiluted sexual extremity. Her sexy Aletheia, complete with protruding fangs. The sheer beauty of him thrilled her, especially in his current feral state.

"I used the mating bond to manipulate the shield. I took it into my body. I also severed the link to your brothers at the same time." At her shocked look, he added, "Vane was aware of what I intended. You are mine to protect, Alexandra. He conceded once I reminded him that with the link intact he would know every time I made you come." There was a possessiveness to his gaze that stilled her for a split second.

Then she pinched the bridge of her nose in anger. She could just imagine that conversation. As pissed as a part of her was that he would take control without even asking her, and she was pissed, she looked at the water for a second.

He didn't even tell her what he'd planned, much less ask. "High-handedness will never be okay with me."

He gazed at her for a beat as she took a deep breath and continued. "We have a lot to learn about each other, but that's something you need to understand now."

She had to own that she really didn't want her brothers to know when she climaxed. It felt freeing, yet in a weird way she mourned the loss of any added connection to her family.

Uri nodded and scrubbed a hand over his face as her mind processed more. She looked to the ceiling. That link had been a constant reminder of her failure and weakness. With one more inhale, she willed away the ache in her stomach.

His sexy rumble made her look back at him. "I apologize. I

assumed you wouldn't want that complication." He looked entirely uncomfortable as he admitted he was wrong. She hadn't expected him to utter the words. It pleased her that he did.

She blew out a breath. "You're lucky I'm not kicking your ass. That was your one free pass. This is new to us both; next time ask before you do something that affects me." She had dealt with dominant males her entire long life; he would learn. She realized he was already making a concession by apologizing. That was huge for a male like him.

She closed her eyes and hoped for more, that this bond would be a new beginning, a way to control her powers. She felt like it truly was, and that made her sit a little straighter in his hold.

Uri must have felt her change in attitude because he brought her attention back to his current lack of satisfaction by taking possession of her mouth. She moaned deep as his tongue aggressively probed her depths. She tasted herself on his lips and gasped. In mere moments, she was ramped back up, arching her body into his, holding his head to hers. Pulling lightly at the soft strands of his hair earned a growl against her lips, vibrating them so good. He tasted and taunted her with his wicked tongue. She felt the tips of his fangs, surprised he hadn't nicked her. "Are you going to bite me?"

"In the mating ceremony." His voice was deep and raspy. She wondered what it would be like. His fangs were so incredibly sexy, but she didn't really understand why they kept slipping free. She'd have to ask. He pushed against her, letting her feel the hard evidence of his need while his tongue dueled with hers in a manner that showed just how little control he had. The thought filled her with feminine pride. Loving that she had the ability to make him as wild as he made her. He lifted her with one hand, then moved the cushion to the other side of the small pool and set her on it. There was no step on that side and the water was shallower, positioning him perfectly between her open thighs as he stood in the water.

She watched as he devoured her with his gaze while running his iron-hard length along her pussy, making tantalizing contact with her clit as he moved. After a couple of slow glides, he was coated in the juices of her renewed arousal. His eyes glittered and swirled as the muscles of his arms and chest pulled taut.

"Lay back and hold on to the bench leg behind you." The demand came out low and harsh.

She did as he asked. Lying back with her arms over her head pushed her breasts up in offering and made her squirm. The legs of the bench were a part of the floor. His eyes fixed on the hardened tips, peaked for him.

"I won't be gentle," he said, jaw tense. He reached out to pluck one tight bud, and her eyes went half lidded. He used his other hand to guide his way into her pussy. She felt her body expand to take the massive length. He hissed out a breath through clenched teeth. The tendons along his neck strained, and he looked like a primal beast ready to rut.

"I don't want gentle," she said as she pushed against him. He groaned when she added, "I can take anything you can give me."

Not needing any further encouragement, a groan tore from his throat as he seated himself fully inside her. She wiggled, loving the sensation of being stuffed full of him. She held on tight to the stone leg. It was even more amazing than the first time he took her. An odd primal feeling encompassed her. She wanted him rough and demanding, wild. She was stretched around him and aching in the best way. He was so deep, the press of his sac against her bottom was hot, making her cry out. She pulled him tighter with her thighs, wanting him to move but loving having him all the way to her womb.

The deep rumble of his growl made her pussy quiver.

A small surge of warm liquid slipped inside her, making her take a deep, ragged breath. He pulled out slowly, only to pound all the way back in. They both moaned as he filled her again. Then his strokes became harder, faster, more demanding. Alex never wanted him to stop. She cried out as he hit a spot so deep, so sensitive her eyes nearly rolled back. She watched, mesmerized, as he closed his eyes and pumped as if his life would end without this joining. She felt her walls pulse around him as, panting, she struggled to meet his thrusts. She was as much a wild animal as he was.

Uri's heavy breathing and tight groans mixed with the sounds of wet skin against skin were all her mind could focus on. He wrenched her legs from around his waist, putting them up on his shoulders. He felt even bigger and deeper inside her. Before she fully registered the change in pressure from the new position, those big hands were caressing her thighs all the way to her feet. She watched as he turned his head and licked her instep. Oh, Gods, the sight of his tongue lashing out between the tips of those sharp fangs, mixing with the look in his eyes as he savored the taste of her skin, had her pushing tighter against him.

He rotated his hips seductively before thrusting again. She cried out when a single fang grazed along the bottom of her foot, only to be followed by the circling of that magnificent tongue.

She writhed and moaned, barely able to breathe through the pleasure. Alex was out of her mind when one large thumb made its way to roll against her clit. All the while, he never missed a beat in the relentless pounding of his hips against hers. She crested in a blinding rush, her body bowing as she screamed her release.

She registered him shouting out at the same moment. Her shield seemed to pulse between them but not release. She felt Uri's euphoric release inside her mind. Feeling his climax pushed her into another world-shattering orgasm. Her body tightened over and over against his still-hard shaft, and he shouted again, bathing her womb.

It was beyond anything she'd thought possible. She didn't realize males could have multiple orgasms, but she'd felt the warm liquid filling her a second time. It somehow soothed her aching inner muscles. It was incredible, magical. She'd never truly been sated on her own, had only been able to take the edge off.

He lifted her into his arms, lowering them into the soothing water. For long moments she settled against him, held gently in his embrace with her cheek cradled into the curve of his neck. She was lulled by the rapid beat of his pulse. It relaxed her, and she cuddled into him, sated and content. It felt so right, perfect.

Her heart stilled. "Doesn't the fact that I'm your mate make it possible for pregnancy now?" She held her breath waiting for the answer. Unsure how she felt about that. Or how he felt about it for that matter.

"Only after we've completed the bond, and Sirena says it usually takes at least a decade, or longer."

He tucked her under his chin and rubbed her back in soft strokes for long moments before speaking again. "I need to know what happened to you." It was spoken softly but had the impact of dumping her in ice water; her body instantly tensed.

Crap, why did she have to relive her biggest life-altering mistake with him? She would rather forget about that now that she didn't have the constant reminder that had come with her connection to her brothers.

"I know this must be difficult. I heard enough in your mind to guess, Alexandra." His jaw was clenching so tight, she worried for his teeth. Thankfully, his fangs had retreated. "Part of the mating ceremony is the blood-bonding. In that, I will relive the most poignant of your memories, as you will mine. Trust me when I say that there are things I'm not looking forward to you seeing either. We have both lived long lives. If you've been through what I expect, I would rather hear it before I see it."

Her heart stuttered in her chest. He was going to see it? She felt the blood drain from her body and she grew chilled. He rubbed her back gently and tucked her head under his chin. He whispered into her hair, "Just breathe and tell me." At least she didn't have to look at him. Best to get it over with. She took a heavy breath.

She cleared her thoughts and figured it best to start at the beginning. "I grew up very sheltered. With the Gods falling to madness from taking in dark energies of death and destruction, my mother and father felt it smarter to keep us a secret and hidden away. Especially since our mother always thought my powers would evolve into something amazing. Though, that never happened." She brought her head up and looked at him, finding she'd rather see his face while she spoke.

With a tight nod, he urged her on, watching her with those penetrating eyes that seemed to see everything.

"The news apparently got out about my odd powers and my mother's feelings about my immense potential," she said caustically before clearing her throat.

She needed to stop stalling. "The Tria came for me... it wasn't until later that we found out about the rumors and pieced it together. My mother felt the attack was Artemis and Ares' doing, sending their demented offspring to... breed with me..." She had barely gotten the words out as bile built in her throat, almost choking her at the sickness of the two Gods. "My mother, Aphrodite, and Hades tried to kill them after finding me, but they couldn't. That's why they were imprisoned in Hell. My brothers and I were unconscious and in bad shape at that point, but I heard Drake and Pothos were also there and helped imprison the bastards."

Athena, Aphrodite and Hades had been the only just Gods during very dark times. Though that fact obviously hadn't saved them; they'd been put to sleep by the Creators along with the evil Deities.

"Go on," Uri said in a tight whisper, but she heard his teeth grinding. All during her explanation, he held her in his lap, sitting in the warm water, absently rubbing circles on her hips or on her back. It relaxed her, and she appreciated being soothed.

"That was it. Vane and Erik found me unconscious. I'd hopped into another's head and was lying in one of the hallways in my mother's palace." She tried not to mentally go back there, it was so long ago. "I wasn't inside my body, so I don't remember the act itself. I only remember waking up near death." His body got even more rigid against her. She leaned back into his chest and cleared her throat.

Her stomach churned as she continued. "I was broken, and I could hear my brothers fighting them." She fought back the tears that threatened as she relayed that part of the memory. Uri had gone back to drawing the soothing circles against her flesh, but she had seen the fury in his eyes before curling into his body. She practically whispered the hardest part. "They were toying with Vane and Erik. I'm lucky that was part of their fun. It's the only reason my brothers lived. Gods, Uri, they were so young. Not even twenty at the time and the Tria were so powerful. It was the worst thing imaginable to wake up broken and violated, only to be forced to witness the brothers I loved more than anything being ripped apart. I tried to move… but I couldn't. I couldn't help them." She had to stop and take a deep breath. "Finally, my mother and father, along with their warriors, came. That was the last I saw before losing consciousness. I was told the rest later."

"And…" he encouraged her. She wasn't sure how he knew there was more.

"I guess the worst part was my 'knowing' power had made me want to leave the palace. But I ignored it. I didn't understand the compulsion because I'd never felt the intuitive power until that moment… The whole thing was my fault."

He ground out with force, "It wasn't your fault. They would have found you eventually. Someday, I'm going to find a way to kill those fuckers." He took a deep breath and kissed her temple, still holding tight to her.

They stayed that way for a long time, with Uri just holding her in his comforting arms.

A long while later he sucked in a breath and spoke. "Let's see if we can work with the head-hopping."

She nodded. "Then you can explain that talk of a syringe."

Chapter 17

Guardian Compound, Earth Realm

Arriving back at the compound, they found it full of Guardians. Only Drake and Sirena were absent from the war room. The moment Uri announced that Alex was his mate, the entire place went electric with excitement.

"Wow, damn, it's true, then. Congratulations, man," Pothos said to Uri before winking at her. Even though she'd never officially met him, he was technically another cousin, the son of Hades. "Welcome to the family, Alexandra. Though, I guess you were already a part of my family." His sapphire eyes lit as he grinned down at her. He was Drake's size, and when he wanted, she knew that the son of Hades could pull wings from his back. He looked so much like she imagined his father would look in this era, short black hair, piercing sapphire eyes, and chiseled jaw and body. He wore black gauges in his ears and had a studded belt over his black jeans. Tattoos darted up his neck, and others were visible below the sleeves of his T-shirt.

Vane walked in with Conn as the rest of them were offering their greetings. So many wore surprised looks. This was a big deal. He was the first mated Guardian and it had been to a fugitive Demi-Goddess hiding from exile in Earth Realm. Alex felt a little shell-shocked herself. She saw Conn officially introducing her brother Vane to the others. She wondered how they could get along so easily. Vane had always been such a menace to Conn's computer systems.

She shook her head, knowing she'd never understand the complexities of male bonding.

Both Sacha and Bastian, the beautiful, exotic Kairos Guardians whose race was known for their teleportation abilities, moved forward. They were reserved, their movements graceful. Regal. As they welcomed her into the Guardian fold, Alex wondered if they were siblings. They looked so similar and could easily be a part of ancient Egyptian royalty with their black hair, dark eyes and tanned skin. Sacha was shorter, with her hair in a long braid, and had delicate features, whereas Bastian was tall and muscular like the other male Guardians. They were kind and soft-spoken, with a respectfulness that seemed a part of their DNA.

Dorian came up next. The Nereid actually looked more surprised than the others, or his was just lingering longer. He slapped Uri on the back. "Damn, who would have thought! I'm happy for you, man." Dorian wore a bright orange hoody over worn jeans and a green T-shirt. She narrowed her eyes, wondering if the sweatshirt did in fact have muscles drawn on it. She looked up into his smiling face. His blue-tipped blond hair was spiked high on his head, and his aquamarine eyes were stunning. He was tall, like Uri, but a little leaner, not that the male lacked in muscle.

When Conn introduced Vane to Brianne a few feet away, Alex felt tension in the air and frowned. Alex noted Conn's expression echoed hers. There was some crazy chemistry between her brother and the female Guardian. Had they met before? Brianne had her titian hair up in odd Princess Leia buns. The female Geraki was stunning, with pouty lips and shining amber eyes. Her race was able to transform into an extinct bird of prey, or partially transform so that she could use her powerful wings to take to the air. That explained the brown leather halter top with matching pants. She imagined Geraki didn't like having their backs confined in any way.

Brianne's earlier whoop of excitement, when Uri announced Alex was his mate, was now subdued. The female Guardian's entire focus was now solely on Alex's brother.

Before she could think on it more, Drake and Sirena walked in.

Sander groused, "Why aren't we doing this in Tetartos?"

Sander had dark almost chocolatey skin covered in tattoos, a shaved head, and hazel eyes that reflected his perpetual bad attitude. She and her brothers had learned a great deal about all of the Guardians in the last centuries. And she had to admit, the Phoenix was not her favorite.

"Because I'm in charge. Sit your ass down. All of you." Drake's voice could have chilled the room with its icy irritation, and Alex exuded a lot of restraint in not grinning. Everyone found seats. Uri pulled her chair close so that he could put an arm over the back of it. She took a deep breath and inhaled his wonderful scent. His warmth flowed over her and soothed her as Drake began telling the others about Erik's horrible situation.

"Sirena believes the moment we get to Tetartos, Erik and Sam's mind link will fully connect and he'll be able to locate her... as well as Cyril and Elizabeth." They would most likely only have one shot to get Sam and the others out and get their hands on Cyril and Elizabeth before the two found a new hiding spot.

Alex had lost all hope of staying clear of exile when she found out they would need to help get Sam from Cyril's clutches. No way would she or Vane let Erik go alone. They would be together in Tetartos. She only hoped something bad wouldn't come from leaving Earth because she still felt they were needed in the human Realm.

The whole thing left her uneasy, but she couldn't see a way around it. Uri had said that Sirena didn't think she would get any of his Guardian powers, but she held out hope that maybe she'd gain the one that would allow her out of the Tetartos confinement spell. She blew out a breath, because in the end it just didn't matter if she was trapped in the other Realm. She would deal with any cosmic consequence that came her way from denying a *knowing*, because there was no way in hell she wouldn't be there for Erik.

Drake explained, "We have no choice but to go in blind. Sirena and I have gone over all the alternatives, but based on Erik's situation, we'll have to play it as we go. Sirena thinks he'll go wild when we get there. We'll start at the Guardian manor in Tetartos but probably won't have long to wait for him to link with her. It's Sirena's belief that Erik's been burning through energy attempting to link to his mate in the other Realm, knowing she's in danger. She thinks that link will solidify fast once they're in the same Realm. Uri, Alex and Vane will follow him using their familial telepathic bond. After they track him to Cyril's compound, Uri will give us visuals to follow."

Everyone nodded. It would be easier if they had images of inside the compound that Sacha and Bastian could use to get in, but they didn't. Drake explained that even if Uri got views from a guard's mind, they still wouldn't know how many layers the Kairos would be forced to go through, and after several layers, the metal would start to drain their energies. The two Kairos Guardians had equally hard gazes as Drake vetoed that option.

"P, Brianne and I will go up to get aerial views for everyone once we have the location. Jax will bring charges; we'll likely need to blast our way inside. Dorian and Sander, you'll watch whatever entrance we make."

The other male's groan actually made Sander, the ass, grin. What was that about?

"Suck it up, Dorian." Drake's hard stare made the male groan again.

"Whatever." Dorian lounged back, arms crossed over his chest, eyes the color of aquamarines glittering with irritation, while Sander continued to smirk. *Okay?*

"Sirena will stay back and deal with whatever females we rescue. The rest will follow inside. I'll send directions on the fly for the rest, since we don't know what we're getting into," Drake said, not appearing overly happy with the plan.

Gregoire, Conn and Jax nodded understanding. Gregoire looked on when a clenched jaw.

After a little more talk, they got ready.

The rest happened so fast it was like a blur. She, Uri and the others, including Vane and an out-of-it Erik, touched down on a beautiful lawn, a courtyard they'd said was at Drake's manor on Tetartos. Uri quickly procured a spelled vest and was helping her into it. It fit snugly over the black shirt and fighting pants they had picked up at her apartment before heading to the meeting. She felt the touch of Uri's hands over the fabric, and her nipples responded instantly. The back of his big warm hand intentionally rubbed against them before securing the zipper. The courtyard was full of Guardians and her brothers, but no one seemed to notice.

Uri's eyes held so much heat she groaned.

Sirena approached them silently and whispered, "You two will need to be careful in there. Until the bonding ceremony is complete, you'll be hit with bouts of uncontrollable arousal. It could easily distract you." The Guardian healer lifted an eyebrow knowingly and shook her head before turning her gaze to Erik, sympathy shining bright in her violet eyes.

Well, that explained what she'd already learned of the mating frenzy sapping her concentration.

Alex took a breath as she gazed over at her brother. He was still in his own world as he stood with his big body tense, eyes shut. Her heart clenched looking at him.

Uri pulled her into his warmth, his thumb seductively stroking the skin where the shirt and vest met the low rise at the back of her pants. It was a touch that should have felt comforting, but was anything but. It created images of licking every hot inch of his flesh, like he was a freaking treat made just for her.

Shaking herself out of a bout of sexual ADD, she looked at her brother again. His eyes snapped open; he roared, his fury shaking the ground, and was gone. She tracked and followed in his wake. They hit a shield around the facility, and even though she knew it would happen, she, Vane and Uri all groaned at the impact. She felt Uri giving visuals to the others. Erik was in lion form, growling and roaring at the shield. They appeared to be outside a mountain in the heart of some jungle she'd guess would be in South America if the continents had the same names as Earth Realm.

Her muscles instantly tensed when a *knowing* came over her. She found the telepathic links to the dragon through Uri and quickly spoke. *Drake, we need to be in a location down in the ravine. I have an intuitive ability. I know that's where we need to make the hole.*

Drake didn't hesitate. *Jax will meet you there.* She and Uri ported to the area where they needed to blow the hole. Jax was there a second later, laying the charges. She broadcast the information to Erik and Vane as she listened to Uri informing the other Guardians.

Erik was currently banging into an invisible shield surrounding

165

the place. She didn't see any guards, but they'd have to know something was happening. She felt Uri's mind caress hers as she glanced to the winged Guardians in the air and had to admit it was impressive seeing Drake in his magnificent iridescent green dragon form. He was stunning. Brianne had released her wings, soaring in the winds. Pothos flew in the opposite direction, displacing the winds with his massive black wings. The whole sight was exceptional, and she felt a sense of rightness for the first time since setting foot on Tetartos.

Family. That thought expanded her heart as she readied for battle.

Blasts rang out, frightening birds from the haven of the jungle surrounding them.

Chapter 18

Cyril's Compound, Tetartos Realm

Sam gained consciousness again, her mind coming into focus in slow, hazy increments. She didn't even want to think about the long-term repercussions of the drugs they kept dosing her with. She only knew it had started giving her peace in her dreams. Her dreams had given her a protector, a magnificent coffee-colored lion with ice blue eyes. His presence made her feel safe and she didn't care that it was only fantasy.

In her current stupor she wanted to cry at the loss of that small slice of peace. She no longer felt warm fur and the lulling huffs of her dream beast. The cold reality was coming through the drugged haze.

She tried to shake off the madness of the drugs because she needed focus. She needed to get out.

Her holding cell pulsed in and out of focus like the room was made of Jell-O being jiggled with a fork. She closed her eyes against the sight. Actually, it felt more like being in a rubber ball. Her world was that ball, being bounced against the floor over and over, totally in the control of the asshole that kept dropping her.

She blinked and shook her head, hoping the bouncing would soon stop. She knew they'd come; they always did when lucidity began setting in. Her muscles were sore from the constant tension she felt every time she gained consciousness. She forced herself to block thoughts of the other reasons she was sore. That wouldn't help anything. What she needed was to come out of this as quickly as possible.

She took in her surroundings. She was lying naked in the freezing cell again. Better there than the lab. She didn't dare think of that now. She felt fragile, as if she'd break if she allowed thoughts of her abuse to permeate her mind, so she wouldn't. She was stronger than that.

The scent of sterile cleaners filled her nose. Luckily for her, Nazi Fuck apparently didn't like dirty "patients." At least she wouldn't have to smell them on her skin.

Sam forced her thoughts back to her goal. She needed to get out and try to free as many of her fellow inmates as possible. There would be strength in numbers. With no idea what the layout of the facility was, it would be a struggle, but she'd find a way, as long as her tormentors stayed away long enough for the drugs to leave her system.

Her body felt changed somehow; she knew something was happening, just didn't know what.

She didn't hear them coming for her, like she normally did, which had to be a good sign. This could be the opportunity she'd been waiting for.

Trying again to shake off the daze, she used what little strength she had in her weakened limbs to pull herself from the bunk. She had to close her eyes against the dizziness. Steadying herself, she took a deep breath and managed to get upright.

Sam staggered to the sink in the corner of the tiny cell, slamming into the cot with her knee as she went. Standing on shaky legs, she cupped a trembling hand under the faucet, washed her mouth out, and drank, splashing the cold liquid on her face between small sips. She needed fluids. Her mouth was dry from the drugs. She dared not drink too much, but she choked down what she could.

With muscles so tense she could barely stand it, she waited. Taking more deep breaths, she listened for any sounds from the corridor. This was the point when they'd caught her the last time... sweat dotted her skin. Nothing. Her heart beat so loud she could hear it pulsing inside her ears as she hurried to the cell door as quickly as her wobbly legs would allow.

As a child she'd found she had a flicker of ability with metal, one her parents had encouraged her to keep hidden for fear of her being taken and used as a lab rat. Ironic that she'd hidden it and still ended up someone's fucking experiment. If only she could focus it enough now to do some good.

Kneeling just behind where the lock would be, she closed her eyes and focused, not on the cold or the deadening silence, not on the sickening scent of disinfectant... just the lock. *Snick.* At nearly the same moment, she felt an odd snap inside her mind, followed by a pained animal roar. Her dream beast. Had she finally lost her sanity just as freedom was so close?

*****

The low-level pulsing of the alarm was grating on his nerves. Cyril's muscles shook he was so livid. From the main surveillance room, he caught sight of fucking Drake, in all his dragon glory, making deep swoops around the compound's perimeter; he needed to work fast.

How had they found him? There had to be a traitor; it was the only plausible explanation. He seethed at that thought. Once he found out who had betrayed him, they would suffer... he quickly fired off orders while on the move.

169

Elizabeth and Kane, get the Kairos to teleport the test subjects out. I want them guarded while they move the females to the northern facility; then they can come back for the others. Take the back exits from above. The Guardians have accessed the lower level and blocked off the bottom cells. The corridors in C have been compromised.

On our way. Kane's response was quick.

He hated teleporting anyone to one of the alternate locations until he knew who had betrayed him, but there wasn't a choice unless he wanted to sacrifice everyone. *Kane, I want anyone transported to the northern location put on lockdown. Everyone will need to be interrogated once you're done here.* He would need to find the mole quickly.

In his lab he could still hear the low thrumming of the alarm that went with the oscillating red lights in the corridors. He willed the data to back up quickly; he could only teleport so much. A good deal of his earlier data results were already safely ensconced in his eastern facility. He always made sure that backups were sent to the safe location. He fumed as he looked around. He had always thought that if the Guardians found him, he'd have more time after the breach.

Fortunately, he would be able to teleport himself and some data, thanks to the blood of his father, Apollo. But he was highly limited in that particular ability. Something that particularly grated as he moved to destroy anything he wouldn't have time to take. They would not get any of his information.

He would be forced to transport everything from cold storage himself. He only had a few Kairos, as the race was rare. Those he did have would need to first get his test subjects out, then what warriors were left. All knew the exit plans.

170

Angus, send down as many troops as possible to the breach in Section C. Send in waves of Mageias first. Maybe we'll luck out and they'll injure one. If nothing else, it will slow them down. We need to back them away from the corridor leading to the holding cells.

He barked orders to the fidgety lab techs working frantically around him. "Get the vials into transport cases, now. I want them in the exit room within five minutes." He'd need to make several trips. He cursed his limited teleporting capabilities. He wasn't sure there was time to get everything. The data and vials were most important, but he'd like to get a couple of the techs if there was time. If not, he'd kill them before letting the Guardians get their hands on one.

*****

Sam listened to the loud droning of an alarm. What was happening? Was this why the guards hadn't come?

She wished the drugged haze would leave her soon and her sanity would start returning. The animal roar of her brilliant protector had changed to growling and snarling in her mind and was making escape harder. She just couldn't concentrate.

She made it out of her cell and over to the next, embracing the delusion of a protector coming for her only because it made her feel a little stronger. Her body was still moving in slow motion, but she was moving. She leaned her head against the cool metal of the cell door that held another inmate, one that was currently unconscious. She tried willing the chill of the metal to bring her further into alertness. It wasn't working. Sam couldn't focus her powers enough; she was too weak for this. Slowly banging her head against the door was having no effect. Should she just try to leave without rescuing any of the others? They were still out cold, so she'd have to leave and find help for them.

She'd been forced to just sit there and breathe for too long, working to calm herself. It was odd that her heart could beat so fast while her limbs could barely move. The hallway looked so long, spanning what seemed like miles ahead. The growling seemed louder as the drugs slowly left her body. Shit, she was hoping it would go away, not get worse.

Sam held her hands to her ears, it was getting louder by the minute, but she was just crazy enough not to want it to stop. It seemed her mind was heading toward its breaking point. Her entire focus was on that desperate noise. Was this the end of her sanity? She looked down the hall and she knew she needed to go in that direction. Her legs still shook as she moved. She lost herself to the snarls inside her mind. She moved in the direction they seemed to lead her.

Chapter 19

Cyril's Compound, Tetartos Realm

Alex moved in a blur of motion at the breached tunnels hidden in Cyril's stronghold. Uri found himself at once aroused, filled with pride, then fucking horrified at her recklessness. She launched, teleported, and snapped necks at a rate that should *not* have made him want to fuck her up against the nearest wall, but she was incredible.

He'd never before been forced to fight with an erection, and he hoped the thing would calm the hell down, because his semi-hard cock was not making the battle easier. Sirena wasn't kidding about the crazed distraction of the mating frenzy.

Before they'd even left the manor, his mate had been sending him visuals of her sucking his dick dry. He had been so caught off guard by the sights in his mind of her swallowing him down that he'd barely registered that Erik had completed his link with Sam. He'd been one step behind her as they teleported to Cyril's stronghold.

He watched her take down another guard that dared go near Erik. The sounds of a low alarm, shouts of Mageias, and the slashing of blades filled the space. It wasn't as easy to tune out the odor of burnt flesh, courtesy of a Mageia skilled in launching fireballs.

Their bond was distracting as fuck. He felt the mating connection like a living thing. Each time she tapped into his powers, they swelled for her, just like his unruly cock. He felt her use his own bond with his fellow Guardians to link with them. Hell, he'd even felt when she *knew* the spot to blow a hole in the mountain. That particular power was impressive. When they completed the mating ceremony, he wasn't sure what it would become.

This was not the time or place to think about their connection; he had to get his head back in the game. Guards were flooding the tunnels in all directions. Whatever warriors Erik didn't lay waste to, Alex or Vane, who flanked their brother, took out with their blades. Uri covered the rear, irritated that Cyril's first line appeared to be predominately elemental Mageias. He envied his mate and her brothers' ability to dispatch the mortals. He and his brethren weren't so lucky, not with the curse of tenfold the pain.

The area they were in appeared to be a cafeteria or mess hall of some sort. Tables that were once laid out in lines were now overturned, damage wrought by the first air elemental that had come through. Erik was like a bullet, destroying anything in his path with single-minded focus on finding his female, his massive jaws tearing into anyone who dared block his path.

The Mageias seemed to have had their powers enhanced in the labs, effectively slowing him and his brethren. He growled as a blast of fire licked over his shoulder before he quickly took the bastard down with silver cuffs that would inhibit their powers.

Snarling in fury, he teleported behind an Aletheia who dared near Alex. In a flash of movement he grabbed the male by the throat. One harsh snap and sharp slice from his blade, and the male fell to a bloody heap on the ground.

Alex teleported behind another Mageia, slicing skin and bone until his head rolled to the ground as Vane snapped the neck of another who ventured too close to Erik. He dodged fireballs, still watching the back of his female. Another fucking air elemental whipped into the room, pulling power to suck air from their lungs before Erik's claws slashed through the mortal's chest, barely hesitating, too focused on a destination only he knew.

The corridors were crowded and loud with cries of battle rage. Erik had just gone through a tunnel to the side when Uri heard a furious roar and smelled the blood mixed with burnt flesh and fur. Without looking, he knew Erik had been hit by a fire elemental. Vane was there in a flash, slashing with his blade until the elemental littered the floor next to the others who'd already fallen.

Vane and Alex were a sight; hand-to-hand was not a problem for them. And Vane seemed to relish the fight; the male was impressive.

Once Erik accessed the tunnel to the right, he was a blur of movement, bounding down the nearly empty tunnel. Vane, Alex and Uri were forced to cover the influx of fighters at the corner. They didn't want to let the battle get past the connection of paths leading four ways. There were fucking keypads to what appeared to be emergency doors hidden in the walls there. He quickly communicated the need to guard that spot or risk losing their exit.

He heard Alex using his link to Drake and Conn, giving them a mental image of a location she believed might hold Cyril. Another *feeling* she had about a tunnel they'd passed a few minutes before.

Her worry for Erik was relentlessly sliding through their bond, but she stayed near him. Stayed fighting against the hordes of Cyril's warriors that wouldn't stop coming. She and Vane were the only ones who could effectively dispatch this fucking many Mageia, and he knew they were aware of that shitty fact. And there were dozens mixed with Immortals. When one fell, another fought in its place, no matter how many dead bodies piled in the converging tunnels. He called for Gregoire, Sacha and Jax, who'd been battling soldiers in another tunnel.

When the other Guardians teleported to them, Uri directed Jax and Gregoire to follow Erik. Jax had the explosives in case they were needed.

Uri linked with Vane and Alex to inform them what the hell was going on as more cries of Mageia filled the space. He felt Alex's relief that Erik was getting backup while Vane issued a grunt of acknowledgement. They were right in the middle of a cluster-fuck.

Sacha stayed to help fight back the horde coming at them. They still needed to make sure the enemy couldn't throw the doors closed. Sacha and Bastian were the only ones able to teleport through metal, and they wouldn't be able to take passengers. Blowing doors might take time they might not have if Cyril decided to blast the place to rubble now that his location was compromised. He had no doubt that could and would happen, sooner than later.

Alex and Vane were picking off elementals, leaving full Immortals to Uri and Sacha.

The hall they fought in couldn't be more than six or eight feet wide, making it a bitch to use blades, though his beautiful mate wasn't fazed by it. She used sleek fighting skills, opting for her long daggers. She slid low to hamstring a fighter only to come up and slice his throat before bashing the idiot behind him with the dying male's head. She hadn't been kidding about her abilities. He was enthralled by her graceful movements.

They were making progress in pushing the army back, thinning it. At that thought, a fire elemental in the furious rush of warriors landed a fireball against Vane's shoulder. The Demi-God roared while busy cutting down another Mageia.

Uri felt Alex's rage slamming through the link. Right before his eyes, she teleported into the middle of the enemy. Air hissed from his lungs as they surrounded her. He was already en route to her, his ears buzzing in the split second she took slicing the fire elemental's throat. He used his weight and fury to slam the masses away from her before teleporting them back beside Vane, bleeding from a cut to her stomach.

Uri's vision was burning red when he scented her blood and saw the cut on her stomach. He snapped the neck of a big

Hippeus as he demanded, *How serious is your wound?* He was barely able to get the words out through the telepathic link; he was too enraged at the scent of her injury.

It's fine. Just a flesh wound. You didn't need to come after me. I was just leaving.

He couldn't even speak. He was so damned furious she'd pulled such a reckless fucking move.

An Ailouros he was fighting obviously saw his distraction. The male sneered as he landed a bloody claw mark down Uri's chest. The bastard was fighting in a partial cat form. The cut barely stung, but getting caught off guard battered his pride. It didn't matter the cats were of the warrior class of Immortals. He was a fucking Guardian. The bulky bastard was a cheetah or some shit with speed and a good reach. Fighting in close quarters was a pain in the ass, but he finally saw his opportunity to finish it. He teleported behind the cat and smoothly avoided a head butt before snapping the male's neck. He had a bit of time before he'd have to take the asshole's head.

He looked around at the mass of fighters, who were already starting to lose their nerve. When they saw the cat go down, some finally began retreating. The lifeless bodies of Cyril's warriors littered the floor, forcing them to fight over bodies in order to hold the line they needed to protect their exit route.

Drake, Bastian, and Conn must have cut a swath through their end since no more enemies were coming from that direction.

He felt Alex's need to get to her brother.

"You and Vane go. Sacha and I can hold the route open."

She gave him a grateful smile and ran in the direction Erik had gone.

Fuck, he didn't like her off without him.

Sander, can you get down here and keep this exit clear? His need to protect his mate was growing fiercer by the minute. It didn't matter that the tunnel looked empty.

On my way.

Once the other fighters realized that their buddies had retreated, the stragglers fell back as well, but Uri wouldn't leave Sacha alone to cover their exit.

"I've got this. Go to your mate."

He appreciated Sacha's assurance, but he wasn't leaving her. If the enemy returned with reinforcements, she'd be by herself. The fucking Mageia had made this battle far harder on his brethren than Alex and her brothers. The minute he saw Sander's dark skin come into focus, he felt for Alex's location. She was panicked.

He was nearly blinded by worry as he ported through the halls to get to her as quickly as he fucking could.

Chapter 20

Cyril's Compound, Tetartos Realm

Sam watched as the door slid open at the end of the hall. She froze and quickly flattened her body against a cell as four guards poured through. Her heart threatened to leap out of her chest as she looked frantically for another exit she already knew didn't exist. She couldn't understand their shouts through the snarling and growling in her mind.

She was caught and nauseated at the thought of what they would do to her. They hadn't noticed her, yet. Instead facing the opening they'd just come through as the one with long blond hair furiously mashed at the keypad next to the door.

Just as the door started to slide shut, her dream lion launched through in a majestically fierce blur. Suddenly the roaring came in stereo through her mind while vibrating off the icy walls of the corridor. She stumbled, knowing the wild sound was coming from the beautiful beast currently ripping the throat from one of the guards. She fought the dizziness while horrified by the sight of guards throwing balls of fire at her beast.

It was real. Not a figment of her fragmenting mind. She'd already seen and been through enough to know supernatural things truly existed, yet the battle before her was nearly unfathomable. The violence should have repelled and sickened her, but she didn't care. All she could think about was saving her wild beast.

She yelled for them to stop and moved forward as quickly as her weakened state would allow, hoping at least to distract them. She wasn't sure what was happening to her, or why she was so overcome with need to protect him, but she knew she had to. She had to get to him; the harsh scent of his singed fur made her stomach turn, her movements more urgent. There were bloody gouges in his dark chocolate coat and the bastard guard even managed a hit to his beautiful black mane.

Shouts echoed off the cold walls, but she couldn't make out the words. A blast at the door rocked the ground beneath her feet, and suddenly two big males came through the haze of dirt and stone. Her shout of warning seemed weak, choked from her dry throat, and she didn't know if her lion heard her over the shrieking guards. The majestic beast made fast work of one who'd tried to sneak up on him.

The blond guard seemed to be biding his time, moving in for an opening while eying the newcomers. Both new men were huge, yet moved with blinding speed as they took on the guards. She breathed in relief that the two were obviously there to help her lion.

Finally, the last guard fell and she nearly collapsed with relief.

Steadying a shaking hand on the wall, she fought for the balance to move again. Her body nearly denied her, but she finally found her footing and staggered toward the injured animal. He needed her; she felt it. He turned from the last downed guard and faced her. Brilliant, ice blue eyes caught her gaze as he prowled toward her with pure animal grace. The snarling had stopped at some point and all she heard now was her own deep breathing as she moved. Just before they met in the middle, she saw a shimmering, and the most godlike man she'd ever seen replaced her lion. He shared the same ice blue gaze, but these held pain and something else that made her heart lurch.

She sucked in a deep breath at the sight before her. He was pure perfection, with short dark hair and penetrating eyes. The blood coating his tan flesh made her as angry as the gouges marring the dips of muscle covering his nude body.

She had to have lost consciousness again, for she'd never felt such a strong pull toward a man, nor had she ever seen anyone that could compare to him. Her mind had to have conjured him up from her deepest darkest fantasies.

He got close before, towering over her, he lifted a hand to stroke her cheek. Such a gentle touch, it made her body weak with comfort... and need. An intense feeling of safety settled into her bones and warmed her chilled body.

On a deep, gravelly whisper, she heard, "You're safe now." Then he collapsed at her feet. She huddled down next to him. *Please don't be dead, please don't be dead,* ran over and over inside her mind as she lifted his head onto her lap.

Suddenly, a dark-haired woman rushed into the hallway beside a guy with long blond hair.

She gave what she hoped was a fierce look to the newcomers. "He needs a hospital. Now! We have to get him out of here." She looked around, daring any of them to deny her. If this was real, he needed help. Somehow she felt connected to the lion man.

The blond guy and the woman were leaning over her in a split second. "Erik will be okay. I promise. He's our brother, and he'll be fine," said the woman. How could they know that? She was going to have to trust them, because she felt like her body was slowly shutting down and spiking all at once.

The other woman kept talking through Sam's shakiness. "I'm Alex, and this is Vane," Alex said with a gesture to the blond with long hair. Vane was already crouching to them, touching Erik's head, gazing intently at his brother.

A loud explosion rocked the entire room, coming from behind the metal of the wall next to her. More dust fell, and she heard movements in the other cells.

"Fuck. We need to get a move on. Everything's going to be fine." A look of reassurance shined in Vane's pale blue eyes as he said the words.

Another guy came in with a rush of speed, barking orders, "Jax, get some charges on these cells. We need to get the females out of here before they get through that wall." The woman, Alex, looked to the new guy with a grateful expression, which settled Sam's nerves a little. He had to be a good guy.

"I'm Uri," he said as he pulled off his black long-sleeve shirt and handed it to her.

How had she forgotten she was nude? Her face heated as she quickly donned the shirt. It had rips down the front but was long enough to cover her to her knees. She used the hem to wipe some of the blood from Erik's skin.

"We need something to stop the bleeding," Sam slurred, knowing she should have thought to do that sooner.

"I'm working on that, Sam. Don't panic. He'll be fine," Alex said while holding her hands over the wounds.

Before Sam's eyes, the wounds stopped bleeding... closing up. "This is the best I can do for now. I need to save energy to get you both out of here." Alex frowned and bit her lip as if the decision was difficult for her. "Vane, you're going to have to carry Erik out of here; I can get Sam."

How did Alex know her name?

Locks started blowing with loud pops, and she heard another large explosion hit on the other side of the wall.

Uri told the others, "Vane, Alex, get your brother and his mate out of here. They're almost through."

Mate? What did that mean? She shivered; her body was so cold. Her mind was beyond processing any more. She couldn't focus on anything other than the warmth she felt coming from Erik's body, assuring her he was alive and okay as all the heat drained from her own body. Her vision started getting spotty, and she shivered as she broke out in a cold sweat.

"Shit, she needs Sirena. Get them out of here while we get the females." She thought that came from Uri, but couldn't be sure.

Chapter 21

Guardian Manor, Tetartos Realm

Uri's back hurt like a motherfucker.

They almost hadn't gotten out of there at all; it had been close. The last lock hadn't blown all the way through. He'd just gotten a redhead out of her cell when he had heard Conn's telepathic, *Fuck! Uri, Sander, get your asses out!* Sander had been left guarding the tunnel that was Uri's exit. After quickly scooping up the female, he'd started teleporting in stages. He heard the blast and managed to protect the female in his arms, but he'd felt the searing heat and impact as he was teleporting out. He knew his skin was flayed, he could fucking feel it. There was likely debris in the wound too, which was just lovely. That would need to be ripped out.

He took stock of his injuries; some bones were broken.

The soft breeze in the courtyard of the manor felt damn good. He inhaled the sweet scent of the trees and grass and heard the light tinkling of the fountains. Hell yeah. Gone was the acrid stench of smoke, blood, and death.

He was weakening, just beginning to double over, when Drake took the redhead from him.

He hit the ground on his knees, and Alex was there behind him. He heard her breath catch, most likely seeing the damage. He felt her light touch to his bare stomach; she felt amazing even in his current condition.

185

A split second passed as all hell broke loose.

Trying to concentrate on knitting bones and flesh, he didn't register what was happening around him. When he heard a snarling growl and felt pissed hellhound emotion coming through his blood bond, he looked up. Shit. Havoc was in front of him, spewing flames at Drake's feet. The Guardian leader moved clear just in time for his boots not to get torched.

His chest lurched as he moved to get the damn animal out of incinerating distance. Alex let her shield loose with enough power that it covered the three of them. Blasts of fire hit the barrier before dissipating safely away, and Havoc was crouched a few feet in front of him, but the beast was fucking whole. Relief hit hard, along with weakness that made him grit his teeth.

"What the fuck?" yelled Sander.

"Shit, it's not a hellhound attack; the hound's Uri's. Hold your fucking fire. Literally, you fucking dumbass." This was from Jax.

Uri noticed Drake didn't stick up for the beast, no doubt he'd have been happy if Sander had fried Havoc's ass. Smoke billowed from their leader's mouth, making the female in his arms cough.

"Dorian, come take this female to Sirena," Drake bellowed, his voice booming in the mostly quiet courtyard.

Uri noticed most of the Guardians, with the exception of Sirena, Gregoire, Conn and P, were there in the courtyard with them. The others were likely taking care of the patients, or working on data in Conn's case. They all sported looks ranging from shock to, in Dorian's case, amusement as he took Drake's bundle and left with her through one of the French doors.

"What does that mean? *Uri's* hellhound? Did I miss a meeting or

186

something?" asked Brianne, standing there with her mouth gaping open.

The shield released around them, and he felt warm healing coming from Alex's smooth hands. He had to stifle a groan at how good it felt. "Sirena can take care of it. Don't waste too much of your energy," he whispered.

He felt a wave of... possessiveness or jealousy hit strong through their link and grinned to himself. He touched the small hand that still held his stomach while the stubborn female finished healing his wound. It felt amazing, and nothing like being healed by Sirena. Alex's touch, and energy, was like a pulse straight to his cock. He dropped his mental shield and let her feel what she was doing to him. She gasped and moaned lightly, holding even tighter to the skin at the front of his body.

At Havoc's confused agitation, Uri snapped back to reality. Somewhat. He sent a message to the animal meant to calm the protective pup. He would hate to see the bastard grilled by Drake, which was still a possibility. He understood that the beast had assumed Drake was attacking. It was the dragon's proximity to Uri and the hound's issues with that particular scent that made Drake the most likely threat in the hound's mind.

"He thought you were the threat." He bit back a grin at the look in his leader's eyes. He saw Drake glaring daggers at the beast, but there was something else there too... Amusement? Maybe even a little respect?

"I got that. I should be thankful the bastard didn't aim higher. A teleporting hellhound isn't fucking good, Uri."

Uri nodded. It wasn't a good sign that the beast obviously got some of Uri's power in their blood bond. Not if anyone in the

Immortal Realm saw that and thought Uri's blood was the answer to leaving Tetartos.

Shit. He'd deal with that later. The pup was still eyeing Drake closely and he grinned at that. Havoc was smart; at least he hadn't gone for the kill with the dragon, remembering on some level that Drake was not to be harmed.

Damn, he was exhausted and still needed to get some internal damage repaired. He also needed to have Sirena check Alex's knife wound, and get them both refueled.

Havoc was still on alert, even when the animal nuzzled at Alex, making her chuckle low, before vigilantly continuing to guard them. The giggle loosed something in him, soothing something deep inside. He realized he loved the happy sound she made, enjoyed this closeness of having a mate after so many centuries alone.

Drake blew out an irritated breath. "Get Sirena to fix your back, refuel, then I need you to check the memories of the victims and the prisoner we captured while we were there. He was one of Cyril's lab people. Conn went to toss him in holding," Drake said.

"Everyone will meet in the manor's war room in three hours. A lot has happened that you need to know, and we need the information you get from the tech," Drake said with a fierce look.

Chapter 22

Guardian Manor, Tetartos Realm

Alex was exhausted and amped up, all at the same time. They'd gotten Sam out, and Erik was safe. She felt mostly just relieved as they stood in the healer's office.

"Give me your arm," Sirena demanded of Uri, and he shook his head as he presented his vein. "We were going to need to do this anyway to have on record for the mating," the healer pointed out as she took the blood sample. She'd already taken one from Alex.

Sirena had already seen to some of Uri's internal damage wrought by the explosion, as well as Erik's burnt flesh, and even looked at the almost healed cut to Alex's side. Uri had irrationally insisted Sirena look at it even after Alex told him it was fine. He'd scowled at her, arms crossed, until she let them see.

Alex had proceeded to raise her eyebrows when Sirena deemed it was, in fact, fine. Just as she'd already told him. Vane, Jax and Gregoire were also crowded into the room with the healer, awaiting instruction.

Sirena had been divvying up duties to everyone within hearing distance ever since they'd gotten to the large exam room. The space was fairly sparse, as if Sirena didn't spend much time in her Tetartos office. Just beautiful plastered walls and a desk to one side. There were a couple of cots, one which housed an unconscious Erik; then to the other side were floor-to-ceiling cabinets. She did notice a sink and almost jumped up and down at the thought of indoor plumbing. Alex had all these visions of a primitive Tetartos, so seeing modernization thrilled her beyond belief.

Erik's brows furrowed even in sleep. She and Vane were both sending their brother energy as Sirena instructed the nurses coming in and out. Alex heard the healer directing her staff to monitor and see to the comfort of the victims holed up in the guest rooms. It made Alex like the female Guardian that much more.

Directing her attention back to their group, Sirena started with the guys. "Vane, I want you, Gregoire and Jax to refuel Erik again."

The males nodded.

Sirena absently scratched behind Havoc's ear, the hound having parked himself next to Sirena the moment they'd arrived.

When one healer took a look at the beast and shrieked, Jax had gone out and informed the staff that the hellhound was in fact Uri's and not to be harmed. She wasn't sure how that had gone over, but no one had come to see Sirena since.

Apparently Uri had saved the beast's life, which only added another reason for her to care about her mate.

When Alex started to volunteer to stay and continue helping replenish Erik's energy, Sirena shook her head. Alex hadn't even gotten the words out before being vetoed. Sirena gave her a wan smile. "I know you want to help your brother, but I really need you and Uri to continue bonding and get refueled. The more you're together and allow your minds and bodies to link, the better."

Vane groaned and huffed, making Sirena shake her head before she continued, "Those females need what you can do for them once Uri is replenished. First, I need you to get their memories of what happened so that I can figure out exactly what Cyril did. I'm also hoping you can do something to dull the edges of their trauma. I hate for them to suffer if we can do something to help them."

Alex wasn't sure exactly what that entailed.

At Alex's confused look, Uri explained, "I'm able to alter mortals' minds and memories, take the memories, or just blur the lines of the trauma so they'd know what happened, but it wouldn't feel as fresh. I can add some positive compulsions while I'm in there." She could hear the exhaustion he felt through his quiet words. She needed to get him refueled.

Sirena moved on. "My hope is that once you have completed the mating ceremony, your added power should allow you to work on Immortal minds as well." Sirena paused, only to add solemnly, "I believe Erik might need that skill."

Alex knew her brother was going to be in bad shape, knowing what happened to Sam. If there was even a chance they could help Erik, she would do it.

"For now, I think it's best to keep Erik unconscious. Maybe for a couple of days to allow him to recover and delay the frenzy he'll feel when he awakens," Sirena added, shaking her head.

The sadness Alex saw in Sirena's gaze echoed in her own. Sam and Erik had a difficult road ahead, and it broke her heart.

"I knocked Sam out with a spell, but they never last long and are a pain to do. I didn't want to give her more drugs, not knowing what Cyril had been giving her. I got some blood samples afterward and am waiting on the results. You have about two hours before she's conscious."

Sirena was thorough.

Alex felt the delicious heat coming off her depleted mate, who stubbornly stood instead of sitting in a chair. She shook her head as she looked at the proud warrior that was hers. Her stomach tightened just at the sight of him, still covered in blood and grime, his muscles strong and large even in repose.

Alex looked away. She just might jump him in this very room. She had to get them out of there. Her voice came out a little croaked as she asked Vane, "Are you sure you've got Erik covered? I can help when—"

Gregoire was the one to cut her off in his low deep rumble. "Go with your mate. We will take care of Erik." Something about the comforting assurance in the broody male's eyes calmed her. He hadn't spoken much to her, but it seemed he wasn't the vocal kind.

Vane nodded his agreement. "We've got it covered, Alex. Jax owes my ass for taking out a fire elemental Mageia earlier, and once Erik's refueled and comfortable, I'm on data duty with Conn. I'll be checking on him, even though the doc says he'll be out."

That Vane had jumped headlong into working with the Guardians was a good surprise, although it had her feeling slightly bereft. His eyes held an anticipation that felt odd when they'd just left everything behind. She guessed she should be grateful. It would make the change easier on him now that their old lives were officially over.

It was like Gregoire read her mind as he said, "You have nothing to worry about. I've already told Vane that Erik will take my suite. I never sleep here. It's at the end of the hall from Uri and your suite."

Before she could think, Jax spoke. "P doesn't use his suite either, so Vane's going to be in that one; it's next to Erik's new digs. We've got the staff getting everything ready." His wink was pure lasciviousness, which earned a growl from Uri. Jax barked with laughter.

Gregoire shook his head with a tilt of his lips as Uri squeezed her hand, bringing her attention to his beautiful and possessive face. His warmth wrapped around and through her. Alex didn't know what hit her harder, the gratitude that they would provide what sounded like a permanent home for her brothers, or the fact that they said she automatically got half of Uri's suite. She shook her head. Everything had happened so fast, logistics of their mating hadn't even made it into her brain, except in fleeting moments.

"Everything will be fine, little one. Go, take care of your mate," Gregoire said in his deep, soothing voice. There was a flicker of compassion in his gaze, mixed with those shadows she kept seeing in the depths.

"Okay, if you need us, call. We'll get refueled, then work with the females." She tugged on Uri to get him moving.

"Go ahead and leave Havoc with me. If he's not fine here, I'll drop him at your suite," Sirena said as she cooed a little at the animal again.

It was a really odd feeling when Uri communicated emotions and pictures through his link to the animal, instructing the pup to obey Sirena. It was a very different kind of link than what they shared. Simplistic. His skills with the mind were truly impressive, and she enjoyed feeling his powers slowly work their way into her. That was the only way she could explain the sensations in her body. Every time Uri linked with the other Guardians or Havoc, she felt it, and the links were becoming stronger inside her own mind. She'd never been particularly competent with telepathic skills. She could link with her brothers and talk like she had with Uri, because he'd been so close, but that was the extent. Until now.

193

She tucked into his warmth when they slipped into the hallway.

It was awe inspiring to believe that fate had given her a mate whose powers so completely complemented her own. That Sirena thought she would enhance his abilities made her stomach flutter.

Sirena had high hopes for them, and she seemed to want them to complete the bond soon. Alex had to agree. The healer was fierce but compassionate. She knew the female's motives were for the better of the races and she respected that.

She wished she knew more about the ceremony. About matings in general. She felt out of sorts and nervous. She understood that they'd have to blood-bond and had to admit that taking blood was never at the top of her to-do list, but she'd manage. She hoped that her powers would really meld and she'd be able to control them as Sirena and Uri thought. She'd been a failure with her abilities for so long her gut clenched that she'd fail with the way they combined. What if she ended up being the only mate that didn't gain more control of her abilities?

"We have a lot to discuss. After. Right now I need energy and to be deep inside you," Uri growled. He sent vibrations deep into the bond that somehow made her needy entrance pulse and her knees start to buckle.

Chapter 23

Guardian Manor, Tetartos Realm

Uri let the soothing energies flow into him from the manor's underground cavern suite. He felt restoring fuel flow in deep waves to his depleted cells. His body soaked them in greedily, causing tight muscles to slowly relax as the steaming water from the multiple showerheads carried off the dirt and blood from his skin. He'd wanted to take Alex the minute they entered the room. The scent of her slick with need had been driving him wild since they left Sirena's office. He took a great amount of primal enjoyment in seeing his effect on her. His cock was rock hard, but he forced them both into the shower to clean, not wanting to slip inside her tight little pussy while still covered in blood.

He knew Alex was in turmoil. He felt her emotions roll in waves through their growing bond.

He also knew she had no idea what was coming; there was much to explain, most of which he didn't fucking want to tell her. The blood bond would no doubt show her all of his fucked-up past and, truth be told, he dreaded seeing what happened to her all those centuries ago.

He blew out a frustrated breath. They didn't have much time, they needed to get to work within hours, and he had to be wrapped inside her warmth before that happened. The need to fill her with his cock while linking their minds was all consuming. The fucking frenzy was ruling them both, and if he didn't take care of those needs, he'd be useless.

It was still crazy to him that, while he was able to see all of Alexandra's beauty, loyalty, and skill, she saw mostly inadequacy and flaws. He understood when she'd shared her past with him. He understood how that would mold her, but, fuck. She was so much more than what happened. She was more than the unique and wild power she held.

He would someday find a way to end the Tria, but until then, he would have to find a way to get her to see how fucking amazing she was.

He didn't want to contemplate how she saw him. All those females he'd fucked in front of her, getting off on the fact that she was there watching him. Confident that she was just as hot for the game, but now wishing they'd never played it. He ran his hand over his head. He was possessive, which was a completely foreign emotion for him.

He felt her scattered emotions through their bond. She washed while he did, at the second set of showerheads in the cavernous bath. She was so close. He could touch her if he could get his shit together enough.

Turning, he took in the gorgeous picture she made. Her forehead rested on the wall as the warm water caressed her beautiful skin, washing the blood and grime away. Dark strands of her hair ran with moisture, rivers of it cascading down the most firm sexy ass he'd ever seen. His breath stuck in his throat as his cock swelled to painful levels. With her hands braced against the cool stone and the smooth lines of her back arching slightly, it left the perfect track for the water flowing down past twin dimples at her hips to make its way between the mounds of her ass.

He had to close his eyes.

"Mmm, I guess that means you're feeling re-energized?" Her voice came out husky.

His breath left in a rush as she turned to him. Fucking hell. He felt her pushing waves of desire through the link, making him groan low.

Her skin was glistening and flushed from the warm water. Her rose-tipped nipples were tight. Those perfect full tits swollen, just begging for his mouth and hands. In an instant, he had her pinned against the wall, with water flowing around them. He took her soft lips possessively, nipping and then delving into her hot little mouth to tangle with that sweet tongue. She reversed the hold. Her strength had his back to the wall, muscles tight. He tilted his head, interested to see where she was going with this. He could easily change positions, but his little Goddess had something in mind.

She shook her head at him and licked her kiss-swollen lips. "I've been wanting to try something..." The sultry cadence to her voice almost drove him to his knees, but she beat him there. Oh, Gods, yes. Her sweet innocence was somehow an aphrodisiac. He had no problem with her plan. His cock was begging for it. He thought the muscles of his jaw would surely shatter as he looked down. She knelt below him with water and steam gently caressing her soft, smooth skin. Droplets clung to impossibly long lashes that lowered as she licked up his length. How was she even real? It felt like he was in a dream. The best kind of dream.

He touched her silken cheeks with the tips of his thumbs. Never had he encountered skin so smooth. And fuck, her satiny little tongue would be the death of him. His head rolled back on his shoulders for a moment, reveling in the sensation she wrought on his aching body. His stomach and arm muscles tensed with the need to

197

hold her down and possess her. But she'd just begun, and her delicate licks and nips were making him wild, forcing a groan from him.

She made small circles with that delicate tongue, finally reaching the tip, where she swirled, then took him deep inside the wet depths, moaning her way down. The vibration made him clench his fists at his sides, fighting for control. He was losing it already, and he really wanted the first time she took him inside her hot little mouth to last.

He couldn't take it. His balls were already pulling tight. Grabbing the base of his cock, he squeezed to stop from coming right then and fucking there. Through half-lidded eyes, he watched as she indulged herself on his dick, licking and sucking as far down as she could, then moaning deep, making him jerk inside her mouth. Her lips slid back, leaving his cock shiny with saliva. Looking up, her lids were slumberous, desire burning in the depths of her gaze. Taking a deep breath, he smelled the sweet slide of arousal coating her skin, and moaned.

"It tastes so sweet. So good."

Her soft words added another layer his aching body couldn't take. Closing his eyes tight, he fought the desire to pump into her wet little mouth. He didn't want to scare her with his need to be forceful.

She pushed into their link. It felt warm and right to have her blanket his mind. Before he knew what she was about, she showed him. He growled low. The visuals she shared were of how she saw him: large and dominant above her, staring down at her possessively. Then the scene changed, with him guiding her mouth, holding her jaw and pumping against her wet tongue. Taking her just as hard as he'd dreamed of doing. It had to be the most erotic thing he'd ever seen.

Swallowing hard, he looked into her eyes and took control of her movements. Both hands held her jaw lightly while he watched himself disappear between plump little lips. His shaft slid out, then pushed deeper.

"Suck hard." He groaned the words. Her cheeks hollowed out, and he felt her moan again as she took some pre-come in. That she was enjoying it so greedily told him this would be an exercise in control he wasn't sure he had.

"Shit, when I take you back to the tip, I want you to swirl around the head." At her slight nod, he pulled out again, watching as his cock came out slick.

"Fuck, yeah. Gods, just like that. Now take it deep, and when I hit the back of your throat, breathe through your nose and swallow around me." The muscles in his legs twitched when she did as he said and took his length deeper. The extra depth made him close his eyes on a loud hiss.

He was losing his mind. Opening his eyes, he watched as she writhed on the shower floor. The enthusiasm with which she sucked him made him lose every last shred of control. He picked up speed, keeping to shallow strokes, concerned he'd lose it completely if she swallowed him again.

Groaning, he watched her dazed look when he thrust and took control of her movements. His shaft kept slipping in and out of her sweet mouth, over and over.

"Fuck, Alex, I'm close. I want you to come with me. Touch that tight little pussy, and let me feel what it's like through the bond."

She did as he asked. He knew she was as close as he was. He felt as her soaked little pussy sucked at her fingers and pulsed against them as she pushed inside, rolling her hips against her hand. It was incredible how she ached so deep inside, using the same moist digits to circle her hard little clit, all the while sucking him in. He was inside her mind, being driven mad until he finally couldn't take it. He shouted as he climaxed on her tongue. He kept at it until he filled her up, and reignited when he felt her release. He pulled from her lips. His legs nearly buckled as she sucked and licked every bit of come from his still half-hard cock. It was one of the most powerful orgasms he'd ever experienced. When she rested her head against his leg, panting to catch her breath, he stroked her cheek reverently. He would always cherish her. She was his. For eternity.

Quickly shutting off the water, he gently lifted her in his arms, grabbing a couple of towels on the way. He set one towel down on the bench before lightly setting her on top. As gently as possible, he used the other towel to wring some water from her hair and started to pat and rub her body with the soft cotton.

She stared at him, not speaking, just watching as if she'd never seen him before.

There wasn't an inch of skin he didn't want to discover with his hands and tongue. He couldn't wait for the time when he could truly linger for days. He would worship those high full breasts and the sexy curve of her hips all the way down to that mouth-watering ass and those long legs. He'd take her body to peak after peak until she begged him to stop. But now that they'd taken some of the pressure off, they had shit to talk about.

Chapter 24

Guardian Manor, Tetartos Realm

Alex had known the talk was coming. She and Uri needed to get things straight, but he was taking such sweet care of her, and she could get used to it. Her heart almost stopped at the look in his eyes, as if he'd never seen something he cared for more. She was in redline territory. She swallowed and was forced to close her eyes, not sure if she should trust herself.

He cleared his throat and began, "You'll see my memories when we finish the mating ceremony; the blood-bonding helps mates know each other fully. But there are things that I'd rather you not see. Things I'm not proud of. My time in the labs wasn't pretty," he growled. "I want you to ask me if you see something you don't understand."

She was trying to hold a little of her heart back, but he was making it next to impossible to do that.

If she didn't hold a little back, she couldn't help but worry what would happen when the newness wore off. They had an eternity together and his race was not known for their devotion to one person. She admitted, she'd never seen a mated Aletheia, so she didn't know if that changed anything. But if he ever tried to take other lovers, she would be devastated, and she couldn't guarantee her temper wouldn't manifest violently. She knew it wouldn't be good.

"Let's start with what you're thinking right now." His eyes were narrowed on her face. "I've been getting your emotions, and so far I could guess what might be going on in your head, but I'd rather you tell me," he continued.

He was right they needed to talk this out, but when she hesitated, he blew out a breath and went on, "I'm new to this shit. I've never been in a relationship before, much less something with the intensity of a mating. I know you have even less to go on than I do because at least I've seen matings in the Immortal Realm. This is going to be something we're just going to have to figure out as we go. There is no precedent for *us*." He paced a little.

She cleared her throat. "I agree."

"I can't pretend to know what you're going through. You've been uprooted from your home, lost your link to your brothers, and now have a mate you don't know. I get that this has to be hard for you. If we start out talking about shit as it comes, I think we'll be better off. I assume when the link completes, it won't allow for lies, but I want you to always tell me your concerns so we can figure it out as we go."

She had to admit to being relieved at seeing him flounder like he was. It was also comforting that he was right, their bond shouldn't allow for lies. "I agree. I know humans play games in their relationships, but I don't think I could deal with that, so honesty is a must for me." She gave him a slight smile. He'd wrapped the towel over her shoulders after drying her, and she cuddled more snugly into it. He picked her up before she knew what he was doing, and carried her to the bed. She could get used to being pampered by him.

"With the mated pairs I've seen, it always seemed that their powers complemented each other. Each pairing seemed to meld

202

differently, depending on their individual strengths, but there was always something peaceful and right about the match."

She really was lost, looking at his beautifully pensive face. She was gone for him. Hell, she'd even given him a free pass when he'd taken her brothers' link away; that had been the first sign that she cared deeply for him.

It wasn't altogether fair to let him deal with all the uncomfortable stuff. She took in a breath. "In the spirit of honesty, I'll let you know my main concerns. We don't know each other, other than what my stalking revealed about you." She laughed a little, trying to lighten the mood, but it was far too close to the truth.

His lips curved, so she continued, "Since I don't know you, and obviously had no prior experience, I would feel better knowing if this is something you want. That *I'm* what you would have chosen." She shook her head when he went to speak. "I'll warn you now that I'm a bit bitchy at times and may have a bit of a temper." She gave him a grin and continued, "I can be opinionated and may or may not have a shoe problem that you'll need to support wholeheartedly." She looked into his eyes to glean his thoughts without entering his mind. Was he trying not to laugh?

She needed to get to the heart of it. "I know we need to finish this, whatever that means. Erik needs us, and the added powers will be an asset to the Guardian cause. I think it's only fair to tell you that I might also be possessive." She looked down at the soft black comforter and rubbed it between her fingers. Dreading the main part of the confession, she figured it best just to get it over with. She blew out a breath. He waited, watching her with narrowed eyes. "Okay, I'm afraid if we do this and you ever get bored... and you tried to seek other lovers, I would most likely... level something. Probably you." She hated how insecure that made her sound, but she had agreed to be honest.

To her surprise, he barked out a laugh, bringing her shocked gaze back to his glittering eyes. For a second she reveled in the rich sound, before she realized he was laughing at her. Did he think she was joking?

"I'm really not kidding. I mean, I've had centuries full of fantasies that I'm more than happy exploring. Those clubs you like give a girl a lot of ideas, and I would be okay doing things with other people, together, but so help me, if you ever took someone outside of our...." She squeaked when she was suddenly on her back under a very serious and highly aroused Uri. His cock was a hot pulsing weight between her spread thighs.

Swirling mercury eyes held her in their thrall as he pinned her arms to her sides. "First of all, I want this for purely selfish reasons that have absolutely nothing to do with your brother or the other Guardians." His hips bumped that amazing erection into her sweet spot, making her moan.

"Second, I agree to your terms that neither of us take other lovers. I find I am also feeling possessive tendencies I've never before experienced." He really was lethal. She already wanted him so badly, and he was cutting down all her defenses.

"What would make me want someone other than the fierce, loyal, blindingly beautiful, strong not to mention intelligent mate that was gifted to me? So, just understand that I have *no* intention of ever letting you go. You're *mine*. And I'm not sure how I feel about ever allowing another to touch you, so if that's in your fantasies, we'll need to talk about it." Piercing silver eyes held her in place while he let her feel the truth of what he was saying. Her head spun, and things tightened down low at his possessiveness.

"Third, I will gladly provide you with all the shoes you'd like as long as you always model them for me. Naked." The devilish grin he sent her was positively roguish as he rotated those amazing hips. They were both nude, and the feel of him against her pussy drove her wild, making her slick and swollen for him.

Her hips had a mind of their own, grinding into him. The movement earned her a tight growl that served only to make her body tighten and her pussy quiver. Why did his more primal responses drive her so insane?

"Fuck, female, you'll be the death of me. I feel like I'm losing my damned mind. But right now, I have every intention of spanking that ass a nice bright red," he growled while leaning in to nuzzle her neck. Reflexively, she tilted her head, wanting more.

Wait, spanking? "Why am I getting spanked?"

"You were reckless as shit today, and you got yourself hurt in the process."

She was flipped over a hard firm thigh before she could even protest that it had only been a flesh wound.

One loud smack issued loudly in the quiet of the room, shocking her into stillness. It stung for only a second then delicious warmth flowed over her skin. She was so focused on the heat leading between her thighs that she was surprised again at the hard strike to the other cheek. He smattered sharp whacks to her bottom and thighs, making her wiggle and moan as he commanded, "Let me inside your mind."

His voice was so sexy and low it made gooseflesh rise as she opened to him. "Mmm, you liked your punishment?" He moved them so he was half atop her, his warm breath tickling against the sensitive skin of her neck. Her nerves were on end. That wicked tongue laved a loving trail as she let him see some of her fantasies. Each time he entered her mind, it felt more and more right. Her body felt the same, like all her cells were somehow realigning into something better.

Strong hands flipped her up and around to straddle his thighs. She moaned again, her ass was so hot and sensitive against his bare skin. Uri lifted her high to feast on her breasts. He suckled at her swollen mounds ruthlessly. His mouth felt so hot, his tongue so wicked.

He kept her off-kilter. She ended up on her back with him above her, dizzy with sensation. He held her tight to the bed as he rubbed his shaft against her slick opening. The blatant show of strength made her heart beat harder, along with a much more primitive response lower in her body. Before she knew his intent, she was moved again, this time with her back to his front, standing in front of a floor-length mirror. She felt him in her mind, sifting deliciously through her fantasies. He growled low when she allowed him to see it all. She wasn't sure he was happy with the last.

"Fuck, you want to know what it's like to have two cocks?" He bit off a curse. "That's one of your fantasies, little Goddess?" His breathing was ragged and she felt him struggling with her desires, which seemed off for who she knew him to be. And then he whispered into her mind, *I don't know if I can allow anyone else to touch you, Alexandra.*

She melted a little. It didn't stop her from fantasizing; in fact it added something to it.

He pushed her hair to the side and started devouring her ear and neck. Her eyes fell closed on a groan as he nipped her sensitive lobe.

"Open your eyes and watch what I do to you." The raspy growl took her to another level.

Eyes open, she took in his massive body behind her, all strong lines and dips she wanted to lick. It was erotic, seeing her much smaller frame in front of him as he stroked up her body with one hand to plump a breast and pluck at her nipple. His hair was wet and falling against his forehead as he scraped a distended fang along her collarbone. Those sexy fangs made her crave dirty things. He groaned in response to the visual of him doing just that. "Yes, in the ceremony," he whispered against her skin. "Now, watch. Will you give me everything, my little Goddess?"

She groaned. Her breathing was ragged and getting more so as she watched his eyes. She almost always masturbated in front of a mirror. She had loved to watch as the toys disappeared inside her body.

"Give me everything... tell me I can have you any way I want."

She groaned. "Yes."

"Good. Now, spread your legs and bend forward."

She hadn't even realized he'd moved another mirror and a large armchair until he sat behind her. Her body grew flushed, and her pussy ached. Taking in a deep breath, she did what he said and was rewarded with a wet tongue against her lower lips. Alex arched her back to give him better access as she watched in the mirror. Her breasts shook with the movements of her hips.

"Look through my eyes."

She groaned deep as he pushed the visual of what he was doing inside her head. He had her pink cheeks spread wide, so she saw her back entrance as he licked her slit. Moving up, he stuck two big fingers in her pussy. The digits came out shiny with her desire. Then he licked at her ass, making her writhe with the eroticism of it.

He growled, "I'm going to take you here. I want all of you, Alexandra." Just as he finished the words, he sent more visuals of what he was doing. It was like watching a video inside her mind, as he used both hands. One fucked her pussy. The other used a single digit slicked with her desire to pump inside her ass. Seconds later the visual was gone and she heard a drawer open; he was using telekinesis to get something. The sounds of a lid unscrewing made her curious. And then his hand was gone, and when the digits came back, they were sliding something cool over her ass.

"Push against my fingers," he growled.

Oh Gods, it was so hot to be fully possessed by him. He pulled the fingers out of her pussy and back hole and stood. She felt empty and needed him inside her with a desperation that bordered on insanity; she ached for it. He moved them again, to the bed, his chest against her back as he looked at her in the reflection in the mirror. Twining his fingers through hers, he brought her hand to his lips and he sucked the digits as he watched her. She moaned at the wild sensations it wrought. How could it make her so damned wet? She saw him smile before he stopped and moved their twined hands down her body. He slid her slick fingers inside her. "Leave them there."

She sucked in a breath as he shifted her knees wider, her ass higher. Her cheek rested against the blankets as she faced the mirror and watched him. Her other hand gripped the material in a fist when she felt the head of his big cock pushing into her ass from behind. It was so different and so intense that she almost lost her mind. Her body was stretched, so full of his thick cock that she gasped. The cream had to have something magic in it because she swore it felt far better than it probably should have. She expected pain, but there wasn't any.

"Arch your back and watch through my eyes as I claim your tight little ass."

She did and almost came at the sight of how he filled her. At how it felt to have her fingers in her pussy and his cock sliding into her ass.

"That's it. The cream will let you take my whole cock. Push back, and work yourself slowly onto it."

So much. So good. She was panting as she pushed.

"Are you wet? Are your fingers slick?" He growled. "Fuck, you're so tight; you suck me in so good..." They both groaned as she writhed into him.

More visuals of her taking him like that swam in her mind. It was utter torture that he entered her so slowly. She pushed back as forcefully as she could manage, earning a smack to her already heated flesh. It only fed her desire. She gasped and tried again to get him to take her like he'd promised. The sharp sting of another smack made her moan deep. All the sensation was too much for her. She needed him deep. He massaged the cheek he'd spanked and finally gave her what she wanted, thrusting so hard she barely kept her balance with the one hand in the blankets. Even with him holding one hip. He slammed all the way in. Gods, he was so big she was near bursting, and it made her wild.

He circled his hips and pounded deep, taking her with a fierceness that made her ache. She moved her fingers, it felt so good like this, she was so wet, she wanted more. He leaned down over her, caging her as he pushed into her from behind and it was too incredible. His warmth, the way he groaned behind her, it was perfect.

"Come," he demanded and that was all it took to send waves running through her, she clenched and bucked as they sent her reeling. She felt again as her shield pulsed but didn't release. And then he shouted and she felt warm come bathing her and it was enough to send her over again.

She lay there panting as he gently eased from her. He was gone a moment, but she'd yet to find the strength to do anything but move the hand that was beneath her when she'd collapsed. Seconds later soft wet material slid between her thighs and the crease of her bottom. Instead of awkwardness, she felt cared for. A moment later he lifted her up only to lay her so that her head was on his chest.

"How do you feel, little Goddess?" His voice was so calming and sweet and she felt warm breath in her hair before he kissed it.

"Incredible." She'd never imagined this. For her his touch was comfort and a sense of freedom all at once. It was odd, but having never been able to experience touch, this seemed a thousand times more potent than she could have imagined. It was perfect.

She paused for a second before looking up at him. "What does the ceremony entail?"

He eyed her for a moment. "There are several parts to it. First, I'll take the mark of a mated male. Then we blood-bond. And after that is the consummation ceremony."

She frowned a little. "A mark? What does that mean? And why would you even do that?"

He took a deep breath. "It's a tattoo. Sirena uses her healing ability to make the mark permanent on the mated male's chest."

Her father had no such marking. "When and why did this start? How do you feel about being branded?"

He barked out a laugh before leaning down to give her a fleeting kiss. "I'm actually happy to have a mark that says I belong to you, Alexandra." That made her chest clench, more so that she could feel the truth of his words through their growing bond.

"What will it look like?" she asked.

"It's twin serpents entwined by their tails in the mark of eternity."

She still felt like it was odd, but she couldn't deny the appeal of him being marked as hers.

He must have seen or felt her confusion. "Things are different in the Immortal Realm than they are in Earth. Immortals have lived in peace for centuries and matings are so incredibly rare and beautiful. There may only be a few within each century."

"Why wouldn't a female take the mark as well?" Curious and intrigued at the thought of marking herself for him.

He groaned and she felt it vibrate from his chest through her body. He seemed to like the idea. His eyes flashed with emotion she couldn't understand, but she felt it. "It has a lot to do with history..." He didn't seem happy about what he was about to share, which had her worried for a moment.

"When the Immortals were enslaved by Apollo and Hermes to make up their fucking armies, we were used as breeders."

She knew that, but when he said "we," it brought so many other questions. Before she could voice them, he nodded. "Yes, I was a breeder too."

"Do you have children, then?" They would be thousands of years old if that was the case.

His eyes hardened for a split second. "No. Any young that came

211

from my time were destroyed when Ares and Artemis leveled Apollo's warrior camps. It happened right before the Creators returned and stopped the bastards from doing any more harm."

Her heart stopped, saddened by his loss. He brought her hand up to his lips and kissed her palm. "It was a very long time ago."

Were they feeling one another's thoughts now? It almost felt like that.

"Immortals hold animal DNA because of Apollo's experiments to make us stronger." She knew that aspect, her brothers' lion halves were a byproduct of her father's time in Apollo's prison. "Immortal males may have always been protective, but I think the animal DNA made those instincts even stronger... Being forced to have sex with the females... Ones who were forced to be used... And then having our children ripped away to warrior camps. We failed our females and our young. So when the first of our kind found mates, they used the ceremonies to... atone. It wasn't just a vow of protection. The mating ceremonies are in no way like the mortal's marriage."

She saw him struggling with finding the right words. "How else is it different?"

"The blood bond will allow us to share our memories. It's a way to draw the pair closer. To experience our pasts and start new."

She nodded.

He blew out a breath. "But the biggest difference is the consummation. Before our souls connect, I'll claim you in every possible way, but it's all for you, Alex. A mated male, even the most possessive, will usually allow this one night to give their female all her fantasies. All the female's desires are met before she begins an eternity with her male. That means if you truly want two cocks, love, I will find a way to let you experience it. It's seen as a huge honor to be chosen to participate in something so sacred, you would have your choice of males." He actually looked pained when he said the words. She was fully aware that he'd seen her fantasy of being sandwiched between him and Gregoire.

She stared at him, unsure of what she wanted anymore, but it definitely wasn't to hurt him. She swallowed. "Are you saying that mated pairs, even Aletheia, don't participate in orgies after they're mated?"

He took a deep breath before raising an eyebrow at her. "You seem to know my race's penchant for play all too well. How is that?"

"There were Aletheia in my mother's army." She saw his question. "My father was incredibly protective. Males were afraid to get within a foot of me," she said sardonically. It was very true. And she was focused on becoming a warrior and caring for her brothers when they finally came. She could honestly admit to never having interest in any male other than Uri.

She saw the moment when that fact hit him. His eyes grew softer and he turned her into the bedding. She was half beneath him when he took her lips, his tongue devouring her, making her dizzy. There was so much intensity in the way he held her so gently, in the way he claimed her.

Chapter 25

Guardian Manor, Tetartos Realm

Sam quickly threw on the robe she found after waking clothed in what looked like scrubs. She clenched the material, trying to remember what had happened. The room looked like a fancy master suite of dark browns and hardwood covered in expensive rugs. She eyed a tray that was left on a table at a seating area in front of the fireplace. It contained what looked like soup, water, juice and tea, but she was too leery to touch it. She wasn't sure where she was and her adrenaline was pumping.

Her heart stilled when she heard a knock at the door. She looked around for a place to run.

"Sam, it's Alex and Uri. Are you okay in there?" Alex and Uri? Her head started spinning with the realization of who they were. It really hadn't been a dream. She closed her eyes, her mind immediately going to Erik as her heart clenched in her chest. Their presence here meant he was also real, not some product of her imagination. They'd saved her, so why did she distrust it all so much?

She sucked in a breath and willed her shaking hands to stop. She had to know if her mind was playing tricks on her. That meant braving the door even though her heart was beating a hole in her chest.

The first thing she said when allowing them to enter was, "Is Erik okay?"

Erik's sister seemed to try for a smile, but the effort... Her heart plummeted. They'd been wrong. His wounds had been too great. She felt herself pale and almost fell into the nearest chair.

Alex immediately walked around and sank down in the chair next to her, taking one of her cold hands in her warm ones. Alex's bright blue eyes had gone wide. "No, no. He's fine. He's alive. I didn't think about what my face was indicating. I just don't like to see him hurt. He's going to be fine. He's recovering from his injuries, Sam. I promise you he's okay."

The two sat with her for a while, softly explaining a world of Immortal beings, telling her she was a Mageia. To her it all sounded like the same thing as a witch. It was too much to process, but that didn't stop the questions firing from her lips. They'd patiently explained that she would be in a kind of protective custody there while they searched for Cyril, the one she knew as the Nazi Fuck. Her heart stuttered when they'd told her he'd escaped. She felt bile burning her throat.

"Sam, we have a way to access your memories if you'll allow it. I really hate to ask this of you, but we need to catch him before he does this again." She felt Alex's regret in asking her.

Hatred and fear filled her at the thought of that bastard out there abducting more innocent women and using them as lab rats. Doing things...

Could she deal with one more violation? Having them in her mind would be exactly that. She closed her eyes for one heart-pounding moment before swallowing. "Do what you need to." The idea of allowing them inside her head, seeing what she went through, nauseated her, but she had to do it. She could never live with herself if someone else suffered because she didn't have the courage to do one simple thing.

215

Uri nodded at her, and she swore she saw something like pride shining in those metallic eyes. "You're very brave, Sam. It will be fast, but I have to ask…"

"What is it?"

"Would you like me to take the memories away? I can erase them, but it would be like a hole in time. It's your choice."

Her lips parted. They could take them. Take the fear?

"If not, I can also dull the impact. Make them fuzzy so that you'd know what happened, but you wouldn't feel the anxiety. The fear. We've done this for some of the others who were there with you. None of this was your fault, Sam. If we can ease the trauma, let us do that for you."

Alex squeezed her hand. "You're not alone. You were incredibly strong to find a way to free yourself. You can do this. Either way is your choice. I hope you'll allow us to blunt the memories if nothing else. It would have the effect of years in therapy. Nothing invasive."

She swallowed. She didn't like the idea of a hole in her memories even though she hated them.

"Don't take them away. But I don't want them paralyzing me anymore." She closed her eyes, almost feeling like a coward. There were too many emotions. The biggest was shame. God, she hoped they would take that away, but it was hard to ask them to. When Alex squeezed her hand again, she eased some. A glance into the other female's eyes showed something more.

"I understand more than you know, Sam. We will be gentle. Thank you for being brave enough to let us do something to help."

She didn't feel brave. She felt terrified, but it seemed to be over almost before they started. The odd feeling of someone inside her mind wasn't as unpleasant as she'd worried it would be. Then she opened her eyes and she felt relaxed. The thick blanket of shame and panic was no more than a thin sheet slipping away.

Her muscles finally relaxed and the ache in her bones eased.

She sucked in a breath.

"How do you feel?" Alex asked, searching her eyes.

She shook her head in awe. "It's there, but the weight of it isn't so heavy." She blinked back tears.

Alex hugged her and they stayed for a little longer.

"If you push the button on the wall, they'll bring you anything you need. More food, toiletries. Just sit tight. You're safe here and we'll be back.

She was basking in her newfound courage up until the next knock. This time she opened the door to the blonde doctor she'd seen when they brought her in.

"Hi, Sam. Do you remember me? My name is Sirena and I just want to check on you."

She smiled hesitantly as she let the doctor in.

"Are you feeling up to a short chat?"

She stilled. "Is it about the blood samples you took?"

Sirena nodded. "I know this is all a big shock for you, and I promise we will do anything in our power to help you through this."

Sam cleared her throat. "What did he do to me?" Something felt odd inside her. And she knew it wasn't normal.

"I don't want to scare you, but, yes, your body is changing. You are healthy and will be fine. But there are going to be big decisions you'll need to make going forward."

"Oh god, I'm pregnant?" She barely choked out the words, feeling her world falling apart around her.

"No. You're not." Sirena shook her head but seemed to hesitate in continuing. This couldn't be good.

"You're sure? Wouldn't it be too soon to tell?" Sam croaked the words she feared most as she searched the other woman's eyes, trusting her on some instinctual level.

"I'm positive." Sam blew out the breath she hadn't known she was holding when Dr. Sirena continued in a low serious voice, "Do you know how we found your location?"

Ice blue eyes filled her vision. She knew somehow that Erik was her savior, but she wasn't sure how or why, and Alex hadn't explained that part.

Her stomach clenched, remembering his strength and the heat that pulsed from him in waves, finally warming her after being cold for so long. She hadn't even had time to thank him before he'd passed out. Why did she feel like she'd known him her entire life? Like she was connected to him. It made no sense.

She whispered, "It had something to do with Erik, didn't it?"

"Yes, Erik was the one who found you."

"How?" Then she asked what she was dying to know, "Is he really okay?" She hoped Alex hadn't lied to her. She wanted to see for herself that he was whole. She ached to know why she'd dreamed of him. She wanted to know why and how she'd felt safe in the middle of hell with him. It made absolutely no sense.

"There's a lot to it. Erik sacrificed a lot to get to you. To get *you,* specifically, out of there." Sirena's words held a depth of meaning Sam didn't understand.

"Why? I've never met him. Why would he come for me? How would he?"

"Did Alex explain that one of her powers is being drawn into others' minds?"

"She was in my mind after I was taken. She said as much." The impossible was truly possible. Creatures of myth existed, but weren't quite the same. "I don't know if I can fathom half of what I feel like was the kindergarten version she explained to me." Sam rubbed the bridge of her nose. Her head was spinning with everything she'd learned. Had she not seen fangs and lion men and fireballs, she wouldn't have believed any of it before.

"Well, that's how they found out about you," Sirena said.

"I'm not sure what to think about that," she said honestly. "I don't even know why I was taken. Alex said it was because I am this Mageia thing. A witch." She shook her head and then thought about something else. "Are my parents okay? They have some ability with plants." Her mind reeled with all the questions she didn't know if she wanted answered. "I have to talk to them. Tell them I'm okay."

"Your parents should be safe. He seemed to be targeting a certain age range, but we'll send someone to check on them and let them know you're okay as well. There's no phone service here."

"What did he do to me? And how do I even protect myself against his powers if he finds me again?"

After a brief pause while Sam took a deep breath, Sirena continued, "You're safe here, Sam. But there is *one* way for you to get the power to protect yourself, and by doing so, you'd also be helping Erik."

Sam's eyesight blurred. How could someone she didn't even know find her, risk his life for her? There had to be more to it. "What haven't you told me? Stop trying to ease into whatever it is," she asked through clenched teeth.

Sirena's eyes softened. "You're very strong, Sam. But I fear you're going to have to be stronger."

Air stuck in her throat. "What does that mean?"

"It's complicated. Part of it has to do with what you are." The doctor searched Sam's face, looking for something. "You were taken because you are a Mageia that has a rare compatibility with Immortals. That compatibility is what makes you Erik's destined mate. I wouldn't have told you any of this now. Not after all you've been put through, but there's more to all of this, and it's put you both in an untenable situation. The moment you and Erik touched, it put things into play that can't be stopped."

"What things?" Sam demanded. "Destined mate?"

"It's a soul mate. Your souls call to each other, and when a mated pair touches, they're thrown into a mating frenzy. You won't feel the effects as strongly or as painfully because you're mortal. But he will. He'll go nearly mad with the need to *be* with you physically. That's why I intend to keep him asleep. You need time to heal, but I can't keep him knocked out forever. And when I wake him, it's going to be bad for him. It will start to become a problem for you as well. In days you'll want him uncontrollably... and it will eventually be painful if you don't have sex with him." Sirena shook her head. "I'm sorry,

220

but that's the reality. If I could kill Cyril for what he's done to you, I would. You shouldn't have to deal with this now. Not after... everything. The monster tainted something incredibly rare and beautiful. I'm sorry."

Sam's stomach clenched. He wasn't okay after all.

And it didn't look like she was going to be okay either.

Chapter 26

Guardian Manor, Tetartos Realm

Alex sat next to Sirena with Uri in the seat at her left. They were in a war room that looked almost identical to the one on Earth, waiting for a few more Guardians to show up.

She and Uri had changed, checked on Erik and Sam, then sifted through the minds of the lab tech and victims, and arrived with barely time to find their seats in the meeting. She was still reeling from everything they'd done in record time.

She zoned out, pondering how much she had misjudged Tetartos. She'd expected something primitive. She hadn't imagined the opulence of the manor, with its massive courtyard and several wings. When they'd gone to Uri's suite, Havoc greeted them with a raspy woof and wiggle, expecting to have his ears rubbed. It was odd, but the beast was so like a puppy would be except for his red eyes, oddly soft fur over shiny black skin, and the potential of flames coming from his mouth.

Alex had asked Uri how big Havoc would get, and he issued one word, "Big," with a grin. She was looking forward to heading back to his suite after only getting a quick glimpse. It had a sunken living room done in black and grays, and huge

French doors opened out onto a big balcony. A kitchen with mottled black and brown stone sat to the side of the entry, and a huge bedroom, with a spacious seating area, was to the left. The closet had only a few clothes for him, and she was happy to see some of her clothes had been brought over from her Earth apartment. Along with shoes. Thank the Gods. She had smiled at the sight, enjoying the view of his big clothes and boots next to her much smaller things. Her stomach had tightened a bit at the domesticity of it. She wanted it all.

Vane prowled in beside Conn a moment later, holding a laptop. Her brother narrowed his eyes at Uri after greeting her, then sat at the opposite side of the table between Jax and Conn.

Jax was grinning like a freaking kid with a secret, and she felt Uri stiffen next to her. A second later she heard him telepath, *That video better be in our apartment at the end of the meeting, or you and Conn will both meet my ass at the mats after this is done.* She was catching Uri's words to Jax, just as she'd accessed his Guardian links during Sam's rescue. Then it hit her that the video they had to be talking about was of her and Uri in the holding cell. Alex's cheeks heated, and she sent a death glare to Jax, only getting a wink and devilish grin back.

He has a copy of one of Brianne's chick flicks. The only copy of the video is in your apartment. Conn winked at her, his amber eyes glittering with mischief as he sent the message over.

She choked back a laugh at the wolf's antics. Her brother raised an eyebrow in confusion. Jax just leaned forward to turn

223

and glare at Conn, who flipped him off. Jax sat back in his chair, mumbling about assholes.

Thankfully, Vane didn't seem to be paying any real attention anymore. He was concentrating on the laptop he'd opened up on his knees as he lounged back. His muscles were tense, and she suspected he was doing everything he could to avoid looking at Brianne. Something was up there.

Finally, Drake entered the room with a few others scattering into chairs.

"Uri, Alex, report," Drake ordered.

Uri began telling the group everything they'd done to dull some of the mental effects for the victims. It warmed her chest that he included her as if she'd contributed something monumental. She had only helped with some intricate work inside the minds, by accessing Uri's power. It was invigorating and enticing, this feeling of swirling and swelling of her life force trying to combine with his as their abilities blended. It kept her in an aroused state that was unlike anything she'd ever experienced. It wasn't just her body, it was her entire being, as if he were stroking her inside and out.

She heard his frustration when telling the other Guardians that they were unable to do anything substantial for the redhead. Her mind was in tatters, and the pieces inside kept moving around. He informed them that they would try again after their mating was complete. Uri had been gentle with the females. If she hadn't already been losing the fight against falling deeply in love with him, his care for the damaged

Mageias would have pushed her over the edge.

Uri sent what felt like a caress to her mind through the bond. It was highly erotic and had her clenching her stomach. She sent a growl back. The last thing she wanted was to get hot and wet in a room with her brother.

He chuckled through the link.

Uri sobered before continuing his report, "At least one of the Aletheia that raped the victims seemed drugged. Eyes glazed and dilated. He also spoke inside the victims' minds, encouraging them to relax and not let Elizabeth get off on their pain. All the women remember being raped with Elizabeth present. One of the males slipped them Aletheia venom so they would enjoy the experience. It confused and upset the victims more to be aroused by what happened to them. I'm not sure if it matters, but it seemed that both Aletheia present at all the rapes seemed to hate Elizabeth. Who knows what their allegiances are. They might be captives, too."

"Fuck," Drake said, pacing, which Alex realized was his norm. She had yet to see the Guardian leader sit.

"We got a lot of intel from the lab tech. He's an earth elemental, been with Cyril since he was a child. His memories were tampered with, so how he got to be in Cyril's employ is a mystery. Sirena will be digging into the family tree. He doesn't know Cyril's current location; backup facilities were kept secret, which is fucked. He doesn't have a lot on Cyril and Elizabeth themselves, not being in the inner circle, but he is aware of vials of Aletheia semen being traded for test subjects on Earth.

The name Cynthia was in his memories." She felt Uri's fury all over again with that knowledge. He seemed to know the female and had said he'd checked her mind when the first females had gone missing.

"Is it the same Cynthia who rules the west coast covens?" Jax growled.

"He didn't have a last name or any more information. It better not fucking be her. But Sam remembered Mageia chanting a spell to send her to the other Realm, so it would track. She's a fucking bitch with Mageia at her beck and call. I checked her mind when this all started and found nothing. It was just a surface scan of her thoughts, so it looks like time I check her fucking blood memories." Alex sent him soothing energies, trying to calm his fury, knowing it was tinged with guilt at not having known.

"She's smart and powerful with a lot of fucking money," Conn ground out. "Let me do some digging into her life."

Uri continued, shaking his head. "The lab guy also knew that Elizabeth is the one able to contact Earth as well as the Tria..." There was a short pause as the table went quiet before the occupants erupted in a variety of expletives. Who knew the extent of Elizabeth's power?

"Added to that shit, it turns out Elizabeth has been luring Mageia from the covens on Tetartos over centuries. Until this last year, when they started getting them from Earth." More noise followed until Drake's booming, "Quiet!"

"The Tetartos covens have finally put in higher security

measures. I should have insisted on working more with them. The leaders can be such pains in the asses," Sirena volunteered. She looked concerned and just as furious as Uri.

"The lab tech's mind confirmed that the tests they're performing focus on the mating spell. He's a total zealot, refused to speak. Cyril promised all in his compound that his research would find the key to allowing Immortals and Mageias to choose any mate they wished to have. They were working on a serum that would trick the DNA into thinking there's a match. It seems that instead of getting rid of the spell, he's basically attempting to deceive it." Uri waited as the room quieted again. "I've sent Sirena all the memories we got from him so she can decipher the medical shit."

Alex felt the rage all through the room.

Uri's voice held disgust. "It gets worse. When the serums he's using fail, they cause brain damage. Those Mageia whose minds are no longer working are kept and used as payment to the Tria for some kind of service."

"Fucking hell," Drake said as the room's noise volume reached epic heights.

Uri's voice dropped dangerously low. "And this is only one of the experiments they've been working on. There are several, but our guy only worked on one other." Uri paused again. "They've been using their own warriors as lab rats to find a way to sever telepathic links. The problem is that they weren't able to find a way to reverse the effects, so the Aletheia he's injected are messed up and now practically vegetables."

"Shit." Drake's response was echoed down the table. All were grim.

"Well, now we can guess what was in the syringe the demon-possessed had," Gregoire said with a menacing scowl.

Uri nodded, but Alex remembered that they had never gotten around to discussing the syringe. He was so damn distracting. Gregoire must have caught her look of confusion, because he explained for her.

"Uri was attacked a couple of nights ago by a trio of possessed with a syringe, but we weren't able to recover it. Havoc took one down. We still don't know if the hound was how they found him, since Havoc is blood-bound to Uri, not the Tria."

Sirena explained to the others who had only seen Havoc in the courtyard, "Drake and I okayed the pup's presence. It appears that hellhounds are not evil by nature. Havoc feeds off dark energy, metabolizes it, without being affected at all." Sirena took a breath. "The demon-possessed probably did track Havoc's aura. I could see that being plausible. The possessed brought in was too new to have any real knowledge. Uri interrogated him. The fact that Havoc teleported to Uri in the courtyard is something I'll have to look into. Hell beasts don't teleport, the Tria send them, so it has to be Uri's blood, which is something that can never leave this room." If the Immortals in Tetartos learned that Uri's blood had that power, it could be very dangerous.

Sirena turned to her and Uri. "When will you two complete

the bond? I recommend you do it quickly. The distraction could be dangerous."

"Tonight."

Alex's shocked expression shot to Uri. They hadn't discussed doing it tonight. She raised a brow at him. He grinned wolfishly back. A laugh escaped before she knew what was happening. She shook her head. They needed to do this. There was no turning back, and she wouldn't want to if there was. In truth, she was excited that he wanted to finish their bond.

"Okay, let's finish this meeting. Looks like there's a mating ceremony to prepare for. Sirena, do you have anything to add?" Drake said, grinning at Alex with affection.

She grinned back, thoroughly enjoying being a part of the fold. She could truly get used to this.

"Only that we need to get Erik and Sam to finish their mating soon, for both their sakes. I don't think Sam would be able to handle the mortal mating ceremony, and the Aletheia semen will only stay in effect for a few weeks at best. After that, the process will need to be started all over again. So the quicker we can get them mated, the better for them both," Sirena remarked to the table.

Alex was confused again. "I think I missed something?"

Sirena said, "Part of turning a mortal into an Immortal is that they need to be filled with Aletheia semen, which has regenerative power that helps initiate the change. That already happened with Sam's rape. The next issue is that mortals can't digest any Immortal blood other than that of an Aletheia. So in mortal-Immortal matings, we add Aletheia blood to the Immortal mate's for the blood-bonding. Erik's blood will have to be mixed for Sam to be able to take it and complete their bond. After that's the consummation. In the end Sam will become Immortal and mated. Since Cyril has already begun the process, we need to get them to complete it. Otherwise she will need to have sex with another Aletheia."

Alex's mouth gaped at that. They said it was a process, but that was extreme. She shook her head grimly at that information. There was no way it was happening. Not after what Sam had already been through, and Alex couldn't imagine Erik being okay with sharing her.

Drake nodded with the same look of understanding. "Conn?"

"Cyril wiped his research and data files before we got there. All I got was a month's worth of video surveillance in DVDs. Cyril had all the labs, corridors, outside, common areas, training area and holding rooms monitored. No clues on where he went. If he hadn't blown his exit, Sacha or Bastian might have been able to track him, but now it's doubtful," Conn said as he leaned back, tapping on the table with his thumb. He was in another flannel, this one in green and black, sleeves rolled back revealing the tattoos covering his arms. He must like to pull at his hair as he worked, since it stuck out everywhere. "I gave Sirena the videos from the labs. Vane and I have been going through the other files. It'll take some time to get through it all. We haven't found anything useful yet."

Drake continued down the line. "Gregoire, Jax?"

"We didn't get shit at the location where Uri was attacked. Nothing was left behind, and there was no video surveillance covering the exit road. Too many options after that," Jax provided.

Gregoire was sprawled out in his chair, spreading his big body out like the warriors around the table all seemed to like to do. He was large all over, and she'd seen a lot of him in those clubs. His equine half was definitely dominant in the lower part of his anatomy. Her brain was officially fried if she was thinking of that. It was all the talk of her mating ceremony and what Uri had shared, making her think of it now. She felt Uri's heat and essence mingling with hers from inches away and couldn't wait to get him alone. She had been trying to avoid looking at him for fear she would jump him.

Jax began, a distinct scowl painting his beautiful features. "Sirena asked us to check on Sam's parents' home and we found something interesting."

"What?" Uri asked.

"There were two Mageia parked outside, watching the house."

Uri snarled, "Cynthia's?"

Jax shook his head. "I don't know, man. I have their license shit for Conn to check."

"This is bullshit," Vane snarled.

"Don't," Alex bit off. She could feel Uri's own frustration and guilt, and her brother didn't need to make this worse.

This is not Uri's fault. He already feels guilty enough, she sent to Vane.

But he talked to the female.

"Just stop, Vane. We still don't know that it's her," she snapped out loud. "Even if it is, we could just as easily blame my lack of skill with head-hopping for not getting to Sam or the rest of the females sooner. If I'd asked better questions when I was in their minds, it might have made a difference."

Vane bit off a curse.

"That's enough. This isn't productive!" Alex pointed out in irritation before snapping at Jax, "Did you talk to her parents? Maybe this is a coincidence?"

Jax nodded. "They didn't know them, but they were definitely there for something." Drake nodded so Jax continued, "Drake didn't want us to take them in, so I got close enough to hear them planning to take Sam's parents somewhere."

Conn spoke next. "If this is the Cynthia we think it is, I need to gather more information before we go after her. Like who she had helping her. She is a staunch believer in security. We'll need to plan if we want the element of surprise. The crazy bitch has made a lot of dirty money over the decades, enough to fund an escape."

Alex shook her head as Uri seethed. She wanted to ease

his guilt, knowing she'd feel the same way in his situation, but it wasn't his fault. Seeing him like this was rough. She sent him soothing energy before turning to Jax. "Where are Sam's parents?"

"Stashed in a safe house. The elementals didn't even know we were there. Hopefully, they'll be watching the house for a while before they figure it out. I put a tracker on the car when they weren't looking."

Conn was tapping away at a laptop. "The car is registered to a corporation owned by Cynthia."

Silence filled the room and she grabbed Uri's hand in hers.

Smoke lifted from Drake's lips as he spoke. "We need to bring Cynthia and her inner circle in. We will raid all of her locations to get the information we need. Hopefully, she kept some kind of records, since she is apparently resistant to mental scans. In all reality Cyril or Elizabeth likely helped her with that."

"I underestimated her." Uri cursed before adding, "She looked far too fucking young when I did that scan. I assumed it was good plastic surgery; now I know she was getting Aletheia semen from Cyril. If that piece of shit is selling off her own damned kind to look young, she deserves a slow painful death."

The air in the room buzzed with energy as Drake growled. "I agree. Conn, put a hold on checking Cyril's security footage and get all the data you can on Cynthia's location. The raid needs to be precise; we'll be spread thin. I want to hit as many

233

locations as possible at once. We need to strike soon. We'll meet back here at eight a.m. tomorrow to go over strategy. I want everyone fully refueled and ready."

Vane growled in frustration. She knew how he felt. Alex wanted in on the raids just as much as he did, but they were both stuck on Tetartos. She blew out an irritated breath.

"All right, does anyone else have anything to report on the rest of the patrols?"

"Same shit in Hell," P said.

Alex's eyes started to glaze over a bit as the others reported.

Her mind fixated on the fact that she would be mated in a matter of hours. Her stomach fluttered with anticipation.

"Mating ceremony at eight p.m. I'm assuming we are all invited?" Drake grinned at that.

Looking around, she saw that everyone was up, moving around them. There was some backslapping for Uri, and happy grins and hugs from the females. Her heart clenched a little that Erik wouldn't be there. Guilt hit with the impact of a boulder at the fact that she was happy while her brother suffered.

Vane pulled her in for a hug. His frame was familiar and comfortable as she rested her head on his chest and closed her eyes, just as she had always done throughout her long life. Vane had always given her such free affection. *Erik would want you happy, sis. You've been alone too long. You deserve to have*

234

a mate of your own, even if he pisses me off. Uri seems solid. I'll admit that if I couldn't tell he loves you, I might not be so okay with you mating the asshole. The guy makes it pathetically clear he cares for you, so we're good.

When he pulled back, the sad little grin he gave her made her eyes blur. She blinked back tears and gave him a watery smile that she hoped showed how much she loved him. Uri sent a soothing caress through the link. Was Vane right? Did Uri love her? The warmth of it made her skin tingle.

Chapter 27

Guardian Manor, Tetartos Realm

Sam found herself in a hallway one floor up, in a wing opposite from her own room. A slew of butterflies had set up residence in her stomach, and her mind wouldn't stop the constant rerun of all Sirena had told her.

Could she do this? She remembered the pain etched in his gorgeous face as he moved toward her, completely nude and absolutely perfect, even with the wounds riddling his body. His beautiful ice blue eyes had searched her face before he gently touched her cheek. Her breath caught at the thought of being near him again. He'd made her feel safe in that hell; his warmth had surrounded and caressed her cold body. Even unconscious, his presence had been a balm. He'd come for her, believing she was some kind of soul mate. Sirena had said that he'd been desperately trying to find her from the day that Alex had come inside her head. How long ago was that? Days? It felt like she'd been in the clutches of that Nazi Fuck for a lifetime.

Her feet moved quickly and of their own accord, seeking him out. She badly needed to see him and was drawn to where Sirena had said Erik was recovering.

Sam didn't think it was possible for her heart to beat any faster. All she knew as she padded down the halls and passed the staff that busily cleaned and bustled about was that she had to know he was truly okay. Had to feel his skin. She became aroused every time she thought of being intimate with him.

Shame hit her like a blow. Knowing her body responded when the bastards had violated her was what she struggled with most, even though Sirena had explained that they'd drugged her. It still left her feeling dirty, though she was grateful that Uri and Alex had dulled the terror, the debilitating panic; she felt she could move past it all.

She took a calming breath, wondering about the man she would see any moment. She replayed his words over and over. *You're safe now.* He was beyond her dreams physically, and she owed him her life, but she didn't know anything about the man, or he her. Would he want her, knowing how damaged she was? A part of her understood what Sirena had told her; this was fate, supernatural, not something either could fight. She would do what needed to be done. Repay her debt and take the power she needed, but she wouldn't entertain thoughts of fairytales after what she'd endured.

She shivered, suddenly freezing again no matter that she'd lingered within the heated shower until her skin wrinkled, finally getting some warmth into her cold bones. She closed her eyes and could almost feel his warmth beckoning.

Sirena said that if she were strong enough to help Erik, she would, in turn, gain the power to protect herself from Cyril. The gut-clenching desire to be strong, powerful, after having been at the mercy of that bastard and his bitch was tempting, but she was lying to herself if she said that was all this was about.

She stopped and rested her forehead on the door she knew had to be his. Her heart continued to batter her chest. Her daring was gone, but her body and soul ached to go through that door. Taking deep breaths, she tried to calm herself. Erik was supposed to be asleep for a couple of days, according to the doctor. That would give her a little more time to adjust, and seeing him sleep, maybe helping in his care would be comforting.

Click.

She jumped back as the door popped opened. Uri and Alex stood just inside. Alex gave her a radiant smile and hugged her close. "We were just about to head your way," Alex said gently as she ushered Sam into a huge suite. Thick, shaggy wool carpet sat beneath massive furniture done in brown and black in the sunken living room. There was a beautiful wood fireplace next to French doors leading out onto a big balcony. A wet bar was on one side with a table, and to the right, she saw a small kitchen with an island that faced the living room.

"We just came to check on Erik." Alex studied her for a moment before asking, "Do you want to see him?" The other female gave her hands a light squeeze that bolstered her.

Sam took a deep breath, knowing she could do this. "I spoke to Sirena. I'd like to do what I can to help."

Uri gave her a warm smile filled with concern before saying, "We would really appreciate that, but has Sirena told you what will happen when he awakes? He won't be himself, Sam. He would never harm you, but I don't want you to be frightened by anything." He searched her face as she felt her cheeks overheat. The one part of her body that wasn't cold.

She cleared her throat, guessing Uri knew about everything. "Yes, she explained." Shit, it wasn't like she was a virginal teenager, but the whole thing was overwhelming. Sirena had already explained that it would be impossible for him to hurt her; he would seek her pleasure beyond all else. For some reason she believed it. *You're safe now,* played again in her head.

Uri nodded once. "You don't have to do this and you can choose to go back to your room. He'll be out for days." He was assessing her, giving her an out, which she appreciated, but she had no intention of taking it. After a second he continued, "Alex worries about him being alone while we work, so thank you. I'll let the others know you're going to stay and watch over him. If you need anything, push the intercom button, and someone will come." He nodded to a red button by the front door. "There's one by the door to the balcony in the bedroom, as well."

She lifted her chin and gave him an awkward nod.

"I'll have someone come up with food and drinks for the fridge," he said.

"Thank you."

"I'll have some clothes and toiletries brought up for you," Alex said.

It warmed Sam to see that they seemed to genuinely care for her comfort. She tried for another smile. "I'd appreciate that. Is there anything I need to know to take care of him?"

"His wounds are healed. He won't need anything but to have you close until he wakes up."

She nodded at Uri's soft words, hoping it came through more confidently than she felt.

Alex added in almost a whisper, "You were incredibly brave to come here and face the unknown. We understand the nightmare you've been through. If you change your mind, no one, especially not Erik, would think less of you, Sam."

Sam saw hope war with concern in Alex's beautiful features. Mind made up, she said, "I'll be fine. I'll ring if I need anything. Just, go find that bastard and take him down."

Uri reached out and squeezed her shoulder, and Alex pulled her into another sisterly hug before leaving.

Sam felt her chest warm while new purpose and desire fought for control of her entire being. She moved toward the doorway she knew led to him. She felt him, felt the deep pull of him in her soul.

Chapter 28

Cyril's Secondary Compound, Tetartos Realm

Cyril was out of his mind with rage. He paced the confines of his new suite—one that lacked his father's ornate bed. Fury radiated through him. His most prized possession lay in rubble, along with the rest of his old compound. Once the last of his troops made it through the secret tunnels out of the mountain and teleported here, the charges had been set. He would not have the Guardians gaining any more information.

He needed to figure out who had betrayed him. Kane and Angus were charged with checking everyone's minds. He wasn't sure he could trust either of them, so there were checks and balances.

His data had survived, but he hadn't been able to get the last lab tech out, the male had been gathering video surveillance DVDs on the other side of the room. Cyril had been in the process of teleporting his second-to-last tech out of the cavern when the door closing the area off from the compound blew. Cyril had seen the silhouette that could only belong to Drake enter the room. Before Cyril teleported, he'd telekinetically hit the charge to blow the area. All he had heard was the loud click of it engaging before he was gone. Still, he couldn't be sure the tech died. He couldn't be so lucky that the dragon had been destroyed.

It infuriated him that he lacked the skill to teleport more than one other being at a time. As soon as he got the mating serum correct, he would mate a Kairos, among others, and would acquire

241

every skill he deemed important.

He was so close. Though now he was forced to hide all his data until the new compound was safe. The mole had to be ferreted out immediately.

Elizabeth, in my room, now. He needed to relieve his anger, and her body would provide an outlet. That would help. Kane and Angus had already cleared her mind, fortunately, because her skills were still needed.

His muscles shook with rage. So much had been lost. A large number of his army was dead. The Guardians had their hands on all of his subjects, including Nine. His hands clenched. The bastards would soon regret their interference. He would set his new plans into motion, soon.

Chapter 29

Guardian Manor, Tetartos Realm

A trio of females had taken Alex to prepare her for the centuries-old mating ceremony. They'd bathed her skin as was tradition of old, before massaging her body in light oil sweetly scented of almonds.

The tranquil bathing house honored each of the elements, just as the temples of ancient times had. French doors opened to the view of a thick forest of tall redwoods mixed with fern and moss. The water in the marble bath was flowing from the long delicate fingers of rose stone Nereids. Potted flowering plants and trees filled the inside of the room. She could smell the earthy moss, which settled her nerves. It had begun to darken outside. The scattering of billowing clouds were backlit with the blush of dusk in coral and peach, slowly darkening as it brightened one last time. She lay beneath the talented touch of the three preparing her. Flickering candlelight licked at the stone and water.

Anticipation filled her. She still felt the tantalizing touch of Uri's essence rubbing and twining with her own, even though he was nowhere near this place. She heard the water of a nearby fall as she lay face down on the cushioned table, getting all of her muscles worked out. Thala, Pela and Areth were a relaxing presence, friendly. Not speaking, just quietly humming a soft tune.

Alex felt limp as Thala massaged her way down one arm all the way to her fingertips. Pela's strong hands loosened and relaxed muscles in her neck and back. The third and quietest of the three, Areth, used a firm touch to relax her thighs, down her calves, to the soles of her sensitive feet.

"Time to get your hair done so we can dress you," Thala said, grinning, as they helped her stand.

"Thank you, ladies, that was amazing," Alex said as she beamed a smile at all three. She stretched her arms up. Her body felt incredible and loose.

Sitting her on a velvety side chair in front of a small table, Thala worked on her hands. Areth worked at her feet, and Pela worked on her hair.

When they finally finished, Alex was dressed in a gown of beautiful nearly sheer silk in a blue that matched her eyes. The dress was cut and draped in such a fashion that it held itself in place, but one small tug would have it on the ground. The light fabric lovingly hugged her curves with its strapless floor-length design. It was decadent to feel the silk slide along bare skin.

All three smiled delightedly at their work. The soft click of heels signaled the arrival of Sirena, Brianne, and Sacha. Brianne made whooping noises as she entered, and they exclaimed at how beautiful she looked. They each chatted and thanked Pela, Areth and Thala for their work.

The three Guardians were dressed in short ivory gowns that covered one shoulder and flitted in the light breeze. They were stunning. Brianne looked tanned under the pale dress, and her flaming hair fanned out in wild waves down her back. Sirena's pale locks were done in more sleek controlled waves and curved bangs. Sacha looked like an Egyptian princess, with straight bangs and almost hip-length ebony strands. The transporter Guardian even wore a gold band on one arm. A true display of power, as metal encasements dampened their abilities.

Sirena brought with her a gorgeous green bottle labeled in black. "This is specially blended wine made only on Tetartos." The female shared with a smile. She had apparently gotten her hands on a much-coveted year, if Brianne's squeak of pure glee was any indication. Each took a small glass. Pela, Areth and Thala declined an offer to join them. With wide grins the three females left in a breath of air, leaving just the four of them to their decadent treat as Sirena went over the last details of the ceremony, which Alex altered slightly, to all three Guardians' delight.

After enjoying the rich, sumptuous flavor of the drink, which was unlike anything she'd ever tasted, Sirena asked, "Are you ready?"

"Yes." And then they teleported her away, reforming on a rock ledge high above a crashing sea highlighted lovingly by the moon's caress. The excited Guardians chattered as they ushered her through a tunnel that looked to be plated in gold and lit with a thousand candles. Words of love and wisdom were etched in the old language all along the cool surface. It touched something deep inside. A reverence settled over her, feeling the magic in this place.

Her gaze instantly found Uri in the back of the cavern below a high vaulted ceiling with a diamond-drop candle chandelier. The room was absolutely stunning, but nothing compared to the sheer primal beauty of her mate. Her chest swelled, and it took everything in her to slow her movements and enjoy the moment, savor the sight of Uri waiting to pledge his life to hers. The wide expanse of his chest was bare, and the light flickered over every dip and line of muscle. His shoulders were so impossibly tight that it looked as though he was having trouble staying where he was.

Black silk pants hung low on his hips, revealing the V of muscle that begged to be lavished by her hands and mouth. She heard as he sucked in a deep breath; a shiver of a growl echoed in her mind, sending tremors down her entire body. Silver eyes swirled as he stood in front of the other Guardians. Her brother stood with them, all dressed in black, but only Uri was without a shirt. Vane smiled lovingly at her before his gaze moved to Brianne, a wicked glint in his eyes.

She felt a fleeting pang of regret that Erik couldn't be there, but took comfort in the fact that he had a brave and strong mate by his side, willing to ease his pain when he finally woke. Sirena assured her that a mated male wouldn't be able to hurt his mate. Alex knew her brother well enough to know that was true.

If all went well, there might be something she and Uri could do to also lessen the pain of memories past.

Her breath caught in her lungs as her soul pushed against the bonds of her body. The feeling had been getting increasingly forceful of late, somehow anticipating the completion of the bond? Demanding that ultimate bond. She bit her lip, stifling a groan and willing her lower body not to dampen with need in present company. It was all she could do to stay focused on moving toward him.

She watched Uri's chest heave, his eyes full of delicious promise. They just needed to make it through the first part of the ceremony.

She heard some choked coughs, a groan, and female giggles chiming lightly in the room as she finally arrived in front of Uri.

She took his hands in the center of the room. Sirena stood to one side and Drake to the other.

You look beautiful, sis. Congratulations. Vane smiled from behind Uri.

Thanks, I love you, she sent back as she fought tears.

Uri sent her love and comfort through their link, giving her the distraction she needed. She gave him a grateful smile.

She felt the joined strength of the Guardians around them, and Vane slightly behind Sirena. The room was filled with the scent of candle wax, but nothing compared to the hint of port coming from her mate. The stone and dirt floors were slightly rough on her bare feet. Uri's large palms grasped her much smaller hands. Their warmth grounded her in place.

Drake smiled down at her from his superior height. He'd shaved his scruffy chin, combed his hair, and he looked the part of the regal leader. Gregoire had also cleaned up. His red-tinged, brown beard was trimmed on his sun-kissed skin, making him even more handsome. He gave her a fond smile.

"The blood-bonding will be in a private temple after the vows are given." Drake's eyes twinkled and it made her heart swell to think that she and her brothers had an extended family.

"Uri will begin." Drake's command brooked no argument.

Suddenly it was if they were encased in magic. The only ones there.

Uri held her gaze as his deep tone echoed off the walls, vowing to honor and care for her, body, soul and in blood for eternity. He spoke the words in the old language. It was as if words said in this magical place had power of their own. Her heart swelled and tears threatened as Sirena moved forward. She held Alex's hand above Uri's heart and Sirena's warm power flowed through Alex's own palm and into Uri's skin. Sirena was enabling Alex to permanently mark Uri's flesh with the symbol of a mated male: the thick swirls of two scaled serpents entwined together by their tails, a double eternity

247

symbol that declared his eternal devotion. It appeared along his skin in slow, detailed increments. She saw incredible beauty in the features. Two sets of gray eyes appeared, jewel-like and alive upon his skin.

She was mesmerized by it all, loving how Uri's muscles twitched beneath her touch. He sent her the emotion of it. The reverence. She felt the pain, bordering closely on pleasure, as the symbol developed, more enduring than a tattoo. If his skin were damaged and needed to be regenerated, this tattoo would always reappear. The erotic pressure of their merging essence was a sultry dance under her skin as she forever branded her mate. Their mingled breaths came out in ragged bursts.

It was beautiful.

Once done, Uri grasped her tightly and pulled her in for a deep kiss, practically devouring her lips, possessing her mouth as she now possessed a piece of his flesh. Cheers mixed with groans from her brother.

She pulled back and grinned at Uri, who was looking toward the exit.

"We're not done," she murmured.

Everyone stilled in confusion. Alex clearly repeated the vows Uri had given to her. The room vibrated lightly under her toes. The magic of the place seemed to approve. Uri's eyes took a decidedly more feral turn, shoulders and chest bunching and flexing as he listened to her words. Just as he would have grabbed her again, Sirena grasped Uri's hand in hers and positioned it over Alex's chest. This time he growled deep in his throat as well as through the bond. Alex settled her hand above that of both Uri and Sirena, showing him, with all the love in her eyes, how important this was to her. He stilled, jaw tense, as Sirena's power flowed again.

The room was silent. All watched as a more delicate version appeared on her skin. The markings were plum colored and graceful, from what she was able to see through Uri's eyes. The dragonlike serpents twined in swirls over the upper swells of her breasts.

She sent the delicious pleasure-pain through their bond as he had done with her, and he groaned aloud. His lips were open, taking deep breaths, as he watched the symbol meet in the valley of her chest. He had never appeared as fierce to her as he did when Sirena's hand fell away. Hard silver met and held her gaze before she was whisked into his arms and into the tunnel leading out. Cheers and whoops abounded at their backs. Once at the exit, he gently leaned down and kissed her markings, making her nerve endings trill in delight.

Their minds stayed entwined through the teleport that took them away. An erotic fuzziness filled her being until they touched down as if they'd completely combined while teleporting. Oh, Gods, how she loved and wanted him with near blinding need.

He sucked in a breath before speaking. "This is just a quick stop along the way. Vane shared the location and some mental images of your private cave on Earth. I moved your things here. Along with the toys I found."

She was looking at an identical reproduction of her private cavern island location. Her eyes filled again as she continued to stare. She heard his ragged breath and knew it cost him to make this detour.

"I would have shown you later. But after you gave me your gift, I had to give you yours. I can't give you back a life on Earth, but I could bring some of it here, love." He spoke softly as he held her tight, cradled against his chest, her heart melting with joy and love.

"Thank you," she whispered.

Uri took her mouth again, this time a slow, seductive plundering. She moaned and wiggled to be let down. She could hear the break in the surf and the whoosh of the sea as it hit the cliffs. She loved salt air and wanted to soak it in with him.

When he broke the kiss, she smiled up at him. "You found my stash, huh?"

His eyes glittered wickedly, but she noticed his jaw tic. "Oh, yes, and we will have to see what you can do with them, later. Right now we need to meet Gregoire for the rest of the ceremony. It's tradition to have someone watch over our blood-bonding, but I also planned to have him stay... If that's still what you want?" He looked into her eyes as if seeing inside her soul. She could feel how much he didn't want to share her, but he didn't voice it. He was giving her a choice, giving her all her fantasies as he said he would. For this night she could experience it all. She flushed with desire, but also hesitation.

Pulling him down by that silky dark hair, she took his mouth, enjoying the sweet port flavor of him. Using one hand, she touched the freshly shaven skin of his jaw, loving the movement it made as their tongues tangled. He pulled her tighter, deepening the kiss, as his hands smoothed over the silk that covered her lower back. *Just this once. Anything you wish, Alexandra,* he whispered into her mind.

Chapter 30

Island Temple of Consummation, Tetartos Realm

Alex saw Gregoire standing with his shoulder resting against a marble pillar nearly the width of his chest. The other Guardian's face reflected in moonlight as he looked out to the sea. The roiling of the surf against the soft white sands surrounding the island temple was soothing. The male's arms were crossed over the large expanse of rigid muscle, his dress shirt having been discarded at some point, leaving him in the same black silk pants Uri currently wore. He looked at them as they approached. The oddly haunted expression he wore was quickly replaced with a hint of warmth. She was still cuddled against Uri's hard, warm flesh, with her arms twined loosely around his neck, playing with the soft strands of his dark hair. He refused to put her down. Instead he took the steps still holding her.

Uri leisurely nuzzled her earlobe and she shivered and tilted her head in offering. "We will blood-bond first."

Uri moved with her into the temple as if she weighed nothing at all, holding her close to his smooth chest. A warm, salty breeze fluttered her hair, which had been left down in long waves for the ceremony. She barely heard the pad of his big bare feet against the marble, mosaic floors. She viewed scenes that depicted lovers sharing blood and bodies, in all positions, before reaching the monstrous bed high on a dais in the center of the room. Her stomach fluttered with nervous anticipation; every nerve ending became more sensitive. The silk of her dress became almost oppressive. She felt herself gasp for breath. Looking up through the domed ceiling of glass to the moon above calmed her. Candlelight flickered against the walls and softly caressed the white silk bed coverings. Nearly sheer ivory curtains billowed from the open walls. The salt air mixed with the scent of expensive candles and spicy-sweet arousal.

Uri set her on the bed, and she looked her fill at the hard shaft pushing against the confines of his silk pants. Her nipples tightened and swelled at the sight of how much he desired her. She saw every indent of muscle that played along his torso. She wanted to feel every rigid inch rubbing along her skin as he covered her... took her.

Uri growled low. "Blood-bonding first." She wondered if he was reminding her or himself. The words came out so primal his eyes swirled like melted silver.

Uri pulled off his pants and got onto the bed with her, a prowling predator. Inches from her face, he pulled loose the tie that held her dress. It fell around her in a sea of softness.

Her lids lowered as she took him in. She was bared to him, their entwined life forces fluttering. She'd almost gotten used to the soft pressure under her skin.

His gaze fell over her exposed flesh. She felt it almost as a touch as he took in her swollen breasts, to the wet lips and inner thighs, down to painted pink toes. With a pained groan, Uri took her mouth in a rough, soul-stealing kiss. Demanding as he skillfully searched her depths.

You are the most beautiful female I've ever seen, and you're mine, his thoughts whispered in her mind.

The look in his eyes as he broke the kiss made her body burn with the heat radiating from his flesh to hers. Her breathing became jagged. It was both arousing and unnerving being nude in front of Uri as Gregoire watched from the end of the bed. It was getting harder to breathe. She forced herself to inhale, only to again take in the scent of Uri's delicious skin, causing her back to arch toward him.

Uri positioned them facing each other, his leg nestled between hers, their heads resting on soft airy pillows while his cock brushed against her stomach and his hand caressed her jaw. She touched the beautiful markings, kissed them lightly, and he growled as he rubbed circles against her own symbol. Gooseflesh rose at his soft touch. Holding her gaze with his own, she saw his fangs had descended, and she licked her suddenly dry lips. She could imagine the eroticism of him taking her blood, but the thought of drinking his was a little disconcerting.

It'll be just a sip, and you'll like it. I promise. The sultry cadence of his voice touched parts deep inside. Gregoire was forgotten. All that existed was Uri. His warmth, the love and promise in his beautiful silver eyes.

Remember that I'm not proud of the things you are about to see. It's all in the past. You are my future. My eternity. His mental voice was somehow unsure.

She grinned at him and then pulled against the velvety strands of his hair she hadn't realized she was gripping. Taking deep possession of his mouth, she poured all the love she felt in to it.

We both have pasts. We'll move through it. Show me what to do now, she said, with more confidence than she felt at her ability to drink blood. She felt his shoulders shake and knew he heard the last part.

He gave her another seductive, searching kiss; then in a flash his wrist had replaced his mouth. She tasted that sweet port that she had always smelled on his skin before realizing what he'd done. It

253

was intoxicating; this was nothing like she'd worried it would be. Her pussy ached, and she rubbed it against his thick thigh. He shifted her so that half his body covered hers, nearly blanketing her with his bigger body. It was a kind of possession on its own, and it gave him better access to her neck. He leisurely licked, kissed and sucked a trail up and down her neck, touching briefly around and behind her sensitive lobe, making her moan and writhe against him. Then he struck, just a light prick, nowhere near painful. She cried out in euphoria as she felt the pull of him drinking from her.

The flashes began instantly. Suddenly she was in his mind millennia ago.

He was in Apollo's lab. How had they imagined they'd be capable of rescuing the imprisoned Immortals? This place was a fortress, and everyone was forced to wear magical metal cuffs. They'd been arrogant and fucking stupid. His body fought the effects of the experiments; he was in agony, had been torn asunder and turned into something else. It felt like acid was flowing beneath his skin; he felt fangs break through the skin of his gums. His body bowed again, and he fought hard not to shout in pain. Hermes enjoyed that too much.

Next flash.

His body was heated, the arousal overwhelming. What the fuck did those assholes do to him? He couldn't handle the need, was no more than an animal in rut. Sweat ran down his naked chest as he tried not to hurt the female they'd thrown in the cell with him. She was in much the same state. Her arousal caused her body to contort with want while anger shone bright within her eyes. The scent of sex and desperation hung in the air of the dank room.

"You must unleash your seed inside her this time, Urian. Tsk-tsk. I think, to punish you for wasting it, I will take you while you do as

you are told. You will finish, or I'll just continue giving you incentive."

Uri saw the unholy gleam in Hermes' eyes as the God came in behind him. The bastard made him sick. His skin flinched as the male touched his back. Hermes was seven foot, with long blond curly hair to his waist, and he got off on the pain of others. He had been fondling his large cock for long moments, his grin showing how much he relished the idea of what would come. Uri just needed to get through this. It was one thing for him to be punished, but the female writhing below him would continue to be used until she was with child. Her eyes flashed; knowledge that neither wanted what was to come was in their depths.

Uri's skin tightened in disgust as Hermes touched him. Hermes enjoyed males more than females. He loved the pain he could inflict. The God could do a considerable amount of damage, causing agony if one wasn't prepared. Uri would never yield; his wounds would heal. He bit his tongue. The drugs would not let him lose his erection even if his body was violated. Someday he would make sure the God paid for this.

Another flash.

Uri looked at the small forms that were miniatures of himself and his brethren. He felt bile rise, nausea riding him hard. He was unable to stop Gregoire in time. They needed an escape route now. The fury that there was nothing he could do made his muscles tense and twitch.

Apollo had done something to the children; they were not right. Dark energies? A spell to keep them loyal to Apollo and Hermes? It was as if their minds were blank.

Gregoire had tried to take one that was so obviously his son, blatant in the child's scent and appearance. The handlers, barely into

255

adulthood themselves, ordered the child, who was no more than eight years, to kill Gregoire. His friend had refused to hurt the boy and did no more than defend himself until his young finally tired. That was when the handlers finally took Gregoire to the ground, chained him, and forced him to watch as his own offspring was beaten for his failure. Hatred burned in the child's forest-colored eyes. The handlers watched without emotion. Other young were brought out to witness the punishment. Uri just clenched the railing as his knuckles turned white. It killed him not to help. But if they were both locked in confinement, they might not get out to free the others.

They had only just found a way into the training centers. It had been almost solidly locked down. Uri hated himself for not being able to do anything, wanted to rip the handlers to shreds, but more, he wanted justice. Wanted Apollo's and Hermes' deaths.

The young were lost to them. He saw it in their eyes, felt it in his broken soul. They were beyond damaged. The knowledge was a blow.

Alex's heart ached as she was hit with another flash into the horror of Uri's past.

He and Gregoire had found a way to get to the female. Blonde hair matted brown with dried blood, her once beautiful face was swollen and discolored, as was the rest of her nude body. They needed to get her out. She'd sacrificed herself for the races. Gregoire's hard glare mirrored the deadly determination Uri felt.

"The escape route has finally been forged," Gregoire said.

"Drake will come back soon. He said he felt certain Pothos had found the location of the box that would call the Creators back. He wants us to free the Immortals as soon as it is in our hands."

"Only Drake and those helping us can know she lives. Charybdis deserves peace for all she has sacrificed. She never knew how close

we were to escape." Guilt was a plague consuming him. He could see it was doing the same to Gregoire. They had been secretly forging escape plans for years. Had they told the female, she might not have tied most of her life's blood into a spell in order to save the Immortal races from being bred like the beasts they had become. She'd been tortured in the most detestable ways when Hermes and Apollo hadn't found a way around the spell. Her bleeding, torn body would heal, but he feared her mind never would. They broke the chains holding her. Uri was repulsed by the bastards. Hatred burned inside his stomach.

"I know where to take her," Gregoire offered with steely determination etched in his tight features.

Another flash. This time the memories felt different.

The Great Beings had chosen him as a Guardian; she felt power like nothing she'd ever thought possible running in his veins. Fury infused him at being denied the deaths of Apollo and Hermes. She felt the warmth of the Creators' love flow into him. Felt their understanding and pain. It had been overwhelming and heartrending. Then they were gone. Duty prevailed.

Again.

This time it was her she saw, thousands of flashes and raw emotion. Always her. In the shadows of clubs, in his yard. The yearning for her scent, her body. The wildness of the frenzy when it came. The pride as he watched her defend her brother. Reverence and joy. Fear when she was harmed in the fight. Peace like nothing he'd ever felt. Love. Sheer blinding love.

Back to herself once again, Alex took a deep breath. She willed the dizziness and tension from her body. Uri was holding her tight, his chest heaving as if he too fought for control of his emotions. His entire body was rigid. He was furious at what he'd seen in her memories.

It's much different being told than seeing it from your eyes and feeling what you felt, he said in her mind, holding her in an almost bone-crushing embrace. He took deep breaths just as she was. His eyes were shut, and she melted into him, needing to comfort him as much as she needed to feel it in return.

My father had not been in the breeding labs, had barely made it through the experiments that transformed him into a half lion, an Ailouros. My mother got him out as he was still recovering. If only they'd have been less concerned with fortifying their army before doing something for the other Immortals. They spent nearly eighteen years in hiding, building ranks when they could have done something! She knew her mother was a bitch, but not this bad. Why couldn't she have saved the others?

Uri cuddled her as he answered, *It was a horrible time. Ares and Artemis with their Tria... Your parents had to have felt the need to protect their children above all else. No more dwelling on this. Sirena said the purpose of the blood-bonding is to bring deeper understanding for a closer bond. This was more like Hell. We have to move forward and not think of what we can't change.* Uri blew out a shaky breath, obviously trying hard to follow his own advice. She saw in the hard lines of his shoulders and the twitching of his jaw that he wasn't finding it easy to let the memories go. She wondered if he'd felt her love in the end, as she'd felt his.

Reaching over, she sifted her fingers through the silky strand of hair that had fallen against his cheek. Touching and soothing the lines at his eyes, she brought his head in slowly so she could take his lips with her own. She lightly rubbed her lips against his, then nipped and sucked at his sexy lower one. She loved that it was so full, enjoyed its softness against her own. She traced along the tip of one fang before dipping her tongue into his warm cavern to duel with his own. He growled low before taking control, turning it into something much more insistent.

He pushed her back against the soft bedding. She felt his heated breath as he trailed a line of open-mouthed kisses from her throat over the soft lines of her mating markings. She felt the tip of his tongue glide over the delicate lines, lovingly caressing the serpents that indicated she was his. He laved the entwined circles, then palmed her tender flesh and rubbed his cheeks along the sides of the chasm. Having his warm mouth so close to her peaked buds was torment. He gave one last seductive kiss to the center of the markings before moving to her agonized peaks.

She moaned deeply, arching into the wonderful wet warmth. Tingling sensations inched over and inside her flesh as their life forces continued to push and pull at each other. She pulled in ragged wisps of air as she rubbed her bare pussy against his unyielding thigh.

He took his time as he nipped and lightly sucked her swollen flesh until she groaned in frustration. He was teasing her unmercifully, making her forget and get lost in the pleasure. Finally, he took a nipple into his mouth. The firm suckling forced her back off the bedding. Her fingers tightened in his hair. Through half-lidded eyes, she saw Gregoire standing back from the bed, focused on both of them, pain sparking in his eyes. Did he wish for a mate of his own?

Uri released the tightened bud with a pop, and she groaned.

"Gregoire." Uri's raspy voice seemed to echo in the room, but she felt the tension in him.

When the other male didn't move, she felt Gregoire's tension matching Uri's. Why had he come? He was obviously struggling with this, they all were. She gazed deeply into Uri's eyes, shaking her head. "I think this is better as a fantasy, love."

When she looked to Gregoire, she saw relief and a hint of warmth in his eyes as he nodded at her. "I'm honored you would have chosen me, little one." He bowed a fraction before leaving. She didn't feel rejected, she felt bad and a little worried for the male Uri considered his closest friend. Gregoire had known hell, and something more was going on with him. She'd stalked Uri for long enough to know that the male had changed in the last couple of decades.

Uri was above her in a second with a frown marring his beautiful face. "This night is yours, Alexandra. Whatever you desire."

"And I desire you. I may enjoy the fantasy of having two males, but reality is... different."

He groaned. "You're certain?" He was searching her eyes and she felt his mind sliding over hers. "Be sure, little Goddess. I will call him back if you want this."

She felt the truth in the words. "I'm sure. All I want is you, Uri. That's all I've ever truly wanted. The fantasy was just that. You're far more addicting than anything I could have conjured in my mind."

She felt his muscles ease as he growled low. "Good." His hands gripped hers and moved them over her head. "Leave them here," he demanded before moving down to nip at a nipple before moving to dip his tongue inside her navel while his hands slid over her thighs and so close to her pussy, but not touching. She arched her body, begging for his lips, his fingers, anything.

Uri growled low as her body moved uncontrollably under him. Her pussy wept, needing Uri's hands or mouth there; instead he was torturing the tiny indent in her stomach. Her nerves twitched with each caress as he teased her.

260

She felt desire running between her thighs down to her bottom. She was wet and dying to be taken.

Mmm, I love how wet and ready you are. Uri's voice in her mind held silken promise.

Inside their bond she felt his primal arousal and so much love her breath caught on a moan.

She groaned in frustration.

Open your thighs wide for me, he demanded and she eagerly complied.

When he lifted his gaze to hers, she saw his fangs. Her breath caught at just how primal he looked. "You've never experienced Aletheia venom, love. You're about to know what kind of pleasure I can give you."

Uri grinned devilishly as he moved between her thighs and scraped his fangs along her mound and then she felt a prick and gasped. It wasn't painful, it was so good. Warmth and pleasure spiked to dizzying heights as she writhed, his hot tongue sliding into her pussy.

She cried out as more intense sensations sparked all the way down her thighs. Son of a bitch. She bucked into his mouth, but he was holding her down as climax after climax rocked her body, leaving her breathless and reeling.

And so incredibly hungry. She moved in a flash and was on her knees. He'd turned to sit at the edge of the bed and it was her turn to devour him.

"Fuck, yes." He growled as she licked her way up his shaft before taking him into her mouth.

Tell me how to make you as wild as you made me, she demanded as she flicked the tip with her tongue.

His hands tunneled into her hair. "Suck it to the back of your throat." His voice was deliciously raspy with need.

She sucked as she stroked him with one hand and toyed with the heavy weight below using the other. The harder she sucked, the tighter he held her hair. He was losing control and nothing made her happier.

"Damn it. Drink it all, Alex. Every fucking drop I give you," he demanded before shouting and jerked inside her throat. She drank every splash of come he gave her and moaned at the sweet taste. He was like a dessert she couldn't get enough of.

He was breathing heavy when he pulled her up to his lap. "Fuck. You're incredible."

He kissed her before he flipped her onto the bed. She laughed as she glanced back at him. He was going through a bag by the bed.

A large clear glass dildo came into view along with a little jar. "You're going to get a taste of your fantasy. I planned plenty of dirty things for you and I'm glad this made it into the bag," Uri said.

"Lay on your stomach with your legs spread." Her pussy clenched at his demand. She felt a pillow slide under her hips and then she was lying there exposed.

The cream came next as he kept her off-kilter with kisses along her spine. Her hips moved as his fingers pushed into her ass. "That's a good Goddess. Take my fingers like you'll take the toy." She groaned as his heat moved from her. And then she saw it. He was feeding her the image of the toy as he caressed it with the cream. It was as thick as Uri's cock at the flare in the middle then tapered before the flat

262

base.

She saw and felt as it was pushed inside, her body expanding around it, taking it all the way as her hips pushed against it. It felt full, and good, which meant the cream was doing its job. She was mesmerized as she watched her body fully accept it. Her body was no longer her own; inside and out, she was possessed. She felt her life force pushing to mate with Uri's. She was wild with that and the hard glass cock in her ass. She saw why he'd used the glass. She could see through it, see inside her body. She groaned deep.

Her hips pushed back, begging him to move it. To do something. He lifted her hips and she mewled when she felt the head of his cock at her pussy. Slowly, he pushed into her from behind. She took him, though it was a tight fit in this position, especially with the plug already filling her up.

"Fuck, so tight, so good." He groaned, showing her what he was doing. "Do you like taking two cocks, love? Do you feel full?"

"Yes." It did feel good, but Uri was moving too slowly. She needed more. Finally, he rode her harder, faster. She felt so taken, so hot, she was insensible and wanted him to be as wild as she felt, wanted him to lose control. She was a Demi-Goddess; her body could accept anything he could dish out.

Uri moved to finger her clit while circling his hips behind her. His mind was open, letting her feel how good she was wrapped around him. It was too much. One soft touch on that protruding nub had her over the edge into heaven as she bucked back uncontrollably against him. Uri's pleasure filled her full, leaving that warm soothing sensation in its wake.

They collapsed with Uri at her side. He was stroking her hair and back, leaving her sated and in a kind of bliss she never imagined possible.

They stayed like that until their chests no longer heaved. She stretched, feeling the liquid evidence of Uri's possession slide down the inside of her thighs. So much, she groaned. All the while, Uri traced circles along her spine. Then she registered the full feeling still stretching her.

"Um, did you forget something?" She wiggled her bottom, as it was still propped high with pillows.

He chuckled. "No, love, I didn't forget anything. I like you with a plug in your tight ass." Uri's voice still held that delicious rasp as a warm palm stroked her bottom. In a second she felt him roll the plug as she groaned. "I'm a little jealous, because I want my cock in here again."

Her breathing started to stutter as renewed arousal assailed her.

He had her up and in his strong arms an instant later, taking her to a corner that housed a large shower flowing from the ceiling. Setting her down, he rubbed his cheek against hers, then ordered, "Bend over and touch your toes."

She felt her skin prickle and flush. It was the effect his dominance had on her. Bending all the way over, she put herself on display for him, shimmying her hips a little as she did, eliciting a growl from her male, making her feel empowered and daring.

She felt and then saw through their link as Uri began removing the plug. Her body fought to hold it inside, but she pushed back, knowing that something else would be filling her very soon. Just the thought of what he would do to her made goose bumps line her flesh.

Instead of taking her right away as she thought, he gently

soaped and massaged her muscles, leaving her in an aroused state that was soon bordering on insanity. She tried to reciprocate, but he moved her in circles as he touched her, which soon morphed into licking and sucking at her exposed skin. Her head fell back and to the side, allowing him better access to her neck and sensitive ears.

Alex felt the light prick at her neck, then the rush of warming arousal that drugged her senses. It traveled swiftly through her body, making her moan and wiggle as her essence pushed and contracted against his. The instant near ecstasy could be addicting.

She was lifted again and taken to the bed, where he pushed her legs wide and back, propping her bottom up with pillows. His eyes were on her flushed skin. "Touch your breasts, Alex."

She moaned and used both hands to push the heavy mounds high as she gazed up at him. He used a thumb to lightly tease her clit as his cock pushed at her back entrance. Her thighs were spanned wide, her knees bent up, displaying everything for her mate to see and touch as he slid inside her ass. He rolled his hips as he watched her playing with her breasts.

He groaned, "I love that I can see how wet you get as I fuck your beautiful ass." His thumb collected the moisture and rolled it over her clit and her breathing seized. She was too far gone already. The venom, the feeling of being claimed, of being taken and owned was too much as he pinched her clit and slammed into her ass.

She felt Uri inside her mind, felt his pleasure along with her own. Felt his essence twine with hers until a sense of love and euphoria racked her entire being. His life force pulsed and flooded hers just as his come coated inside her body. She screamed and convulsed until she was swept into oblivion.

Chapter 31

Guardian Manor, Tetartos Realm

Alex paced the confines of the war room in Drake's manor, something she'd been doing for a good hour. No doubt there would be a nice circle in the tile where she made her laps. Havoc had followed her for probably the first ten minutes before realizing they weren't actually going anywhere. He soon crashed out on the couch against the wall. So now all she heard was the snoring pup mixed with Vane's irritating finger-tapping. She blew out a breath; she really wasn't angry with Vane. She knew he was just as frustrated at being left behind.

Her brother sat at the big conference table, going over what seemed like painfully boring DVD surveillance of the hallways and corridors in Cyril's demolished compound. His brows furrowed as his eyes continually scanned the screen. She wished she had something useful to do.

Alex had already gone and checked on Sam and Erik after the Guardians left, only to find Sam curled up against her brother as they slept. Sam was on top of the black comforter, dressed in the yoga pants and a sweatshirt they had sent to Erik's room. Erik had apparently moved in his sleep so that his big body faced Sam's slender frame, wrapping her up. Sam's blonde head had been tucked under Erik's scruffy chin, and Alex's vision had blurred at seeing how tightly her brother held onto his mate even in spelled sleep. She had barely made it out of the room before her shoulders shook and tears tracked down her cheeks. Things would be so difficult for them. Her heart ached as she walked back to the war room. She and Uri hadn't had time before the raids to try their newly merged powers on Erik, and she didn't dare attempt it alone.

Last night she'd awoken to the feel of power surging in her veins and a deep feeling of peace and rightness. Uri had held her in his strong arms as they lay on the temple bed and adjusted to the newness of it all, together. They'd stayed there, holding each other and kissing for hours.

She knew it would take time to fully use all the power inside her. Her biggest experiment had been to attempt teleporting to Earth. Hitting the Realm's confinement spell had been a blow. It had been a crap shoot that she'd hoped would hit pay dirt. It hadn't. She frowned in irritation at that fact.

She touched the link she shared with Uri. She didn't want to interrupt, so she didn't speak. He'd said he would let her know when the first batch of raids were complete. They had surveillance that showed Cynthia—beautiful, blonde, and cold blooded—was at one of her homes. They chose to go in at night, with teams of two each to incapacitate six of her facilities at once. Then they would go into her last two locations after. They didn't have enough damned people to go around over there.

Damn it, when would he contact her? She hated that he was out of her reach. Hated how trapped she felt.

She was sick of pacing. She walked over to the couch where Havoc lay sprawled, and sat in the small corner that was left, pondering the sexy things Uri had done to her for far too long. She looked over and saw Vane's uncomfortable look before he cleared his throat and stared at the screen again.

"Sorry."

"The whole thing is just awkward. I'm truly happy for you. But, shit, you're still my sister. I can't imagine how Erik's going to deal when he wakes up." Vane shook his head. Sadness there, they both knew how pained Erik would be when he awoke, and not because of her mating to Uri.

"I know, but even without your extra-special enhanced animal senses, I've still smelled females on the two of you for centuries." She grinned at his uncomfortable expression. She swore his cheeks even got a little pink.

She laughed as she sat rubbing Havoc's sleek, barreled chest. His eyes slit open before the snores started again. He was so warm.

"I'm worried about Erik and Sam. What if Uri and I can't do anything to dull his memories like we did with the females?" She said it quietly but knew her brother would hear.

"Erik is strong. He's stubborn as hell, but strong. He'll do what's best for Sam."

"That's what I'm worried about. What if he fights the frenzy? Doesn't complete the bond to try to protect her? He could end up hurting them both more by waiting. I can't see either of them allowing the process to restart if they screw up this chance. She's still mortal and will be vulnerable until he completes the ceremony making her Immortal."

Vane looked off, sprawled back in the office chair, but he nodded tightly after a while. "I know, but we can't make his choices for him."

"Sirena explained some of it to Sam. She's willing to complete the bond, in theory. They looked so peaceful when I looked in on them. I just want him happy, Vane. He's been so serious and controlled, nothing like the boy he was. I hate that my mistake cost so much." She felt tears threatening and fought them back as she rubbed Havoc's ears; his warm body was comforting.

"Shit, you can't think like that, sis. He'll be fine. We may still have weeks to figure it out."

Are you okay?

She grinned, expelling a relieved breath at hearing Uri's voice in her head. He must have felt her sadness.

Everything's fine, just talking to Vane about Erik and Sam. Is everything okay there?

That seemed to soothe him. *We've just finished clearing the first batch of locations, but the bitch had a series of tunnels she escaped through. Drake and Jax are tracking her now. Conn and Dorian are working to collect the last data. I'm heading out to the other location with the others. Will be back soon...* His last words were sent with a rush of arousal. Her breath whooshed out.

"Guess Uri's fine." It wasn't possible for Vane's voice to get any drier.

She couldn't help chuckling at his scowl. "Yep," she said with a big smile, which fled when she relayed the rest of what Uri told her.

Vane frowned and leaned forward, thinking, obviously not liking the situation any more than she did.

Suddenly her body stilled and compulsion overwhelmed her. A *knowing* stronger than anything she'd ever known. She was spurred into movement, rushing to the weapons cabinets. It was incredibly powerful and jarring, but she didn't fight it. A relaxed sensation flowed through her veins and her limbs moved almost completely on their own. Her hands pulled the cabinet doors wide and were pulling items out. Both Havoc and Vane jumped up and were at her side in the span of a second.

"What is it?" Vane asked, muscles tensed, ever the warrior ready to spring into action. He accepted the weapon harness and spelled vest she thrust in his hands. She pulled item after item, Sigs with multiple clips, sniper rifle, knives, more clips, heat-sensitive goggles. "Holy shit," Vane said as he quickly donned the gear she gave him. She turned her attention back to the cabinets and started outfitting herself in much the same fashion.

"Out on the balcony," she said, and Vane and Havoc quickly exited the French doors. "Now get on the ground and hold as tight to Havoc as you can." Even the hound, though completely alert, didn't move as Alex went through the motions.

Vane crouched down, and Havoc licked his face as he held to the beast's neck firmly. Vane glared at the pup. "This better not be a joke, Alex." He was thoroughly disgusted and uncomfortable.

That was when the pain hit, nearly exploding in her body and almost taking her to her knees. She knew instantly what was happening. Uri was hit. Her mating bond pulsed as she teleported. When she hit the barrier this time, her body pushed painfully through. It was like every cell was being constricted inside a vise.

She reformed, gasping for breath, on the ground next to Uri.

Need backup. Alex thought the quiet request came from Sacha, but she could barely hear it through the buzzing In her ears.

She nearly passed out with panic as she looked over the damage to her mate. Still panting, she moved her hands over Uri's body, using her small bit of healing power. Checking inside, she found a mess. He would live, but it would be painful. Thankfully, he was unconscious. The fact that he was covered in blood was freaking her out. Metal shards were imbedded in his shoulders, legs, and neck. Bones were broken, organs collapsed.

She heard Havoc growl, guarding the area at Uri's feet.

Vane was also assessing the area for a threat. There was an alarm blaring on speakers all over what seemed like a secluded estate. Heavy stands of large trees were everywhere around the lawn she was sitting on. A tree above them still smoked, and there were branches scattered on the ground. She encircled the four of them with her shield, not willing to act as a target while she funneled healing power into Uri. She could spare only enough that his internal injuries were no longer dire and his own body's abilities could start working on the rest.

She reached for the bond she'd shared with the Guardians from nearly the moment she and Uri's mating began. *Drake! Havoc, Vane and I are with Uri. He's down, unconscious but stable. He was hit hard with shrapnel or something.* She stroked Uri's bloody forehead as her heart's frantic beating started to even out. The constant noise of the alarm was driving her mad.

Shit. I can't contact any of the others. Can you see or get to anyone else? I'm trying to get out of these fucking tunnels to get there. They're thick with metal and spelled. She could hear his anger and frustration in her mind.

Who was with Uri? she asked. She and Vane would need to get the others out.

Sirena, Gregoire and Bastian. I'll be there as soon as I can. Do what you can. Sacha sent out an alert before she passed out. Conn and Dorian are there now. I'll inform them you're at the other location. Watch your backs.

We will.

271

Havoc started growling, hackles up as puffs of smoke came drifting up. He was facing the stucco and ivy exterior of the old mansion, but she didn't see anything. Unless... An explosion hit her shield, almost taking it down, but the metal pieces didn't make it through.

"What the fuck was that?" Vane said. "That came from the fucking house. I didn't even hear it over that fucking alarm."

"Vane, I need you to teleport Uri farther away. Set Havoc to guard him. I can't do it myself and hold the shield over all of us. Sirena, Bastian and Gregoire are here somewhere. Drake lost contact with them." They heard shouts and footsteps coming from the direction of the house.

"Shit, got it. I'll get Uri back, but then I'm going fucking hunting." Vane's expression was fierce. Jaw tense, shoulders rigid. He was itching for a fight. She knew he wanted to transform, but right now they needed their weapons. Alex's stomach clenched in near agony at having to leave Uri wounded. She didn't dare have them teleport far. Seconds counted. She looked inside herself, found Uri's bond with Havoc, and gave the beast thoughts of what she wanted him to do. Protect. Guard.

"Vane, please don't give me your alpha crap right now. We don't want the Mageias to get their hands on the others. You go clockwise, and I'll go counter." Her head was pounding. Uri's pain? Or maybe the blast to her shield? She willed it away as she watched her brother's features. He didn't want her in the mix, but she didn't give him a choice. They needed to end this now.

"Fuck."

She knew exactly how he felt, but footfalls were getting closer, so Vane teleported just as she released the shield. He was taking Uri and Havoc away as she'd asked.

Alex pulled the rifle off her back and teleported high into the trees lining the secluded mansion. She counted: one, two, three Mageias in black with ear protection, how nice for them. They had come from the house, moving stealthily to her previous location. They were being cautious with their movements, but not enough. She hit the first two in the head before the third took cover behind a tree. She teleported again; third down.

The wind rustled through the leaves, the thick branches swaying. She heard gunfire on the other side of the house. Hopefully Vane's.

See any of the others yet? she asked her brother.

Not yet, but five down on this side of the house.

Three here, but no sign of the Guardians. She moved steadily through the trees, no more than a whisper of movement. She paused, attempting to hear through the mind-numbing alarms. She saw movement further to her right, away from the house. There were half a dozen Mageias in all, dressed in black like the others. The ones in the middle were carrying something. Crap, she saw blonde hair; she was sure of it.

I think I've found Sirena, she sent to her brother and Drake.

I may have Bastian. Listen, the alarms have to be so fucking loud to hide the sound of the missiles. That's the only reason I can think of. I think they might be heat-seeking. Don't stay in one place too...

Crap, she moved right before a blast hit the tree she was standing in. Moving fast, she shouldered the rifle and grabbed both Sigs. She shot the two holding Sirena. Teleporting in and out of view, she came in behind another two. Back and forth she moved and shot

273

the other two while they tried to figure out where the threat was coming from. She was spattered in blood but had Sirena.

She teleported Sirena to where she felt Uri and Havoc. To Vane and Drake she sent, *I have Sirena. They are using heat-seeking missiles, Vane. Drake, tell the others not to stay in one place too long.*

Got it, he growled back.

She felt fury radiating through the bond. It would not be pretty when he got there.

Alex reached inside herself for the link to Havoc. Finding it, she sent pictures of Vane coming to them. Surprising a fire-breathing animal was never a good idea, her presence he could feel, not Vane's. She felt her energy stores depleting, even though she had more power flowing in her veins than she had ever imagined possible. She felt like a superhero.

Vane teleported next to Alex as she was settling Sirena beside Uri. A bloody but semiconscious Bastian was laid out next to Sirena and she saw sweat beading on the Guardian's exotically beautiful olive skin. His teeth were clenched against the pain.

"Where was Gregoire?" she asked Bastian as Vane used his minimal healing abilities on the Guardian. Acid eroded the inside of her stomach. She needed to find Uri's friend and get him out before the Mageias did something to him.

"Bastian's got a punctured lung," Vane said.

Do you know where Gregoire was? she asked, using Uri's mental link to the Guardian.

Front of the house.

Drake, how are the others? We're going for Gregoire now.

274

Slow. Let me know when you have him. His anger practically vibrated through the connection.

Alex and Vane moved as quickly as possible around the house. She saw armed guards at the windows and doors, but no Gregoire. Her heart rate sped up. They had to have him. She heard glass break and more gunfire; Vane was picking them off. Whipping on the thermal goggles, she used the strongest rounds she had and found her targets through the walls.

She cleared an opening in what looked like a downstairs bedroom. *I'm in a downstairs bedroom west of the front entrance.*

Shit, don't get shot. I'm in a library on the east side. No Gregoire.

She moved quietly through the house; someone finally killed the alarm. Probably Vane. The lack of noise had her ears buzzing as she teleported around another guard and cut his throat. She didn't want to alert anyone she was inside. She picked off a couple more now that it was so easy to hear their heavy breathing.

My side is clear. Did you find him? Scent him anywhere?

No, but it reeks of death and Mageia. Fuck, I'll check the upstairs, Vane said.

Crap, something wasn't right. Her head was pounding, and sweat was beading on her forehead. Where did they take him? It was quiet; the place was empty. She checked the garage, and there didn't seem to be any missing vehicles. She worked her way back through the downstairs rooms that she had already checked. Nothing. There was an office with video surveillance set up.

Vane, get down here. Help me with this video equipment. She felt his warmth right next to her a moment later. He moved around the room, quickly accessing the computer systems with the speed of

275

a true hacker. Her heart was pounding as she listened to the rapid tapping of the keys.

Before she knew what was happening, her brother was gone. She rushed behind the desk to see that the monitor was showing four men holding a much larger one. Had to be Gregoire. They were getting inside a hatch hidden in the ground outside of the house. Shit, she'd never even seen that spot.

Vane, where are you?

Don't worry. I've almost got him. I'll meet you at Uri.

She blew out a half-relieved, half-irritated breath. Her hands were shaking when she reformed.

Drake, Vane's got Gregoire. Did you get the others?

Good. Yes. Just got Sander; he's the last. Taking them to the Earth compound now. Send me the visual of where you are, and we'll help get the others.

She did as he asked and sank to the ground next to Uri. She was worn through. No way would she be able to teleport them all. Vane set Gregoire on the other side of Alex so she was between them. He was again giving what little healing he could to Gregoire as he had done for Sirena and Bastian.

Drake and the others came a split second later, and Havoc released a growl and steady stream of fire at Drake's feet before Alex realized she hadn't warned the hellhound of their arrival. Jax chuckled.

"Damn it, you little bastard." Drake's loud voice boomed under the trees, but he didn't kill the animal. Havoc proceeded to sit at Uri's feet and stare at Drake.

"I should have warned him that you were coming," Alex apologized. Havoc hadn't aimed to kill and didn't do anything to the others. She had a feeling the hound had better senses than they had imagined.

"We'll discuss how you got here when we get to the Earth compound." Drake's voice was filled with the authority he'd carried for centuries. He gently lifted Sirena, and Alex could see the pain blanketing his features as he saw the damage wrought on the healer's body. Then he was gone.

Chapter 32

Guardian Compound, Earth Realm

Uri was scowling as he lay in the infirmary cavern below the ground, sucking in as much energy as he could force his cells to take, willing his broken bones to knit faster. He fucking hated being laid out. It helped that the others were in just as bad shape. Though that thought made him a surly ass.

The bed shook, and he looked to his mate curled softly into his side like a sleepy kitten. "I have to agree. That does make you a surly ass." She laughed out loud as she lifted her sapphire eyes to his. They were filled with good humor, and he loved her for it. She'd been cuddling up with him, taking in energy that her body desperately needed.

When he'd awoken in that bed the night before, in complete agony, while feeling how depleted her energies were, he'd demanded to know what had happened and why she was diminished. He remembered her slumberous blue gaze meeting his as she groggily said, "Go back to sleep until you aren't grumpy." Then she'd closed her eyes and fallen asleep while his mouth was still open. Just snuggled into her pillow and was out. He'd seen Havoc curled onto the couch next to the wall, snoring, and Uri hadn't a clue what the fuck had happened.

Pained chuckles had come from his left, and he turned his head. "Shit, it hurts to laugh." Gregoire had been on another bed they had obviously brought into the room, as it barely fit. His brother had

278

looked to be in much the same condition as Uri was. He had scowled at the other Guardian before tucking Alex into his aching side. He'd needed to feel her soft warmth, even if it did hurt like hell.

At some point Drake and Vane finally came in and quietly told him what the fuck had happened, while his mate slept at his side.

But now, he was still not completely healed, and it had been an entire night. He would get up and test his knitted bones in an hour, no later. Alex was still chuckling; the sexy sound wiped away some of his annoyance at being injured. He grinned down at her beautiful face and asked, "Are you feeling better now, Rambo?"

Her eyes glittered in amusement. "Much. Thanks. I guess that means someone told you what happened?

"Drake and your brother have both been here. We hear eight of us were taken down, and you and your brother came in guns blazing. I have full intentions of spanking your ass red for that shit." Eight fucking Guardians taken down by mortals. That left a bitter taste in his mouth.

"What? Why?" She looked at him, a cute furrow between her brows, but her body heated against his when he spoke of her punishment. His Goddess was far too much a fan of spankings. He needed to find something that she didn't like so damn much.

"You kept going until you were too depleted to do more. It was dangerous. Vane could have gone in to get Gregoire's sorry ass out." They both looked over at Gregoire, who nodded.

"I do appreciate your worrying for me. But if you were mine, a spanking would be the least of your worries," Gregoire growled, but Uri could see his brother's affection for Alex reflected in the softening of his eyes.

Uri shook his head when she looked ready to deny being at risk. "Don't even try to deny it." He said the last as a whisper against her silky lips. He took her mouth like he took everything, demanding her response. The fact that they were on Earth and would have to go back to Tetartos soon was far from his thoughts. He didn't care where they lived. He would make her happy anywhere; they would build a house of their own in Tetartos. He would bring her shoes and make it his life's work to ensure her happiness.

I love you, she whispered into his mind.

He smiled, cuddling her close, knowing that love was far from what he felt. It was something much deeper, but he would give her the words, *I love you, Alex.*

Chapter 33

Outside the City of Lofodes, Tetartos Realm

Gregoire stood on the bluff that overlooked both the sea and the vast stretch of meadow with a big lake further off. His head ached, his body still not completely healed. But he'd needed to see her. He rubbed his beard. He'd been running in his other form, forcing his body to stretch out the newly knitted bones.

His brother's mating had changed things for him in more ways than one. He wanted what Uri and Alex had. He wanted the female he'd been waiting for.

He'd been living a damned nightmare.

Always keeping his distance, watching over her from afar, never chancing that they'd scent each other. It'd been the longest decades of his life, and he couldn't leave her much longer. Seeing her now brought a glimmer of peace that had always eluded him. She exuded grace and tranquility as she glided across the field. She was small and fast, but he was faster. He shook his head, a small smile tilting his lips.

He rubbed his jaw. He had needs he worried she was still too innocent, too pure to handle.

Fuck.

He couldn't force himself to look away. To leave. There was nothing more beautiful than the sight of her racing with such wild abandon. Her sun-kissed skin glistened in the light while her long chestnut hair billowed behind her. Her face tilted towards him and even from the great distance he saw a crease at her forehead. His eyes narrowed and a muscle at his jaw started to tic. If anyone had caused that frown, they'd pay.

She was his and soon she'd know just what that meant.

Glossary of Terms and Characters for Reference:

Ailouros – Immortal race of feline shifters (lions, tigers, panthers, etc.), known as the warrior class

Aletheia – Immortal race with enhanced mental abilities and power within their fluids, can take blood memories, strong telepathy, race responsible for Vampire myth

Alex – aka Alexandra, Demi-Goddess daughter of Athena, sister to Vane and Erik

Aphrodite – Sleeping Goddess, one of the three good Deities, mother of Drake

Apollo – Sleeping God who experimented on all of the Immortal races millennia ago, infusing them with animal DNA in order to create the perfect army against his siblings

Ares – Sleeping God and father of the evil Tria, the triplets Deimos, Phobos, and Than, who are imprisoned in Hell Realm.

Artemis – Sleeping Goddess and mother of the evil Tria, the triplets Deimos, Phobos, and Than, who are imprisoned in Hell Realm.

Athena – Sleeping Goddess – One of only three good Gods who didn't feed off dark energies and become mad, mother of Alex, Vane and Erik, mate to Niall

Bastian – Kairos (teleporter race of Immortals), Guardian of the Realms, diplomat for the Guardians within Tetartos Realm

Brianne – Geraki (the Immortal race of half ancient birds of prey), Guardian of the Realms

Charybdis – Immortal Nereid (mercreature) abused by Poseidon and then sold and experimented on in Apollo's labs. She gave a portion of her life force to create the mating spell, aka mating curse, so that no Immortal could breed with any other than their destined mate.

Conn – Lykos (Immortal race of wolf shifters), Guardian of the Realms

Creators – The two almighty beings that birthed the Gods, created the Immortals and planted the seeds of humanity

Cynthia – Mageia (evolved human with elemental abilities) on Earth Realm

Cyril – Demi-God son of Apollo, Siren/healer

Demeter – Sleeping Goddess

Demi-Gods or Goddesses – The son or daughter of a God and an Immortal

Dorian – Nereid (race of Immortal mercreatures), Guardian of the Realms

Drake – aka Draken, dragon-shifting Demi-God leader of the Guardians of the Realms, son of Aphrodite and her Immortal dragon mate, Ladon

Elizabeth – Aletheia (race of Immortals whose existence created vampire myth), works for Cyril

Erik – Demi-God son of Athena, Ailouros (lion shifter), Vane's twin, Alex's younger brother

Geraki – Immortal race of half bird of prey, power over air

Gods – Twelve beings birthed by the Creators. Currently imprisoned in sleeping chambers by the Creators.

Gregoire – Hippeus (warhorse shifters, responsible for centaur myth), Guardian of the Realms

Guardians of the Realms – The twelve warriors of different Immortal races who were chosen by the Creators to watch over the four Realms of Earth after the Gods were sent to sleep. They were tasked with ensuring that humanity was allowed to evolve and that the Gods remained asleep in their sleeping chambers. There are three female Guardians; Sacha, Sirena and Brianne. The nine male Guardians are Drake, P (Pothos), Uri, Gregoire, Bastian, Jax, Conn, Dorian and Sander.

Hades – Sleeping God – One of the three good Gods, father of P (Pothos) who is one of the twelve Guardians of the Realms

Healers – aka Sirens, Immortal race, power over the body, ability with their voices

Hellhounds – Black hounds with red eyes who are blood-bonded to the Tria in Hell Realm

Hephaistos – Sleeping God

Hera – Sleeping Goddess

Hermes – Sleeping God and Apollo's partner in the experimentation and breeding of Immortals for their army

Hippeus – Immortal race of warhorse shifters, power over earth

Jax – aka Ajax, Ailouros (half tiger), Guardian of the Realms

Kairos – Immortal race whose primary power is teleportation

Lykos – Immortal wolf shifters with a primary power of telekinesis

Mageia – Evolved humans, compatible to be an Immortal's mate, have abilities with one of the four elements: air, fire, water, or earth.

Mates – Each Immortal has a rare and destined mate, their powers meld, and they become stronger pairs that are able to procreate, usually after a decade.

Mating Curse – A spell cast in Apollo's Immortal breeding labs that ensured the God wouldn't be able to use them to continue creating his army. Charybdis cast the spell using a portion of her life force and now Immortals can only have young with their destined mates.

Mating Frenzy – Starts when an Immortal comes into contact with their mate. A sexual frenzy that continues through the bonding/mating ceremonies.

Nereid – Immortal race of mercreatures, power over water

Niall – Immortal mate to Athena, father of Alexandra (Alex), Vane and Erik, experimented on in Apollo's lab and turned into an Ailouros before conceiving Vane and Erik with Athena

Pothos – aka P, Guardian of the Realms, Son of Hades, second to Drake in power

Phoenix – Immortal race with ability over fire

Poseidon – Sleeping God

Realms – Four Realms of Earth: Earth – where humanity exists; Heaven – where good and neutral souls go to be reincarnated; Hell – where the Tria were banished and evil souls are sent; Tetartos – Realm of beasts – where the Immortals were exiled by the Creators

Sacha – Kairos (Immortal teleporter race), Guardian of the Realms, diplomat for the Guardians within Tetartos Realm

Sam – aka Samantha Palmer, power over metal, Mageia

Sander – Phoenix, Guardian of the Realms

Sirena – Siren (healer), Guardian of the Realms, primarily works to find mates for Immortals in Tetartos

Tetartos Realm – The Realm where the Creators exiled the Immortals to live millennia ago. Once known as the "Fourth Realm" or Realm of Beasts. Tetartos is encompassed in a confinement spell (designed by the Creators) that only the Guardians can move through. Anyone can get into the Realm, but once there they are unable to leave.

Tria – Evil Triplets spawned from incestuous coupling of Ares and Artemis: Deimos, Phobos and Than. They were long ago imprisoned in the bowels of Hell Realm.

Uri – aka Urian, Aletheia (Immortal race whose existence created vampire myth), interrogator, Guardian of the Realms

Vane – Demi-God son of Athena, Ailouros (half-lion), Erik's twin, Alex's younger brother

Zeus – Sleeping God

SETTA JAY

New Releases Coming Soon!

Subscribe to Setta Jay's Newsletter for:

Release dates

Exclusive excerpts

Giveaways

settajay.com

SETTA JAY

About the Author:

Setta Jay is the author of the popular Guardians of the Realms Series. She's garnered attention and rave reviews in the paranormal romance world for writing smart, slightly innocent heroines and intense alpha males. She loves creating stories that incorporate a strong plot accompanied by a heavy dose of heat.

An avid reader her entire life, her love of romance started at a far too early age with the bodice rippers she stole from her older sister. Along with reading, she loves animals, brunch dates, coffee that is really more French vanilla creamer, questionable reality television, English murder mysteries, and has dreams of traveling the world.

Born a California girl, she currently resides in Idaho with her incredibly supportive husband.

She loves to hear from readers so feel free to ask her questions on social media or send her an email, she will happily reply.

Website: http://www.settajay.com/

Facebook: https://www.facebook.com/settajayauthor

Twitter: https://twitter.com/SETTAJAY_

Goodreads: https://www.goodreads.com/author/show/7778856.Setta_Jay

CPSIA information can be obtained
at www.ICGtesting.com
Printed in the USA
FSHW02n2015140818
51449FS